Sottopassaggio

BIGfib

Nick Alexander

Nick Alexander was born in Margate, and has lived and worked in the UK, the USA and France. When he isn't writing, he is the editor of the gay literature site www.BIGfib.com.

Sottopassaggio is Nick's second novel. The other titles in the series, *Fifty Reasons to Say Goodbye, Good Thing – Bad Thing, Better Than Easy,* and *Sleight Of Hand* are also available, as are the standalone novels *The Case Of The Missing Boyfriend,* and *13:55 Eastern Standard Time.*

Nick currently lives in the southern French Alps with two mogs, a couple of goldfish and a complete set of Pedro Almodovar films. For more information, to contact the author, or to order extra copies please visit his website on: www.nick-alexander.com

Legal Notice

Sottopassaggio – ISBN: 978-2952489911
Cover image © Couperfield/Shutterstock.com
Text by Nick Alexander, Copyright © 2005, 2012.

Acknowledgements

Thanks to Fay Weldon for encouraging me when it most counted. Special thanks to Davey, without whom Tom would have been speechless, to Rosemary and Liz for their help with the final manuscript.

Thanks to everyone who has filled my life with these stories and to everyone who shared their memories with me when I ran out of ideas.

Thanks to Apple computer for making such wonderful reliable work tools, and to BIGfib Books for making this physical book a reality.

Sottopassaggio

A Novel

"Life is what happens to you while
you're busy making other plans."

– John Lennon

Prologue

A son, remembering packed lunches and childhood picnics, makes a flask of coffee for his mother and tells her to be sure to drink it as she undertakes the long drive back to England. He is worried about her leaving, for she is not, emotionally speaking, in the best of ways.

But she reassures him. "I don't know how I'll be when I get there, but the drive will do me good," she says.

As he waves her off, he has one last moment of hesitation, but his boyfriend slides an arm around his waist and says, *"Don't worry she'll be fine."*

He hands the flask of coffee through the window, kisses his mother on the cheek and, as she drives away, he makes a meow sound, mimicking Riley, the caged cat next to her on the passenger seat.

As Sarah drives, she marvels at her convincing acting.

"He shouldn't have let me go," she thinks briefly. "He should have realised."

She discounts this as a bad thought. It's not her son's fault after all if he can't read her mind, is it? It couldn't really be his fault if his imagination isn't big enough to see the terror of driving back alone to all that mess. Could it?

After half an hour on the monotonous Italian motorway the cat quietens and Sarah's mind drifts over the absurdly dramatic events of the last few months. Her shocking realisation that she didn't, or perhaps *had never* really loved her husband of twenty-seven years, and then in the middle of that crisis, her son's revelation...

And now this so-called holiday. "Out of the frying pan and into the fire", she thinks.

Away from Pete and the terrible drama of "home", to be sure. But two weeks of trying to get her mind around the fact of those two together, trying to think about her son, trying find a new way of relating to him while also trying not to think about it; specifically trying not to think about the sex thing, the reality of their two bodies together.

But more than anything else, she has spent the time trying not to think about what she will do when she gets back, *if* she gets back to Wolverhampton.

As she drives past motorway exits for Monaco, Nice, then Antibes, she pictures each of those places, memories from twenty years ago, before Pete decided to hate travelling. She is tempted to leave the motorway and re-visit them all, to never go home. She wonders if French hotels take cats and briefly her hatred focuses on Riley; it becomes the cat's fault she can't do what she wants.

The desire not to return to Wolverhampton is overpowering. She could just carry on, just drive and drive until…

Until what though? Until her bank account is empty? Until *both* their accounts are empty?

The future strikes her as deep and dark and endless, and she wonders if she can face it.

"Am I capable of doing any of this?" she asks out loud. But what is the alternative?

As tears well up in her eyes it starts to rain. She swallows determinedly and in strangely symmetrical acts, she brushes away the tears and flicks on the windscreen wipers.

A sign shows that she will have to change motorways soon, to turn the wheel and swing north towards home, or continue straight-on towards Marseille, Perpignan, Barcelona.

A tiny smile spreads across her face as she contemplates the choices. Wolverhampton or Barcelona. It seems absurd that she will choose England as she knows she must.

Outside it gets darker and the rain gets harder and starts to hammer against the windscreen. She flicks on the radio, which glows cosily and scans briefly before settling on FIP FM. A woman is talking with a late night voice even though it is mid-afternoon. Sarah doesn't understand the actual words but the language, the foreign-ness of it sounds beautiful.

Another sign announces the beginning of the A7 and she braces herself to turn the wheel towards home. To turn her wheel away from the adventures she always dreamt of, and towards the resumption of her life in Wolverhampton, her trips to the shops with her husband, and to establishing some kind of platonic relationship with the man she secretly loved all these years.

It's still too painful to even *think* his name. Having had his life of adventures without her he has now returned and will be living down the road! "*How absurd!*" she thinks. "*How selfish!*"

She thinks about what it means, this turning of the steering wheel, for turning onto the A7 is hugely symbolic.

It is the final and ultimate acceptance of her ordinariness. It is acknowledging, once and for all, that at fifty-six she isn't going to become anything else. That it's too late for adventures, too late to leave Pete, and too late for the lover. Only she doesn't feel old inside; inside she doesn't feel like it should be too late at all.

She glances at the cat. "It's not a life of Riley at all," she tells it.

The cat replies with a plaintive *meow* and Sarah nods.

"You know that already huh?" she says.

As she stares out through the windscreen at the road, her eyes start to tear again, and through two layers of running water it's hard to see the road works.

As she enters a tunnel, a sign tells her to move to the right-hand lane for the A7, so she waits until the end of the road works and then slows and slips in behind a truck.

"Am I doing this then?" she asks, suddenly shocked by the loudness of her voice as the noise of the rain bashing against the windscreen ceases.

The tears start to flow again and she's having trouble seeing in the darkness of the tunnel. She puts on her hazard lights and starts to slow and shift onto the hard shoulder.

As the car halts, only feet before the exit from the tunnel, she thinks of another option she hasn't considered – turning around and going back. But it's not really an option; her son will be flying home at the end of the week and his *lover*...

She swallows and re-phrases the thought. His *friend* will be heading back to wherever it is his parents live, and another different family will bring their own set of hopes and fears into the villa.

She pulls a tissue from her sleeve and blows her nose. She opens the cat's cage, but it doesn't move. As she reaches into the glove compartment for the flask of coffee, a passing truck blares its horns at her, and she is momentarily aware of the danger of where she has chosen to stop, glad yet again that she traded the tiny Daihatsu for a Volvo.

"OK, just a minute," she mutters, filling the cup and trying to consider her options.

"But I don't want to do any of it," she thinks. "I'm sick of it. I'm tired of it all."

A motorcyclist with a dirty visor is travelling back from a romantic weekend.

Riding much too fast in his haste to be home, he misjudges the bend inside the tunnel, misses the grey Volvo parked on the hard-shoulder but clips the crash barrier beyond, loses control and skids across the tarmac, out of the tunnel and into the safety of the bushes.

A yellow *Calberson* delivery truck, with a tired driver who spent the weekend arguing with his wife, swerves to avoid the motorcycle and starts to skid and jack-knife across the glossy wetness of the three lanes.

Behind him, a juggernaut swerves bravely towards the hard shoulder and for a moment the reactive, nervy driver thinks that he might make it. For a few exhilarating seconds he thinks that he might be able to squeeze his huge articulated truck through the tiny space, but as he glides through the gap with only the slightest of scrapes, as he squeezes past the yellow *Calberson* truck on the left, and the crash barrier on the right, he sees a parked Volvo on the hard shoulder, then glimpses the terrified eyes of the woman within. As he ploughs into, then over her grey Volvo, sweat pours from every pore of his body.

In the terror of this collision he forgets to steer and as his truck piles into the curved wall of the tunnel it starts to tip and slide and scrape and he thinks he knows from other accidents he has witnessed that he will die right here right now. He feels terror then a strange silent peace as he gives up and slides into grey.

Behind that, a little white Fiat with a rain-spotted windscreen starts to skid. Inside it are two young men who, as chance would have it, are, at this very instant full of more love and hope for the future than either of them have ever experienced in their entire lives.

Cesaria Evora is incongruously singing her heart out through the car speakers, and the two men hold their breath and stare wide eyed as their car slews hopelessly towards the rear of the juggernaut, now on its side.

A split second before the moment of impact, the driver – Steve –

removes his foot from the brake enabling him to steer to the left. His half of the car will be stopped dead by the huge piercing bumper of the truck while the passenger side of the car will rip and sheer and twist and fold, catapulting to safety two freak survivors of the year's worst traffic accident; his most loved possession, a saxophone and his passenger, Mark.

Surprise

I don't know how I ended up in Brighton; I'm in a permanent state of surprise about it. Of course I know the events that took place, I remember the accident – or rather I remember the last time Steve looked into my eyes – before the grinding screeching wiped it all out. I remember it so vividly and with such a terrible aching pain that I feel as though my heart will stop every time I run the image through my mind.

As for the accident itself, I'm no longer sure what I remember or have dreamt, what I have been told or read in the newspaper clippings Owen, my brother, collected.

The headline I remember is, *French M-Way Pile-Up. 27 dead, Hundreds Injured,* but only one death mattered to me, and only one of the injuries. I know that could sound callous, but my heart just doesn't have space for anyone else's pain.

I know how I got from there to here as well, how I got from that unrecognisably deformed Fiat near Fréjus, to this sofa in Brighton. I know the mechanisms of humanity that dialled numbers, rushed people to the scene, cut me from the wreckage and drove us all, sirens screaming, to hospitals around the area.

Intellectually at least, I understand the unravelling of obligation, shared history and love that made Owen, my brother, leave his wife behind in Australia and fly half way around the world to sit holding my hand before scooping me up and bringing me here.

But it all seems so unexpected, so far from how things were *supposed* to be, that I am at a total loss to see how things will pan out, to see how things *can* ever pan out again.

I had a life and a job and a new boyfriend. I was supposed to hear him play saxophone, supposed to spend a dirty weekend of sex and laughter before sitting at work on a Monday morning pretty much like any other, and trying not to fall asleep at my computer screen. That's all that was supposed to happen.

So I am surprised, and my surprise is confounded by just how familiar Brighton feels, just how like Eastbourne where I grew up, it is; by how normal it feels to be sitting in this bay window, in this seaside town and to be hearing the sash windows rattling behind me as a distant seagull screams. How *obvious* it seems, to be sitting here looking at Owen opposite reading *The Guardian*.

It's all such a surprise, and so unsurprising, that I sit in numbed, stunned disbelief as I try to work out whether I am having trouble believing that I am here, or trouble believing that I was ever *there*. Did those twenty years since Owen and I last sat on opposite sofas in a seaside town really happen at all?

I open my mouth to ask him but think better of it. He's worried enough about me as it is, and, logically at least, I know the answer.

As if he has captured my thoughts Owen looks up at me and frowns.

I wonder what he is going to say to me, wonder what he will ask, how I will reply, what reassuring answer I will find to his concerned questioning.

But Owen just smiles at me. "You want a cup of tea?" he says.

I exhale. "Yes," I reply.

The reply came a little too quickly. I sounded breathless and I realise that I am also frowning, so I force a smile.

Owen raises an eyebrow at me, shakes his head and sighs. I think he's decided that I'm taking the piss but he says nothing.

He stands and turns towards the kitchen.

Family Ties

I sit and stare at the spring light falling through the bay windows forming hard geometrical squares on the varnished floorboards. Particles of dust jump and float in the light, pushed by invisible currents of air.

I drift, thinking of the same squares of light on another floor in another time; a carpeted floor dusted with Lego and Meccano from the big wooden box. I can almost feel the tension in the house, the alertness that I, that we all grew up with, our hidden antennae constantly scanning the horizon for the next breach of the peace.

I pull Owen's dusty bike from the cellar and pump the tyres. The bike, which is filthy, but apparently new – the tyres still have those little rubber mould-marks on them – sits next to an equally unused ab-machine and a sprung chest expander. I grin at the idea of Owen buying this stuff.

It's another grey day. I had forgotten just how terrifyingly grey England can be, even in springtime. Out of sheer habit, not from here but from Nice, I head down to the seafront and west.

The sky and sea are a uniform grey and the seafront is quiet. A very workaday atmosphere has descended upon the town. Men in suits stride purposely, replacing the casual strollers of the weekend. I reach the pier and move onto the cycle path.

I pass the *Grand Hotel* where Margaret Thatcher was nearly bombed out of existence, and remember actually being disappointed that she had escaped unscathed.

Opposite the Odeon, a man is painting the railings, slowly covering the faded blue with fresh paint. I smell the paint and remember when they repainted the railings of Eastbourne, remember the fuss that my parents made when they changed the colour, and I realise that these towns, Eastbourne, Brighton and Nice for that matter, are profoundly similar.

Of course working-class Eastbourne is clearly not Brighton, and gay-trendy-Brighton is clearly not poodles-and-gold Cote d'Azur, but these south-facing coastal towns, with their big facades and their pebble beaches; well there's a symmetry that cannot be denied.

I wonder just how much the destiny of a life is influenced by the desire for one's lost childhood; even Owen, I realise, lives on the seafront of south facing Melbourne, cycles along his very own east-west cycle path, halfway around the world to recreate the experience of his earliest memories.

When I get back home, Owen has returned. He's listening to classical music and leafing through a mass of paperwork spread across the dining table. He looks up as I enter and frowns.

"Hiya," he says. "We need to talk."

I make tea and sit opposite him. "This music's lovely," I say. "It seems really familiar."

Owen stares into the middle distance, still thinking about the documents before him, or searching for the name of the composer, or lost in some other reverie, I'm not sure which.

"Corelli," he says eventually. "Dad had it," he adds. "This very recording in fact."

I nod. "So what do we need to talk about?" I ask.

Owen stares into the distance again, apparently lost in the music, which is swelling to a sumptuous climax.

As the music wanes he snaps back into the room and looks at me.

"I spoke to the estate agent," he says. "About this house."

I nod.

"The guy is coming around to do a new valuation of the house but basically everyone agrees that it's not the best time to sell right now. They all say that house prices are still rocketing and that the best place for my equity is right here." He taps the table to show where *here* is.

I nod again and sip my tea.

"I don't want to rent it again though. It was so much hassle last time." He looks around the room before adding, "So I guess, what I need to know is if you're going to stay here. Or are you going back?"

I open my mouth to speak, but then close it again.

"Maybe you haven't decided yet?" Owen prompts.

"Yeah..." I say.

Owen nods. "I have to get back to Melbourne," he says.

I nod.

"I'm missing Beverley and we have that trip planned for the beginning of May," he says.

"Trip?" I question.

Owen nods. "We've rented a camper van. We're driving along the south coast. I thought I mentioned it."

I shrug. "I don't think so, but yeah, that sounds great."

I picture our father's camper van parked outside the house. Forever gleaming. Forever outside the house, always ready for the imminent, but never actually realised trip across Europe.

"So?" Owen nods at me, his eyebrows raised.

I frown at him.

"Will you be OK?" He leans across the table and stares into my eyes.

I glance away to avoid the intensity of his gaze. Since the accident expressions of love or sympathy just make me cry, and I'm exhausted with crying.

"If you need me to stay longer," he says.

I sigh. "No, I'm fine," I nod. "You've done so much already, I'm sorry to have…"

"No, this has been good." Owen lifts a pile of papers from the table. "I had to deal with all this," he says.

I nod.

"So?" Owen asks.

I realise that this is the third time he has asked the question. I look at him blankly and perform the mental equivalent of pulling straws.

"Here," I say. My voice has an unintended aggressive quality.

Owen smiles at me, encouraging me to continue.

"I can't really think about anything else right now," I say. "I need the space I guess."

Owen wrinkles his brow in concern and sighs.

The music is swelling again and I can feel pressure building behind my eyes, so I force a smile and stand.

As Owen shuffles paper behind me, I stand in the window and watch the sea and think about the dozy dreamlike quality within my mind.

I once dreamt I was falling from a skyscraper and when I awoke, I was convinced that I knew something new; that I knew how it feels to fall from a skyscraper, and though it was only a dream, though it never happened, I can still remember the sickening, free-fall sensation today.

Right now, I feel as though I have dreamt my own death; I feel like I know how it feels to have died.

I feel detached from the outcomes I always worried about, detached from the endless goals I was building towards, a relationship, a good job, a home of my own... They're all gone, all irrelevant. Equally all of the options seem to fit just fine. Here or Nice, what's to choose?

I lie down on the sofa and close my eyes and listen to the rise and fall of the music and the rustle of paper behind me. The feeling of dozing while someone works nearby is reassuring and wonderful. It will be hard when Owen leaves.

As I doze I forget where I am, and then as I linger on the edge of dreams I become confused about which sofa this is and I think I am back home in my flat in Nice, and then that I am on the sofa of our childhood home. As sleep overtakes me I think that Owen, behind me, is my father.

When I open my eyes everything looks more, almost too much. Too much *like itself*.

The information from my senses seems fresh and different; everything looks a little sharper, like when I took acid.

The colours are brighter, the sounds more distinct, and the floating dust strikes me as a little more beautiful than usual, perhaps a little less usual than usual. I yawn, stretch, then sit and scratch my head.

Owen looks up from his paperwork. "Nice sleep?" he asks.

I cough. "Yep," I say standing and heading for the door. "It was good."

Spinning Free

A grey Saturday morning, Owen and I alight at Victoria and trundle through the London underground with his suitcase.

We are talking about which museums I should visit after his departure and are completely unprepared when suddenly, mid-phrase, the moment is upon us; Owen must take the right hand path, I must take the left hand one. This suddenly is where the lives split. It's obvious and natural but we're not ready.

Owen looks at me shiny-eyed. "Um, I have to go this way," he says.

It's a strange moment, and the simple division of the tunnel belies the profundity of the moment.

We were born from the same womb, shared a house, toys, and even at times a bedroom. From that simple accident our lives will forever be intertwined. We will be together, then apart, then together again, as chance and need dictate, and right now, right here, one path leads to the Piccadilly line, Heathrow airport, then Singapore and Melbourne, and the other to the Northern line, to something called, "Life in Brighton."

It's arbitrary that I have decided to go back to Brighton, to live in Owen's house rather than return to Nice. It would seem more logical if Owen went back to his old house in Brighton, but bizarrely that life fits me too. I'm perfectly at home lying on his sofa in his lounge listening to his records.

In fact, it strikes me that any of these lives, in Nice, Brighton or Australia would suit either of us, and I have the strangest notion that in some way our lives are not only entwined, but almost interchangeable. We are in some profound way the same thing; we are at some level a single set of desires.

We are the lives our parents accustomed us to; we are their preferences for seaside towns, their love of France, their unrealised dreams of cross continental camping trips. We are the dreams they built for themselves and also, maybe more so, we are the dreams they didn't managed to realise, the ones they saved for us, passed on through their angst as the only route to true happiness, to true self realisation. We are that vision of a shiny camper van waiting to go somewhere else, somewhere better, somewhere happier.

I swallow hard. I feel shaky and scared but I bluff through it. "Yeah," I say, "I know."

Owen and I hug rigidly. "You look after yourself," he says.

I nod. "You too!" and aware of a tidal wave of emotion swelling suddenly from a distant undersea tremor, I whack him on the back, force a grin, and head off down my tunnel.

I don't look back until I hear his suitcase trundle into the echoing distance.

Slightly dazed, I wander along the tunnel towards the Circle Line.

I think about Owen heading off at a different vector, being pulled back towards his wife, his projects, his camper-van, and I think, not for the first time, how amazingly centred heterosexual lives are when compared to mine; just how many ties and stays – mortgages, dinner parties and schools – straight families have holding them centred, bang in the middle of their lives.

My own life seems so fragmented, so un-tied to anyone or any one place, that spinning like a top, or perhaps circling like an electron, the slightest nudge and I could oscillate out of control and spin off into space. I could end up just about anywhere. The possibilities are infinite, terrifying.

The greatest tie for most is the responsibility to feed and clothe and educate. It's something I will never have, and something I will never have to worry about either. My straight friends are so often jealous of my freedom, jealous precisely of the free-electron aspect of my existence, and I wonder briefly who actually gets the better deal.

I descend a small flight of steps and catch a glimpse of a poster advertising the National Gallery, which my father loved with a passion. As a child of course I thought it was boring and would watch my own feet scraping along the floor as he dragged me around the building.

As I head out onto the deserted platform, I decide, in memory of my childhood, to take my eyes, which are in some way his eyes too, not only to the Tate Modern, but to the National Gallery as well. I wonder if other peoples' childhoods are as intense, as all consuming as mine was. Can they too pause at any moment and sense in every atom of *their* being, the events of childhood that made them what they are today?

It's a shame we didn't organise this differently, I realise. Owen would have loved to visit the National gallery too. It's going to be hard without him. I knew that of course, but it's just hitting me now, quite how difficult everything will be.

I wonder if even Owen realises. I wonder if *even he* understands that I can do anything, go anywhere, and that in some way it matters not one jot. For what's the point in going to the National or the Tate on your own? What's the point of spending a day in London if you have no one to tell about it when you get home?

I take a deep determined breath. I will snap out of this. I will make this OK. I will get myself to the National, and then the Tate, and then back to Brighton, and it will all be *fine*.

The platform is deserted. There are only four of us: three standing waiting for the train, and a wide-eyed tramp on a bench muttering to himself.

"I can do this. It's easy," I tell myself. "Life is just one step at a time."

Wind from the tunnel blows a crisp packet along the floor and a distant screeching announces the train's arrival.

As the headlights of the train appear in the darkness, I absently note that at exactly the same moment the two other people standing on the platform move in opposite directions. The man in the sombre suit with the fluorescent pink tie steps backwards, and the ashen grey woman in the woollen coat forwards; it looks almost as though their steps have been choreographed.

As the train bursts from the tunnel, at the precise moment its leading edge thrusts into our presence becoming a rumbling, shrieking reality, the grey woman – for everything, her clothes, her hair, even her skin is grey – takes another step forwards. It's one step too many.

With unexpected grace she drifts and tips and pivots over the edge of the platform. In a strange weightless movement, drifting like an autumn leaf, she tumbles and vanishes beneath the hulk of the train.

The train shudders to an early halt halfway along the platform. The man in the suit sprints past me, tie flailing, to an intercom beside the tramp. My own mind is empty, possibilities of action have not even started to form, so I stand mouth open, staring at the space where the grey woman once existed as the image of her fall, of the weary elegance with which she tumbled out of life plays over and over in my mind.

A driver jumps, green-faced and shaking from the front of the train. Two staff in yellow jackets push me towards the exit. A tannoy bursts into life with a recorded message.

"Evacuate the station," it shrieks.

People from other platforms are flooding up the escalator, running terrified from an unknown menace.

"A track incident," the tannoy echoes. "Please leave by the nearest exit."

I let the machinery carry me slowly upwards and watch the people stream past.

"Why did she do that?" I wonder. "What can make someone so desperate, so completely hopeless that falling in front of a train seems like the best option?"

As I reach the top of the elevator, and am carried by the panicky swell out through open ticket barriers and into the dingy daylight of Leicester Square I think, *I can't tell Owen.*

Owen has gone, and I realise with a shudder that there's no one else I want to tell, no one I *can* tell. I lean back against the wall and watch people gushing past, streaming away from me, trying to put maximum distance between themselves and the unknown horrors of the tunnels.

It's such a brutal thing to have witnessed; I'm amazed to have seen such a thing and to have been simply ejected onto the pavement. Surely that can't be right?

Some distant part of my memory conjures up my own accident. It's not a visual memory but a physical one, the subsonic thud of the impact.

My hands are shaking so I thrust them into my pockets and stare at the crowds and wonder if it's actually possible to survive this world alone. As a single soul, isn't the world maybe just too hard-edged to actually *be* survivable?

I lean against a wall and stare numbly at a man selling newspapers. Stupidly I look at the posters to see if the tube suicide is already in the headlines.

I watch a Japanese woman fighting her way through the sudden crowd with a mass of high-class shopping bags and I see the tramp from the platform as he appears at the top of the stairs.

"Was he watching too?" I wonder. "Is he feeling shaky and alone as well?"

Carried by the crowd, he drifts along still muttering to himself. But as he passes in front of me, moving from left to right, I hear his voice.

"She had nobody," he says.

I'm not sure if he's talking to me or just rambling.

"That's why she did it," he says. "She had nobody."

I watch, frozen, as he disappears around the corner. My mouth fills with saliva and for a moment I think I might vomit, but then the feeling passes, and I cry instead, salty tears dropping shamelessly onto the tarmac as a hundred indifferent strangers stream past.

Double Entendre

I spend my days wandering along the pier, surfing the net, sleeping rather more than is normal, and watching English TV – a novelty.

I feel lonely and disjointed, as though this isn't my life, which of course it isn't.

I read Owen's old books, listen to Owen's old records, look through Owen's old windows at the sea. It's not even Owen's life that I'm living. It's his past.

I battle on, waiting for the wind to change and for things to start to feel like they fit, but on Friday as I stand looking at the sea, I realise that I haven't actually spoken to a human being for three days. I haven't uttered one word since the woman in Safeway said, "That'll be twenty-two-fifty."

I know that this isn't healthy. I know from experience that the time has come to be brave, and acting quickly, before I have time to chicken out, I swipe my keys from the counter and head out the door.

The *Bulldog Tavern* is shouting, heaving, laughing.

It's only eight pm and my initial shock at how busy the place is fades as I remember that unlike France it will close at eleven pm. Back in Nice, people don't even go out until midnight.

The noise and the laughter are also a big surprise after years of living overseas. French bars are such a serious affair; here people look like they are actually having fun.

As I push towards the counter, I scan the diverse shapes and forms around me, none of the homogenous thin, olive skinned posing of the Côte d'Azur here. There are fat guys with beards and thin guys in suits, and old men in leather, and, more than anything, I note that there are lots and lots of people, of all shapes and sizes, with buzz hair cuts and goatee beards. I have slipped, unnoticed, into the fold.

I randomly select a pint of bitter and move back to the centre of the room in order to free up the limited access to the bar.

For a while I fidget, unable to choose a point amongst the crowd and a position, leaning, sitting or standing that feels comfortable. I finally settle against a pillar, hanging up my denim jacket and placing my pint on a little shelf.

I have never been good at hanging around alone in bars, it has always made me feel self conscious, but by the time I have drunk half a pint the place has become so full that it would be impossible for anyone to realise that I *am* alone.

I note a few people watching me. I guess that Brighton remains a small town, and I am fresh meat after all.

"Here we go again," I think. The thought depresses me.

I glance around the room again and my eyes settle on a couple against the opposite wall. They are the most identical pair I have ever seen, the same height, the same shaved heads, matching goatee beards. Even their jeans are the same tone of blue. They look slightly ridiculous but, it has to be said, *cute.*

One of them winks at me and, slightly embarrassed to have been caught staring, I turn away and face the other side of the bar.

I end up wedged between a fit-but-knows-it guy in cycle shorts on the left, a very ugly man in beautiful one-piece motorcycle leathers behind, and a diverse group of slightly drunken men in front.

To distract myself from the two clones and they from me, I stare vaguely into the group in front as though I am involved in their conversation. They are talking about someone's holiday plans and whether his boyfriend will cancel just before the departure. Most people seem to think that this is what will happen.

I'm so pushed into the group I start to feel as though I *am* involved and the main man, a big guy with a beard and a beer gut glances at me with smiling eyes as he entertains everyone with his spiel. After a while I realise that he does think that I am with them.

His neighbour – a thin guy in a suit – asks him how the man in question managed to take four weeks leave.

"Well exactly!" the big guy laughs. "Especially because his boss is his ex... I mean, they're not exactly on the best of terms."

"Apparently he put the form in on the day Joe went on holiday, so it just slipped in without anyone noticing," comments an older guy in a leather jacket.

Without thinking, I lean forward and comment, "fnarr, fnarr," a mocking laugh I recall from way back that indicates an unintended double entendre.

It's the beer talking, and I immediately realise how rude this is, especially as I don't know anyone in the group or even who they are talking about. But a couple of the guys laugh heartily and the others smile at me.

"Try that in France and you're dead," I think.

The guy in the suit says, "I can't believe you missed that one Burt; you're losing your touch."

The group opens to let me in; I feel I have to say something.

"Hey, do you know how they say double entendre in French?" I ask.

"Um, double entendre?" asks one.

"Nah, I know this one," says the fat guy. "Jean told me." The guy glances behind him, then shrugs and continues. "Apparently they don't have a word for it in French."

"They don't," I agree.

A man appears at his side. It is one of the clones. His double is just behind him holding two pints of beer.

"We say *double-sense*, but that isn't necessarily rude, so it's not really the same," he says, his voice smooth, his accent French.

"We don't really use what you call double entendres in French humour."

"So what you're saying," laughs the guy in the suit, "is that we use your language better than you do."

Jean smiles wryly. "Maybe," he laughs.

The conversation drifts around France and the French. Jean and his twin partner – who amusingly turns out to be called John – take position either side of me and chat. I can feel a move coming and I find the idea amusing and actually quite flattering.

By my third pint I am feeling amazingly relaxed, and this in turn has created a happy feeling of homecoming. It's a surprise to me, but I am realising that despite fifteen years in France it is still only in England that I can strike up an instant rapport, only in England that I can feel comfortable enough to join in an overheard conversation.

As I start my fourth pint, the crowd is diminishing, and the clones are standing either side of me, touching me regularly as they talk, a prod here, a playful punch there.

John tells me that they have been together for eleven years.

I nod impressed. "I don't know how you do it," I say.

Jean winks at me. "We'll show you if you want."

I laugh. "No, I meant how do you stay together so long."

Jean smiles at me. "We'll show you if you want," he deadpans. "The thing is to keep the sex life healthy, the rest is following."

John leans in and says "And our sex life is *very* healthy. With a little help from our friends."

"Here it comes," I think, and I wonder how I will reply.

A strange feeling comes over me. A sensation that I am not myself, or rather that I am watching myself.

I surprise myself by wondering what he would have done, the *he* in question, being Mark.

Mark didn't do threesomes. He may have fantasised about them, sometimes he even almost got involved in one, but he never *quite* did it. I wonder, what with life being so fragile, and what with everything Mark thought so important turning out so elusive and temporary, well, I wonder if he was right.

"We have a great set-up," Jean is telling me with a salacious smile, adding in French, "Notre cave est un veritable Disneyland." – *Our cellar is a veritable Disneyland.*

John, feigning surprise at an idea that has supposedly just popped into his head, exclaims, "Hey! Why don't we go back and have a drink there now?"

Though intrigued by the idea of visiting Disneyland and turned on by the idea of having sex with the identical clone-show, I don't feel ready for anonymous sex. It would somehow seem disrespectful of Steve. Plus a voice within is outraged and imploring me to say no to the proposition. *"Have a threesome?"* It says. *"You are joking?"*

"But maybe random sex would be the best cure for my blues," I tell it. "Maybe it's just what the doctor ordered, maybe it would close a chapter. Don't be so judgemental."

John frowns at me as my weird internal dialogue continues.

"People always say don't be judgemental," I think. "But aren't our judgements about what's good and what's bad precisely what defines who we are? Without judgement who am I?"

I open my mouth to say, "Maybe another time," but Jean interrupts.

"Geez, it's nothing heavy you know," he says. "It's only fun. It's only sex."

And for some strange reason, that clinches it. It strikes me as the most honest statement of intent I have ever heard.

Disneyland

During the walk, the mirror-couple march either side of me.

I could feel as if I have a bodyguard, or perhaps as if I am surrounded, and in different circumstances that could be scary, or exciting, but the air of camp lingering behind their every word, is anything but virile, anything but scary.

Jean is telling me that the lounge still smells of paint, that they only just finished decorating it. John is interrupting him like an excited puppy to tell me that he chose all of the furnishings and made the curtains and cushion covers himself.

My fantasy world is evaporating fast and yet strangely, the simple idea that empty sex with these two might fill some void within me, that it may just help me reconnect with my sense of *me*; the idea that a threesome with John and Jean might act as a kind of unauthorised electric shock therapy is becoming ever more compelling.

"Here we are," John says, indicating with a flourish of his hand that we have arrived.

The house is in the middle of an elegant two-storey crescent. We climb the steps to the front door and as Jean opens the door he places a hand on my arse pushing me across the threshold.

John, who is behind, says, "Ta Da!"

I bet that a few people have balked and run away at this point, not through fear but in sheer revulsion.

The curtains, heavy Dralon, are peach coloured, as is the deep pile nylon wall-to-wall carpet and the enormous sofa.

The cushions have been covered, by John's own fair hands so he tells me, with thick canvas carrying an ethnic print. They would be tasteful were they not, also, peach.

"Sit there," Jean instructs, pointing me to the sofa.

John winks at me and says, "We'll be back in a jiffy."

I force a grin and sit in the sea of peach wondering just how long it is since I last heard the phrase, *back in a jiffy*.

The lounge has been knocked through to the dining room, which has the same colour carpet occupied by glass and wrought iron dining table and chairs.

The bookcases contain sets of identical spines which say more about misplaced ideas of interior design than culture, whilst the surfaces are occupied by a tidily arranged series of geometrically modern candle holders, vases and paperweights; generic items from Habitat or Ikea. Part of the sea of consumer junk that those stores throw at us every year, the same stuff people always seem to give me at Christmas and which I have to wait until springtime to bin.

When the twins return, their outfits, leather chaps, studded posing pouches, big motorcycle boots and harnesses, are so incongruous with the surroundings that it is as much as I can do not to snigger.

They sit either side of me and serve drinks from a pseudo antique bar, which for some reason has mock leaded windows.

"So what do you think?" asks Jean proudly.

"Yeah, great I say," perusing the two.

If one can just ignore the fact that we're sitting in a sea of peach drinking sherry from a mock antique bar, the boys look pretty sexy, but truth be told, I'm having trouble ignoring.

"I'm glad you like it," John says. "It's always so nice when people appreciate all the hard work." He plumps a cushion as he says this.

I assume he has misunderstood. We are talking not about the room but about the outfits they have put on for my benefit, but the couple, at least, seem in tune.

"Took ages to choose the sofa though," Jean says.

I think, "*No. I can't do this.*" I will make my excuses and leave.

But as I open my mouth to say so, Jean interrupts.

"We spotted you straight away," he says. "The second you walked in we both thought, wow!"

"You're new to Brighton aren't you?" John asks.

The flattery calms my nerves. I even blush as I thank them, and start to explain how I came here less than a month ago.

John asks concernedly if I know anyone in Brighton.

"Moving to a new place is hard," he says. "We can introduce you to *lots* of people."

As I start to forget the peach surrounding me, Jean swigs the last of his sherry and nudges his partner.

"Time to take the prisoner downstairs I think," he says.

John stands. "Indeed," he agrees standing.

"Look. Guys..." I say as they each grab an elbow. "Maybe we can do the downstairs thing another time."

Jean laughs at me. "Relax, there's no pressure. Just come and look, you have to see our setup, we're not going to jump you or anything."

I *am* intrigued to see their set-up, and they are so un-scary except in terms of their taste in furnishings that I decide to go see. I'm pretty sure I could take on the two of them if I needed to, even *with* my dodgy leg.

So I follow John to the door under the stairs and then on, down into the dimly lit cellar.

"Best room in the house," he says as he descends before me.

Jean rests a hand on my shoulder as he climbs down behind.

The cellar is fabulous and I am truly dumb struck. Were these not Mr and Mr Peach, I *would* be afraid.

The rough stone walls are dimly lit by the flickering light of fake torches. In the middle of the room, suspended from the ceiling, is a complex set of pulleys and chains, the kind of thing you see at a *Kwik-Fit* garage.

Along the wall is a huge tool rack containing a selection of toys worthy of any sex shop: clamps, rings, leather gear, hand-cuffs and a full set of dildos, carefully laid out from small to large.

It reminds me of my father's tool bench and spanner sets, and I briefly wonder if the one dildo the boys can never find is the one they use the most.

"Wow," I say, touching a hanging chain. "What's all this for?"

Jean laughs and slides a hand to my arse.

"If you want to know that then you are obliged to participate!" he laughs, his French accent suddenly quite strong.

I laugh nervously but pull gently away. "I'm not sure that right now is..."

"Lache toi!" he says. – *Let yourself go!* "It's just a new experience."

"Yeah, but I'm not sure it's an experience I want to have," I say. "I'm not sure that this kind of sex is..."

"Who said anything about sex?" he says. "Just try on the gear and we'll show you how the pulley works. You decide where you want to stop."

For the first time since the accident my dick twitches, and bizarrely there are no voices in my mind raising objections, so as Jean lifts a huge mass of leather straps and buckles, I shrug.

"It's amazing being suspended in this thing I promise you," he says.

"We'll just put it on, and other than that we won't even touch you," John insists.

I look at the complex harness and remember when I was in New York, remember saying no to exactly this. I remember wondering ever since just what it would have been like.

My hesitation is a giveaway and the boys nod and smile as if a decision has been reached.

"I guess…" I say vaguely. "But I'm not sure I want to go any further, really I'm not."

Jean winks at his partner who grins back. "That's no problem," he says.

A wave of heat ripples through my body. It starts at my brow and sweeps down, a wave of panic.

I wonder if I can trust them, I wonder if they will balk at the sight of the scars on my knee and my arm, I wonder if my knee will hurt, I wonder…

But strangely I stay silent. I stand and watch myself let John pull my T-shirt over my head.

"It'll be fine," he says, and for some reason, I believe him.

Jean moves behind me, takes my wrist and starts to buckle a leather wristband around it.

"What's this?" he asks, running a finger along my scar.

"Bad car accident," I say, suddenly embarrassed.

"Don't blush," Jean says. "It's sexy."

"And no risks!" I say. "I'm negative OK?"

John crouches before me and starts to remove my trainers.

Jean, behind me, says, "You don't listen. We already agreed, no sex, nothing but suspension. Relax."

John removes the second trainer and pulls down my jeans and my boxer shorts. My dick springs erect. I feel myself blush.

"Hmm, you're enjoying this aren't you!" he laughs.

Jean leans around me and peers at my dick.

"Hmmm, shame to put that to waste," he says.

They remove my jeans and clip restraints to my ankles. John stands and lifts my arms. His partner, still behind, immediately clips the d-rings of the bracelets to two chains hanging from the ceiling.

It's all strangely business-like, a well rehearsed ritual that feels anything but sexual. As he tugs on the pulleys, stretching my arms taut, I start to feel fear again.

"Look," I say. "I'm not sure actually that I feel that comfortable with this whole..."

As I say this, John clips my feet to two floor chains, completely immobilising me.

"Hey!" I say. "Is anyone listening to me?"

Jean speaks quietly into my right ear. "Just calm down," he says. "No-one's doing anything you haven't given permission for, so relax and enjoy."

"But..."

In a surprise movement, Jean slaps my arse. Hard.

As I open my mouth to shout, he pulls a gag between my teeth.

"Umm," I protest.

"Now shut up and relax," he says, buckling the gag behind my head.

I protest as loudly as I can but Jean just laughs.

"There's nothing you can do now, nothing you can say, so just relax, give in," he says.

For a while I protest through my nose. I thrash around too, but it only makes the men laugh all the more, and slowly an unexpected, nervy calm comes over me. I have given in. I have resigned myself to whatever is going to happen.

Jean pulls a hood over my head. I can still see through the eyeholes but my hearing becomes muffled. Images of the gimp in Pulp Fiction come to mind and I wonder if I will be living in a box from now on. Terrifyingly my dick twitches at the idea. Obtusely I think, "Thank god my mother can't see me now."

John stands in front and looks into my eyes while Jean, behind, finishes lacing the hood and moves yet another chain into place, clipping it to a ring on the top, holding my head upright.

It's weird. I feel like a museum exhibit being dispassionately tended to.

I hold my breath to listen to them speaking.

"In a minute, once he relaxes..." I hear Jean say. "He'll be begging..."

Then, one after the other, Jean covers my eyes.

I hold my breath for a moment, considering the new leathery dark. I shift my weight, trying different ways of standing and hanging on the wrist restraints. My heart is racing and I am sweating in fear.

At the same time, the taste of the gag, the smell of the hood, the very idea of my nakedness hanging before them arouses me.

Nothing happens for a while, and then I feel hands fastening a new series of straps around my legs.

A finger runs along the outline of the scar on my knee; they reposition the strap lower to avoid it. For some reason this attention to detail reassures me. My heart starts to slow.

Someone reaches from behind and fastens straps around my waist and my torso, then another around my neck.

The feeling of skin on skin contact is magnified by the darkness. Just the sensation of their hands endlessly fiddling with straps and buckles feels incredible.

Someone's leg brushes my dick and instinctively I writhe towards the contact eliciting a laugh that penetrates the muffled silence.

For a while some complex operation of attaching goes on behind me, I can feel the four hands working simultaneously connecting chains and ropes to rings on the straps; it feels like they're doing some kind of puzzle, or macramé.

"I knitted it myself," I think.

The process takes maybe ten minutes, though with only the sound of my breathing it has becomes difficult to judge time.

Then suddenly it happens. The weight disappears from my feet. I start to fly.

The experience is amazing, truly out-of-body. With the weight distribution provided by the complex web of straps surrounding my body I don't feel suspended by any particular point, I just feel like I am floating.

I hear vague metallic noises through the hood and slowly I start to lean forwards, to jerkily tilt, a movement that continues until I am horizontal.

My legs slowly spread, I cannot aid or resist, and a bar is clipped between them holding them wide apart. I can feel the cold air against my arse and, in spite of myself; I start to ache with desire.

I float like this for a while, maybe five minutes, dimly aware of the couple moving around me, more and more obsessively aware of the state of my dick, hanging free, now hard, now soft, now hard again.

The dark isolation magnifies the desire for skin-to-skin contact to the point of madness. I feel as if I have taken ecstasy.

I ache for more. My legs are open and my dick is pointing at the ground and I want more. I start to want *anything* as long as it's more. But I can't ask for it.

After a few minutes there is a jerky shifting in the chains connected to the hood and my head starts to lift, to point forwards.

In an unexpected movement that makes me convulse in surprise, Jean rips off the eye patches.

He peers in at me, mere inches away. "You OK in there?" he asks.

I nod as much as the chains permit.

John who is out of sight runs a finger along the crack of my arse as his partner leans into my ear and says, "You want more?"

I arch against the finger as much as the straps will allow and make an "Um," noise through my nose.

John laughs demonically and pulls his partner into view.

The two stand mere inches from my face and stare at each other.

They kiss, delicately at first, then deeply.

John runs his hands down over Jean's back, down to his arse, peeking pertly from his shiny chaps.

The two men kiss and stroke each other, pausing to play first with each other's nipples before moving lower to their pouches. They stroke and rub and caress each other through the leather, before unclipping them.

In an attempt to generate some sensation in my own body I wriggle and writhe and am rewarded by the slightest sensation as my skin moves against the straps.

Mere inches from my suspended face, Jean rolls on a condom, turns John around, and slowly, sensuously they start to fuck.

Occasionally, when John looks up, he stares me straight in the eye. His pupils are dilated and my dick twitches and judders in sympathy.

Live porn. Never has my frustration felt more complete.

Jean starts to pulls on John's harness as he pumps into him and their grunts get louder and start to pierce the material covering my ears.

As if I am a camera, they pause occasionally and change position so that I get a different view.

I tremble and twitch. Whoever would have thought being a truly passive observer could be so exciting?

The grunts and moans increase as the two men slam together, until, in a crescendo of slapping and pumping, tugging and shrieking, they orgasm.

As Jean pulls out and removes the condom, John casts me the broadest of smiles.

I wiggle in my straps to remind them of my presence and Jean responds by standing in front of me. He moves so close that I can no longer see his head, only his groin.

He undoes two zips near my ears. The loudness of the zips after the silence is deafening. He fingers his dick. "You want this now?" he asks.

Despite the shame I feel at my own desire, I nod and grunt.

He laughs. "That," he says, "Is how you turn someone into a sex slave."

He steps back and John reappears at his side, an unfeasibly large dildo in hands.

"You want this?" he asks.

To my shame, I nod and thrash, desperate for them to touch me, to release me from my enforced voyeurism.

Jean puts the dildo down on the workbench in front of me.

"Another time, maybe," he says. "When you know what you want."

The two men move out of sight and I am left alone and suspended. I hang there for what seems a long time, maybe an hour, maybe twenty minutes; it's really hard to say. Time moves strangely when there is no possibility of action.

My state of arousal fades to boredom and with it the voice of reason, temporarily silenced by desire, starts to complain anew, asking how the hell we got into this mess, and what kind of a slut I think I am.

I make some groaning noises but no one responds. I thrash around a little in protest and listen to my own chains clinking, but nothing happens.

I start to worry about getting home. I start to get angry, even a little scared, but just as I begin to sweat again, the chains clunk and shudder and my head starts to rise and my feet move hesitantly towards the ground.

As I am lowered, John removes first the hood, then the gag.

"Game Over," he grins.

I take a deep breath of fresh air, and start immediately to complain.

"Hey don't worry about me," I complain.

But I say it unconvincingly, for the censor is back. The censor is looking at the huge dildo on the table and telling me that I got off lightly, real lightly.

John laughs. "You need to be more careful what you ask for," he says. "Because round here you always get what you ask for. No more, no less."

Past Tense

I sit dreamily at Owen's table sipping my mid-morning coffee and thinking about the episode at John and Jean's house. The whole event has taken on a dream-like quality, as if it wasn't me who did it at all, or at least as if it doesn't matter, as if it had all the importance of eating ice cream.

The similarity of the incident to a near miss I had in New York nearly ten years ago is obvious, and that event became one of my most enduring sexual fantasies.

This time I went further, and it was truly one of the hottest experiences I have ever had, but why *was* it so hot? Is it the frustration of non-completion, or is it something else, something unhealthy? Is it the inherent helplessness of the situation I put myself in that was so exciting – the *danger* of it all?

And if I do go back and complete – whatever that entails – will it lose its power and become nothing but a sullied experience with a couple of unsuitable partners, something I have done with my sexuality that was simply inappropriate? Or maybe it's like heroin – maybe each fix just gets better and better; maybe each trip has to be more and more extreme until suddenly you find yourself doing *n'importe quoi*.

I sip my coffee.

And what about sex as an expression of love in all of that? Doesn't one exclude the other?

I'm interrupted by something dropping through Owen's letterbox. I cross the room expectantly hoping for my first batch of forwarded mail, Owen hasn't lived here for years and his own mail dried up long ago, but it's only a free newspaper.

I return to the table and flick through, daydreaming and half-heartedly reading the adverts. I'm surprised not to have received any of my French mail yet.

I make a "Hum," noise of reflection, and pick up the phone.

Isabelle answers immediately.

"Hello stranger," she says, discreetly rebuking me for not having called more often. "Your cat is on my lap right now," she tells me.

I smile. My cat. Poor Paloma. She seems to belong to a whole different era.

"So how are you?" I ask. "Are you two getting along OK?"

Isabelle laughs. "Yeah. She wakes me up a bit at night, but I'm getting used to it. It's quite nice really. Paloma is having a lovely holiday, aren't you?" she coos.

"But how are *you*?" she asks, her voice suddenly serious.

Me. I pause, thinking about it.

"How am I?" I wonder. I haven't asked *myself* the question.

"I don't know really," I say uncertainly. "I guess I'm fine."

"Are you..." Isabelle says.

But I interrupt her. I don't know what she was going to say, but I can tell from her voice that it's on a touchy feely level, and I very much want to stay in the material world.

"I was wondering," I ask. "Did you find the time to check my post?"

Isabelle coughs. "Yeah. Actually I was hoping you'd phone," she says brightly.

I frown. "Yeah?"

"Mm," she says. "Most of it was just junk. But you did get a cheque."

"A cheque?" I repeat.

I can hear her hunting through the pile. I exhale and bite my lip.

"Yeah, it's from Axa," she says. "Is that Steve's insurance?"

I wince in pain at the statement. "Is it Steve's insurance?" I wonder. "Can it be Steve's insurance? If he's dead?"

"I expect so," I say.

"Maybe it should be Steve's old insurance," I think, but then, it's not like Steve has any *new* insurance. To avoid thinking about the reality of his death my mind is losing itself in a question of grammar.

"It's quite a big cheque actually," she says.

I nod slowly.

"Hello?" Isabelle prompts.

"Yes, I'm still here," I say.

"Ah, here it is," she says. "Yes. Axa. It's..."

"Just send it then," I interrupt. "Or, no... Maybe you could just pay it in," I say. "Oh, I don't know."

"I think I can do that, can't I?" Isabelle says. "If you send me your bank details."

I clear my throat. "Yes. I think so," I reply.

Isabelle sighs. "Well. Do you want me to? You don't sound sure."

I frown. What I'm actually not sure about is if I want the cheque *at all.*

"Mark?"

"Look, I feel funny about it, I mean, should I? Do you think I should? In a way it doesn't seem..."

"Mark," Isabelle interrupts my rambling. "It's not from Steve. It's from his insurance. It's a cheque from a huge company that owes you money for your injuries, that's all."

The accident rips through my mind. I feel sick. My chest feels tight. I shudder.

"I..." I say.

I jerk my foot up and down on the floor and bite my bottom lip and nod at the receiver.

"Just say *yes*, Mark," Isabelle says. "Just say, *yes please, pay it in.*"

"OK, yes please," I say. "Pay it in."

"Good. So how have you been?" Isabelle asks again.

"Fine," I say.

"And your knee, how is it?"

"Fine," I say, my voice rasping slightly. "I keep forgetting about it actually," I tell her honestly.

"And the scar?"

I pull my sweatshirt forwards and glance at the scar on my shoulder.

"Fine too," I say. "So, anything else? In the post, I mean."

Isabelle clears her throat, audibly switching back into business mode.

"Nothing much," she says, leafing through the envelopes. "Oh, yes, there is one I didn't open. A proper letter."

I frown. "A proper letter?"

"Yeah," she says. "You know, handwritten."

I rub the bridge of my nose. "Who's it from?" I ask.

"Well, I don't know," she says. "I didn't think I should... Shall I open it then?"

"Sure," I say. I can hear that she's already ripping the envelope open.

"Oh," she says.

"What is it?"

"Maybe I should just forward this," she says. "Maybe you should read it alone."

"No, it's fine, honestly. Who's it from?" I ask.

"It's from Steve's parents," Isabelle says.

I slowly run my tongue across my front teeth.

"From his *parents*," I repeat.

Isabelle mumbles as she skims the text.

"Oh, I see. Look," she says. "I'm sorry Mark. I shouldn't have opened it."

I shrug. "Just read it?" My voice sounded unintentionally irritable so I add, "*Please*?"

"Well, they're having a remembrance service it says. It's on Steve's birthday. Just his friends and family."

I clear my throat. "A service," I say.

"Do you want me to read it to you?"

I sigh. "No, just, um, send it on will you?"

"OK, if you..."

"Actually, just keep it," I say.

"Really?"

"Yeah," I say. "Whenever it is, I won't be able to go."

"It's the fifth of June."

I swallow. "Really?" I say.

"Humm," Isabelle says, apparently still reading.

"That's the day before *my* birthday," I say.

"Yeah," she says.

"His birthday was the day before mine," I say.

"Yes, I just realised. So you're not going?"

"No," I say sharply. I clear my throat. "I can't go."

"Maybe you should, you know. It might do you good. Will you actually be back by then?"

"I don't really know," I mumble. "Look, I'm sorry Isa, but I've got to go now," I say. "I'll call you later in the week, OK?"

Isabelle coughs. "OK Mark. I'm sorry," she says.

"Yeah," I say. "Never mind, eh? Any others like that, just, you know, post them on."

"OK. Bye then," she says.

I drop the receiver onto the base. I stare at it numbly for a moment, and then, for some reason I start to feel angry; for some reason I start to feel furiously angry.

I pace to the window, and then I pace back again and stare angrily at the telephone. Then I return to the window and stare at the sea.

"Steve's," I mutter. "Steve's insurance, Steve's birthday, Steve's friends, Steve's family."

I shake my head. "Doesn't anyone know? He's *dead*."

Past Imperfect

Steve's telephone resurrection stays with me for a few days, haunting my sleep with tortured nightmares and making my days silent and thoughtful.

I battle along the windswept seafront and walk along the pier. Looking through the wooden slats at the murky depths below, I ponder his death and his unexpected continuing existence.

The more I think about it, the more absurd it seems that someone can simply cease to exist, and the stranger it seems that everything that defined them, everything that *defines* them, from the jobs they did, to the clothes that they chose, from the holiday snaps to friends and family, and above all our memories, our opinions of them, should continue obstinately to exist.

Within a few days I am feeling chronically lonely again but the call has been useful in at least one way. I'm now certain that I'm not ready to go back. I'm not ready to face the concerned glances, the sympathetic pats on the shoulder.

In fact the only people I can even envisage talking to are those who know nothing of this. That I realise, means meeting new people, or delving into the distant past.

Right now through the bay window, I can see a beautiful orange VW camper-van which I think could be Jenny's. Something tells me that only an old hippy like her could have enough respect for the iconic VW camper van to keep one in such perfect condition.

A woman climbs down from the driver's seat, and if it *is* Jenny she has put on a lot of weight. But even after fifteen years, something about the way she holds herself, the way she pulls her windswept hair from her face tells me that it is indeed her. My old friend, my last ever girlfriend, my last ever abortive attempt at being straight.

I run outside to meet her and amid the salty gusts we hug awkwardly. I run my hand along the curved roof-panel of the van.

"I love the van!" I say.

She smiles. "Yeah, isn't it great?"

"It looks brand new."

She laughs. "Believe it or not, it is. They still make them in Brazil."

Then she grabs my arm and pulls me towards the house. "Enough of the car though, I've been sitting in the thing for nearly two hours. What I need is a cup of tea."

Jenny does want tea, but it turns out that she doesn't mind talking about the van at all.

"They're very difficult to get," she tells me. "Nick got this one imported specially from Brazil, cost nearly twenty thousand by the time we got our hands on it."

I pour the boiling water over the teabags. "Worth it though," I say. "The ultimate hippy statement."

Jenny frowns. "I don't think that any twenty thousand pound car can be called a hippy statement," she says. "But we looked at all the new ones, and they're all like ice cream vans, or disabled buses."

"Well," I say, handing her the tea. "You're definitely more Miss Hippy than Mr Whippy."

She glares at me. "Mark," she says. "It's *so* not a hippy van."

I raise my palms in submission. "OK. Just joking."

"Yes, well don't." She says this without apparent irony.

As we sit and chat I realise that the last fifteen years have changed Jenny more than I would have thought possible. Or they have changed me so much I don't recognise her anymore.

In my memories, she was a witty, sarcastic, happy-go lucky kind of girl; a pot-smoking, hard-drinking, man-chasing wench. But I wonder if my memories are accurate. I wonder if I haven't somehow mixed Jenny up with a whole era of youth, a whole era of fun. Maybe none of us are those people now, maybe it's just the mind playing tricks on the past and we never really were.

I wonder when she will ask me why I am back in the UK, and I wonder how I will answer, what I will actually tell her. For the moment she is far too busy telling me about her house.

"Nick wanted a fitted *Smallbone* kitchen," she says. "He just didn't want to settle for anything less."

I have no idea what a *Smallbone* kitchen is, but I nod

appreciatively.

"So we had the whole bottom floor gutted before we moved in. I just couldn't live in a building site. I'm too old for that stuff."

My mind drifts, and I find myself nodding fraudulently as I compare different aspects of old Jenny and new Jenny – the fun, irreverent Jenny of my youth, and this strange Surrey advertising rep.

"Smeg," she says, leaning towards me. "You know *Smeg*?"

I snap back into the room. "Smug?" I ask.

"No *Smeg*!" she laughs. "It's a brand. Kitchen appliances. Anyway, whatever, it doesn't matter. They're very good and *very* expensive. But we thought, well, you only buy this stuff once, don't you..."

I try to remember a rude word lurking in my mind that sounds like *Smeg* but for the moment it escapes me.

"So the oven and the fridge, washing machine, well, it's all *Smeg*," she is saying.

I think about it and decide that I have never heard of *Smeg*. *"Maybe they don't have Smeg in France,"* I think.

But I know smug. Smug is universal.

After an hour or so of uninspiring conversation we head out for a stroll along the seafront. I've been feeling bored and irritable but the wind and the sun blow the feeling away and I consciously decide to re-connect with my old friend.

"So do they still call you Jenny Snog?" I interrupt her. "Or is that all over now you're married."

Jenny freezes, and then laughs falsely.

"Jenny Snog?" she says. "Gosh, I'd forgotten that completely!"

I nod.

"Yes you used to call me that!" she laughs. "God knows why."

I grin. "I know exactly why," I say, deciding to push her, to force her to remember who she used to be. "It's not exactly complicated," I add.

But Jenny now wants to talk about me, snapping a lid on the past.

"So why are you back in England anyway?" she asks. "Don't tell me you got sick of the Côte d'Azur!"

I tell her very little.

"I had a bit of a car accident," I say. "I'm making the most of my time off work by having a holiday," I explain.

But I don't tell her about Steve. I don't tell her that my new boyfriend, the man with whom I was in the first throes of a love affair, was crushed and ripped out of this world. I don't think she, or I for that matter, could deal with it, and even if we could, I just don't have the words to sufficiently describe it.

So we rest on the surface of things. We stick to cups of tea, and brands of skin-cream, to kitchen appliances and local politics.

It reminds me of the conversations I used to have with my hairdresser Daniel. In the days when I had hair, that is.

At six pm Jenny heaves herself into the driver's seat and with the briefest of waves, strains and turns the steering wheel as she pulls away.

I guess I won't be seeing her for a while, and I guess I'm quite relieved about that.

As I climb the steps to the front door, I think, *"Smegma. That's the word."*

I wish I had thought of it before she left.

The Gift

It's just after seven as I walk into the *Bulldog*.

I look around, half hoping, half afraid of seeing John and Jean but they aren't here, in fact, virtually *no one* is here.

Two couples, all four men in their fifties, are sitting at the bar, and a lone man occupies the raised platform at the far end.

It's been a bright bank holiday Monday, and the town has been teeming with male muscle. I'm surprised and disappointed by the lack of action. My walk along the seafront has left me feeling horny and energised.

I order a beer and position myself against the central pillar where I can see the single guy at the far end.

He has a pointy black beard and a pierced eyebrow. He's cute, but apparently too engrossed in his reading to look up at me.

After only a few minutes, I decide that the fun has to be elsewhere, so I cross the bar and ask Mr Pierced eyebrow for a copy of the local free magazine, *Gscene*.

He reaches to his left, smiles briefly, and with a single stroke of his beard, returns to his reading.

It was a good smile, but certainly not a conversation opener, but as I start to walk away, he speaks.

"Legends," he says.

I turn back with an amused frown. "Sorry?" I say.

He places a finger on the page to mark his place, and looks up at me, a cheeky smile on his lips.

"Everyone's in Legends," he says. "It's happy hour till nine tonight."

I nod and let out a bemused laugh. "Thanks," I say.

The man shrugs and returns to his reading.

Intrigued as to how he managed to answer my unasked question, I cross the bar and return to my drink.

Legends is packed. I fight my way to the bar, order a drink, and as I am squeezing my way back through the buzz cuts and leather jackets to a space I have spotted, someone calls my name.

I look over at the crowd in the bay window and catch site of John's grinning face, then Jean's next to him.

"Mark!" he repeats. The group opens, anemone-like, sucking me in.

The couple kiss me hello on both cheeks, French-style, and John runs through a rapid-fire series of introductions.

"Mark, this is Peter, Ben, Baz, Greg..."

He peers behind me, then pushes me gently to one side, "and this is Tom," he says.

I turn to see Tom holding out a hand, grinning.

"We meet again," he says.

I smile. "Yes," I say.

For some reason I blush.

"You found *Legends* OK then," he says.

He turns to John and explains, "We just met in the Bully. I said this was where all the action would be."

The group is funny and masculine and drunk. I stand next to Tom and listen to a series of amusing anecdotes, mostly about the men's various sexual encounters.

As the temperature rises in the bar, the men remove their leather jackets revealing vests and tattoos.

I glance at John and Jean and see that they are wearing their chaps again, only this time over jeans. The memory makes me blush.

Tom, like me, stands at the edge of the group and says little. Occasionally we laugh at the same moment, and I catch him glancing sideways at me, a twinkle in his eye and a bemused smile on his lips. I wonder if his amusement is in some way linked to my presence.

Whatever the reason, I realise that for some reason, his presence in the group is as marginal as my own.

Around ten, John claps his hands. "So are we doing this party or not?" he asks.

Enthusiasm ripples through the group.

I move to John's side. "Party?" I say.

He slips an arm around my shoulders. "Yes, it's Jean's birthday tomorrow. We're having a party for him. You should come along," he says. "Join us."

I nod and glance back at Tom who breaks into an uncontrolled grin.

"A party," I say. "Sounds like fun."

Tom steps forward and leans towards my ear. "It will be fun," he says. "But it's not a hats and jelly party. You know that right?"

I frown. "Well, no... I..."

John swipes a leather cap off the table and flops it onto his head with flourish. "I have a hat!" he says.

I frown at Tom. "I don't..."

Tom laughs. "Lots of gel," he says. "No jelly."

"Gel," I repeat. Suddenly it's obvious and I feel stupidly slow.

"Lots of rubbers, no balloons," Tom giggles.

I nod. "OK, OK! I get it!" I laugh. I bite my lip in embarrassment.

John steps between us. "Who said there's no balloons?" he says. "Don't put the man off, just because you're too uptight to come yourself."

The group are pulling on their jackets and moving towards the door.

"So?" John asks.

I look at Tom who shrugs.

"You're not going then?" I ask.

Tom shakes his head. "I don't do sex parties," he says raising an eyebrow.

I turn to John. "No," I say. "I'll stay."

John nods and follows the group towards the exit.

"Have a good one though," I say.

He glances over his shoulder. "Oh I will!" he laughs.

I watch them disappear out of the door and turn back to Tom.

"Drink?" he asks.

I nod. "Sure," I say. "Bitter please."

As he moves towards the bar I take a last fretful glance out of the window, just in time to see the birthday party disappear laughing down a side street.

A tap on my shoulder makes me jump.

"'Scuse me mate," he says.

I turn to face the man, a skinhead. He has a faded green Mohican, a chrome ring through his nose, and bleacher jeans disappearing into eighteen-hole *Doctor Martins*.

"Sorry mate," he says, grasping my shoulder, "but was that a gift party?"

I frown at him. His eyes are a little wild; his stare is a little too intense. *"Drugs,"* I think.

I sigh. "It's a birthday party," I say, lowering my shoulder in the hope that his hand will slip off.

I glance at the bar and see Tom waving a bank note at the barman.

"Yeah, but is it a *gift* party?" the guy insists.

His breath is dreadful and I instinctively step backwards. I note that he has a swastika on his lapel as well as a biohazard badge. I wonder if the hazard is his breath.

I shrug and move sideways. His hand falls away.

"I'm sorry, I have no idea what kind of party it is," I say. "Except that it's a birthday party."

The skinhead grimaces revealing yellow teeth. "So they're not barebackers? It's not a gifting party, a bareback party?"

I shake my head and glance nervously back at the bar and take another step backwards.

"Bareback?" I say. "No. I doubt it. I would hope not."

"Oh," the skinhead says, clearly disappointed. "Shame."

I wrinkle my nose at him. "Shame?" I repeat.

He nods. "Yeah," he says. "Cos I have it... The gift."

He steps towards me again, and I try and move further backwards but bump into the table. I peer over his shoulder hoping that Tom will appear to save me.

"Oh," I mumble. "Well, um, good."

The skinhead touches my arm again and wiggles an eyebrow. "Good?" he says.

I nod. "Umm, yes. It's good that you're so positive about it... So to speak."

He squeezes my arm and grins at me. I can smell his breath again.

"I don't though," I say, grimacing.

He smiles. "Don't *have* it? Or don't *want* it?"

I cough and glance around, checking out my surroundings in case I need help, but everyone is engrossed in their conversations.

"Both," I say.

At this second, Tom surfaces next to him. He's holding two pints of beer and smiling at me.

"Let me show you something," the skinhead says reaching into his pocket.

Tom frowns at him, then at me. "Who's this?" he asks.

I shrug and stare at him trying to convey my displeasure without words.

"I am the *gifter*," the man says, tugging at a photo in his tight denim pocket.

Tom puts the two pints down on the next table, preparing himself, I guess, to intervene if necessary.

"The gift is inevitable," the man says. "It's only a matter of time; accepting the gift is seizing your destiny."

I glance back at Tom and see he is stooping pulling his coat from a chair.

"Tom!" I say. "Wait!"

Tom straightens up and glares at me. He shakes his head. "Nah," he says. "I'll leave you two to it."

The skinhead thrusts the trembling photo in front of my face. I lean back over the table in an attempt to distance myself from him enough to focus on it.

"It's the final solution," he says. "It's what was always meant to happen."

"Jesus!" I exclaim.

I push sideways and knock over a chair, then force my way clumsily out through a sea of surprised faces.

I glance behind and see the skinhead turning to follow, so I duck out of sight and push out through a side door.

My heart is racing. I need to tell Tom about the photo.

I check both ways and then run to the front of the bar but Tom is nowhere to be seen.

Different Days

I sift through Owen's record collection. He's taken his CDs to Australia long ago, but the vinyl remains, and with it the essence of much of my youth. I slide *Soul-to-Soul Volume One* on the turntable and lie back on the floor cushion, instantly transported back to Cambridge, to the big bouncy bed in the sunshine.

In one of those events that some call telepathy and others insist are the mere workings of chance, the phone rings, and when I answer it is Jenny, the only woman ever to have shared that big bouncy bed.

She is animated and friendly in a clipped advertising kind of way.

"Gosh, it was so good seeing you!" she gushes. "I suppose just being able to pick up fifteen years later is the sign of a good friendship," she says. "I'm sorry I couldn't stay longer."

I frown at the phone. It seems as if something strange happened during her visit; it seems as if we did different days.

I do my best to *ooze* lack of enthusiasm. "Not to worry, it was fine really," I say. "As you say, it has been fifteen years."

"I know!" Jenny enthuses. "There's so much to catch up on. That's why I wondered if I mightn't come down for a whole weekend, Nick's working and..."

"Oh really Jenny," I interject. "There's no hurry, I mean we have loads of time ahead..."

"Exactly," she laughs. "I mean, you're not busy and I'm not working at the moment; so the question is, do I need to bring bedding or do you have some?"

"Bedding? No, look..."

I am trying to think of a lie, a previous engagement that means she simply *can't* come.

"Unless you have something planned for the weekend, do you?"

She has started to understand that I'm not keen, and the realisation that I'm about to hurt her feelings softens my resolve. Plus, I think about the coming weekend. The idea of spending it alone tips the balance.

"Not really," I say. "I guess that'll be fine."

"Great, well, I'll just bring me then; see you Friday evening, about six pm I expect. You can take me out on the town."

I sigh. "Look, can you make that Saturday?"

Jenny pauses. "OK. Saturday it is," she says.

Defrosting

I'm walking towards Safeway, resigned to buying extra food for my weekend guest, when I see Tom heading towards me. He is partially obscured by the crowds of Saturday shoppers.

As he nears I see he's carrying a big box under his arm and whistling.

I choose an expression, relaxed, surprised, happy, and fix it. I add a touch of optimistic bounce to my step and head towards my destiny. Only seconds before the encounter however, Tom ducks left into a coffee bar.

I freeze on the pavement and shake my head.

"Did what I think just happened actually happen?" I wonder. "Did he see me? Did he ignore me? Did he just hide from me?"

A woman bashes my ankle with her pushchair and, ignoring my shriek she thrusts on through the crowds.

"For fucks sake," I exclaim. I turn into Safeway.

I choose the empty checkout. Of course there's a reason the seasoned shoppers aren't fighting to be served by Kelly; she isn't the fastest of checkout swipers.

Kelly has some kind of disability; her trembling stuttering swiping is painfully slow, so I smile at her charitably. She glares back.

I look at my watch wondering if Tom is still next-door, wondering if I should confront him, wondering if Kelly will ever speed up. But Kelly doesn't do speedy, and Kelly doesn't do "smile".

When she finally hands me my ticket, I stride outside, walk three yards and duck determinedly into *Red Roaster*.

I spot Tom immediately, and he spots me too, shifting in his seat, leaning over his book and actually shading his forehead by leaning on his hand. It's such a theatrical gesture it almost makes me laugh.

I walk over, dump my shopping bags, and pull out the chair opposite.

Tom lifts his hand just enough to peer out at me.

"Hello," I say. "Do you mind if I sit here?"

Tom closes his novel and sits heavily back in his chair. He folds his arms and looks at me coldly.

"You *are* sitting there," he says.

"Body language doesn't come much clearer than that," I say, folding my arms to mimic him.

He pulls at his beard and then reaches for a hooded grey sweatshirt on the back of his chair. He's clearly making to leave.

"What's wrong?" I ask, "I think you're being very strange."

"Strange?" he says. *"Me?"*

He grunts. Tom actually grunts at me. I know we're not friends, but surely simple social decency prohibits *grunting* at people?

"What?" I ask.

He laughs sourly. "There's really no point," he says.

I frown at him. "Oh for god's sake," I say. "What's wrong?"

Tom stands and lifts his book from the table.

"Look," he says. "Let's just say I didn't really enjoy the other night very much."

"*You* didn't enjoy it!" I struggle to contain a shriek. "Hey, at least *I* didn't run off and leave *you* with the psycho Nazi bare-backer!"

People around us are looking.

"Yeah, well," Tom shakes his head. He glances around, then pauses, frowns and slowly breaks into a wry grin.

"But, I thought..." he says. He grips the edge of the table and leans towards me. "Didn't you know him *at all*?" he asks.

I shake my head.

Tom bites his lip. "Oh," he grimaces. "I, um, thought he was a friend of yours," he says.

I shake my head and point to the seat. "Will you please sit back down?"

Tom sinks back into the chair and looks at me, giving me a strange sideways glance.

"Oh, come on! Do I look like the kind of guy... Hey, you know what?" I nod at him. "*You* missed *The Photo*."

"The photo?" he smiles questioningly.

"Yeah!" I say wiggling my eyebrows. "Just after you left, the scary-guy showed me a photo."

Tom bites his bottom lip and smiles, his eyes twinkling. "A photo of what?"

"It was a photo of a prisoner of war, or, more like someone in a concentration camp, in a stripy uniform. He actually said something about the *Final Solution*."

Tom wrinkles his face in disgust. "Jesus! That's so fucked up!"

"I know," I nod. "And you left me there! Alone!"

"Still, he's not wrong though," Tom says.

I frown. "*What*?" I whistle.

"I mean about it being the *final solution*. If these people don't stop bare-backing soon there won't be anyone left *to* shag. Hitler must be grinning in his grave."

I nod sadly. "I can't even believe it still goes on," I say.

Tom shakes his head. "More and more," he says. "It's apocalypse now."

It takes an hour for the chill to lift, for me to fully convince Tom of my sanity; an hour during which I am increasingly aware of my frozen food defrosting beneath the table.

But Tom is cuter than ever, and as the frost thaws, as he starts to talk ever more animatedly, to tug on his little beard ever more excitedly, I start to get a vague feeling of tension in my stomach, a strange butterfly feeling I remember from way back.

When we finally push out of Red Roaster into the grey afternoon, he seemingly confirms what I have been thinking.

"I'll be in Charles Street later if you fancy a beer," he says.

"I'll be with a friend, but sure, that'd be great," I grin.

"No skinheads though," he laughs.

"No skinheads," I agree.

I start to walk home but pause. Tom is running back towards me.

"Now here's a good sign!" I think. "He's going to ask for my phone number."

"I forgot my box," Tom says, slapping his head with the palm of his hand. "It's *only* a brand new DVD recorder!"

He laughs and jogs back into *Red Roaster*. Feeling a little disappointed, I start to walk, but then it strikes me – forgetting a two-hundred-pound DVD recorder is probably an even *better* sign.

Incompatibility Issues

Jenny sticks her bottom lip out and wrinkles her nose.

"It's not what I was expecting," she says.

I look at the huge glass-and-chrome bridge, which occupies a quarter of the bar, yet goes nowhere.

"Nor me," I say moving towards the bar. "It looks like the set for a French TV show."

"Or an airport," says Jenny.

"Fun though," I say. "Good atmosphere."

Charles Street is so crowded it actually looks like the security zone at Gatwick. The crowd is an eclectic mix: young and old, gay and straight. Music is booming from a sumptuous sound system and the hubbub of chatter is even louder than the music.

As we push our way through, I scan left and right hoping to spot Tom.

"You see him?" asks Jenny.

I shrug and pull a ten-pound note from my wallet, thrusting it over the bar.

She nods. "Maybe he stood you up," she says. "On your first date!"

I exhale. She's been here less than an hour, but already she's bugging me.

"It's not a first date," I say. "It's not a date *at all*."

I order drinks from the dancing blond barman. He looks too young to be in a bar, but that happens a lot nowadays. It says more about my own ageing than the state of the world's bar staff.

I hand Jenny her *Smirnoff Ice* and pocket the change. "So what about your man?" I ask. "Doesn't he mind you going away for the weekend?"

Jenny swigs at the bottle and shakes her hair, which shimmers, reflecting a violet spotlight above her.

"He's very sweet," she says, her voice incongruously icy. "He's working all weekend... Overtime," she adds with a shrug. "Anyway, how do you know this Tom character?" she asks.

"I don't really," I tell her. "I only met him the other night, via some friends."

"Hmm," she says. "Then maybe he really *won't* turn up."

"I doubt it," Tom laughs, winking at me. "You can't trust his type."

Tom has appeared at Jenny's left elbow. I grin and he nods sideways at her.

"Better than the last friend you introduced me to anyway," he says with a wink.

But after half an hour I'm not sure Tom prefers Jenny at all. To say that they aren't getting on would be an understatement.

"So where do *you* live?" Tom asks.

"Surrey. I drove down this afternoon." Jenny looks around. "God knows why though."

"Oh." Tom looks offended.

"I quite like it here," I say.

Tom apparently feels under attack. "So you live in *Surrey*!" he says. "How *anyone* can live in Surrey I'll never know. It's so smug and superficial isn't it?"

I grimace.

Jenny glares at him, and then shifts to a sweet smile. "Yes, so unlike Brighton, which is *so* working class and authentic, don't you think?"

The ping-pong intensifies throughout the evening. I keep buying drinks in a failed strategy to mellow them out, but though I keep changing the subject Tom and Jenny cannot find it in themselves to agree on anything.

Jenny's eyes become icier with every Smirnoff she drinks and I wish I could vanish, or more specifically vanish somewhere with Tom. I tune in and out of the conversation, wondering if they will come to blows, if there's something I should do.

When I tune in again, Jenny is saying, "So you really spent eighteen thousand pounds on a German copy of a Mini? What's that all about? Couldn't you find any *less* car for your money?"

"Well at least it was designed this century," Tom replies. "Your VW is as modern as Woodstock baby."

I put my drink on the bar. "I have to go to the loo," I say. "Will you two please just *try* and be nice to each other?"

In the toilets I stand between two guys who are more interested in each other than peeing and strangely *I'm* the one that feels embarrassed.

When I return, Tom and Jenny are discussing food.

"I wouldn't really know a lot about *fois-gras,*" Tom is saying. "I'm a vegetarian."

Jenny strokes his black-sleeved arm, and for a moment I think they're getting on much better.

"A vegetarian," she says. "How original. Maybe you can explain what the point *is* of being a vegetarian, I mean if you're going to wear leather? I never *could* understand that."

I make an, "ouch" face.

"You have a moral problem with my wearing leather?" Tom asks, sending me a sideways wink.

"If you're a vegetarian, I do, sure!" says Jenny, stabbing her Smirnoff at him.

"Fair enough," Tom smiles. "Though personally, I couldn't give a fuck what you wear or what you stick down your throat. But that's just me I guess. I'm the tolerant type."

Jenny closes her eyes, and reaches for the bar, seemingly to steady herself. She grits her teeth, and opens her eyes wide. She looks strange: angry, and pale.

"I feel sick," she says. "It's the smoke. I need to go outside."

"Nothing to do with the five *Smirnoffs* then," Tom says.

I look from Jenny's pale face to Tom's cheeky grin.

As Jenny moves away towards the door I start to follow. I glance back at Tom.

"She's sick," I tell him. "Leave it out."

Tom shrugs. "Sure," he says. "Whatever."

"I'll be back."

But Tom looks at his watch and wrinkles his nose. "Another time," he says.

Outside Jenny is vomiting into the gutter. The sight and the smell make me feel ill too, plus I'm furious with her for wrecking my plans, so though I stroke her back, I turn and stare at the lights on the pier instead.

Eventually, when her sickness abates, she stands up.

"I want to go home," she says. She sounds surprisingly sober.

Lost And Found

I awaken just after midday to the dulcet tones of Jenny retching in the bathroom next door. I pull on jogging trousers and shout through the bathroom door; ask if there's anything I can do.

"Yeah," Jenny says. "Fuck off."

Now, I can't use the bathroom, so I can't, *daren't*, drink my morning coffee.

I pull on some clothes and decide to go for a walk. It's a beautiful morning and maybe the sun and the sea will clear the fog lying low in the valleys of my brain.

I make my way down the steps to sea level and start to walk towards town.

The miniature railway rumbles past, tourists sitting placidly in the open sided cars.

The first coherent thought of the day is, *"Jenny has to go."* The second is, *"Tom."*

As I walk, I picture him playing with his weird little beard, picture his cheeky smirk, his sideways wink. I start to smile, and then, as a feeling of warmth rises within me, I break into a grin.

A very old woman walking towards me with her equally old dog gives me a dirty look and moves to the opposite edge of the pavement. There's nothing more upsetting I guess, than having strangers smiling at you. Especially before lunch.

I feel... What *is* the word? I try to work out why everything seems so different this morning. *Contented*? *Warm*? And I feel something else too, but what to call it? Coherent? Cohesive?

For the first time in ages that unnerving feeling of duality, the *this-me* watching the *that-me* is absent. I think about life here, then life in France, but even then, though I can perceive them as two different things, I feel no confusion about it. It seems my mind has finally, or at least, this morning, managed to knit and bind the two together into a coherent whole.

I wonder what will happen with Tom and the warm feeling returns.

I acknowledge to myself that I know very little about him. Other than the fact that he is cute, has a good sense of humour. Other than the fact that he's so cheekily cuddly that I could scrunch him up and keep him in my pocket, I know nothing at all.

I've reached the roundabout at the end of Maderia Drive, so I turn and start heading back up the hill.

A car drives past, stereo blaring, but instead of the usual rap music it's an eighties hit. I only catch a few bars of it, but it's a song I once liked and as I walk I try and remember the opening bars.

Gulls are hovering in the breeze, floating effortlessly above the railings, then turning and swooping back over the velvet green sea.

I walk past a shelter and smile at an old couple staring at the horizon, and as I walk I decide I need a plan of action.

Go home. Get rid of Jenny, *whatever* it takes. Shower, dress and get back to *Red Roaster* as soon as possible. It's the only place I can think of where I might just see him.

As I near the house, I notice that the orange camper-van has gone, and as I slide the key into the door, the eighties song pops into my head, retrieved automatically from some distance database. I even remember the name of the singer. *Bill Withers.*

I start to sing, *Lovely day.*

It takes less than half an hour of sitting outside *Red Roaster* for me to appreciate the limits of my so-called plan; the sun has moved to the right, leaving my table in the shade, and I have read *The Guardian* from cover to cover.

"This is a crap idea," I admit, rolling the newspaper and standing.

I don't know what the chances of bumping into Tom here are, but they're not high enough. I mentally kick myself for not getting his number.

The wind has dropped, the sun is gorgeously hot, and it seems the whole of Brighton is rushing to the seafront.

I do my lap around the pier, refraining for once from buying a doughnut. Owen has no scales, but I'm pretty sure I'm putting on weight, and suddenly it's a concern again – Tom looks pretty fit.

Between the two piers, I pass a group of bikers unzipping their one-piece suits to let out the steam.

A brief pang of desire for my motorbike sweeps over me, and with it a warm feeling for my life in France. I wonder if I could ride it yet, if I'm ready for roads, traffic, tunnels, ...

I haven't driven anywhere since the accident.

I buy a fish and chip take-away and head down to the water's edge. Seagulls swoop and dive and scream at me, able to spot fish and chips at fifty yards.

The sea has darkened into an even more sumptuous green and the sky is almost the same cloudless azure of home; another new thought. I catch myself and roll the word around in my mind, *home.*

I throw a chip to a seagull and realise almost before it has left my hand that this is a mistake. Hundreds of birds – mainly seagulls, but pigeons and cormorants too – appear swooping and screaming and jostling for position.

The number of birds is getting threatening. And embarrassing.

I glance around me and see a few people staring at the spectacle of the stupid man with the fish and chips; the man about to be pecked to death, or carried away, or simply pooped upon by a hundred seagulls.

I think of the Hitchcock film, and the roller coaster at the end of the pier obliges with a soundtrack, distant screams drifting across the water.

The gulls seem to be the most aggressive. The biggest one is standing only feet from me shrieking and I think about moving along the beach, and wonder if the birds will just follow me if I do. That could look *really* stupid.

I decide to throw a stone instead, but just as I reach for a stone, just as I palm it and raise my right hand, a wet, white Labrador bounds into view scattering the birds in a tizzy of terrified squawks.

I lower the stone and turn to look at the owner calling his dog from the top of the beach.

"Come here!" he is shouting, red-faced. "Will you *fucking* come *fucking* here? Stupid bloody dog!"

I decide to reassure him. I decide to say, "Hey, your dog saved me from *The Birds*!" but the dog roars up the beach and runs past him, and as he leaps and reaches and tries to grab the dog's collar, he slips on the pebbles and falls.

He laughs and looks up at me and opens his mouth to speak, but then pauses. Recognition spreads across his face.

"Well what do you know," he says.

And Lost Again

The dog continues to chase the gulls ever more excitedly.

Tom and I lie side by side and look at the sea.

"I don't know if he's like this all the time or just with me," he says.

"Oh, not your dog then?" I ask.

Tom shakes his head. "Nah, I'm walking it for a friend. She's ill... In bed."

"Oh right, good," I say. "I mean good it's not your dog, not about your friend! I'm not really that keen on dogs."

As I say it I realise I have given something away. Why should I care what pets Tom has?

"Hey!" I shout at the dog. "Come here!"

I smile at Tom. "This one's OK though. What's his name?"

"Lad." Tom nods sardonically. "I *know*... Lad the Labrador; sounds like a character from a bloody *Noddy* cartoon."

"Could be worse," I say. "Rupert Everett's dog is called Rupert."

Tom frowns. "Really?"

"Yeah. I saw him in St Tropez wandering up and down the beach calling to it. *Rupert*! *Rupert*! Just in case anyone *hadn't* noticed he was there."

Tom bites his lip. "How dreadful. When were you in St Tropez?"

I tell him I have been living in Nice and that I'm taking time to work out where I want to be.

Tom laughs. "Oh *there*! Definitely!" he says.

It's one of those strange moments when speech precedes thought. Only once I have said it do I realise that for the first time I have re-framed my stay in England, not in terms of the terrible events that brought me here, but in terms of what I intend to do with it, where I intend to go with it. *"And this,"* I think, *"is how we heal."*

"I go to Italy a lot," Tom is saying, "or I used to, near Genoa, if you know it."

I nod. "It's only an hour and a half from Nice."

Tom nods. "Isn't Genoa great? Such a *real* city I always think."

I blush. "I knew this would embarrass me one day," I say.

Tom frowns. "What?"

I reposition myself on the pebbles, imperceptibly sliding closer to his warm, funny self.

I shrug. "I only went to Ikea, then I came home."

Tom laughs. "Shame on you," he says, "though I have actually been to that Ikea a few times myself."

"Really?" I laugh. "How funny. So what takes you to Genoa? Your job?"

Tom laughs. "Nah, my job takes me to Dortmund sometimes, but that's about as exotic as it gets. And believe me, Dortmund *is not* very exotic."

"Germany?"

Tom nods. "Yeah, dreary industrial town."

I nod.

"No, Antonio lives just behind Genoa," Tom says.

I wrinkle my brow and raise a hand to shade my eyes from the sun. "Antonio?" I ask.

"Yeah," says Tom. "Antonio. He's Italian."

I frown at him.

He nods. "My *partner*?"

I cough and rearrange myself, moving imperceptibly back to where I started.

"Your partner," I say.

"Yeah," says Tom nodding. "My boyfriend."

A cold shower makes me shiver. Tom reaches for a stick and throws it.

"Lad! Go dry yourself somewhere else," he says.

Déjà Vu

As I doze on Owen's couch, my right-brain reasons my left-brain into submission. Logically, it argues, I need a friend, even a friend with an Italian boyfriend, as much as I need a lover. I'm probably not ready for any other kind of relationship anyway, it says.

And an evil, bad, bad, *bad* part of my mind that I do my best to silence, agrees I should go for a drink with Tom tonight, but for completely different reasons. It's best to know as much about the enemy as possible, it says. Who knows how solid Tom's relationship with Antonio really *is*, it snidely points out. To prove its point, it has sieved through my conversation with Tom separating out one particular phrase.

"I go to Genoa a lot," he said. "Or I used to."

"I used to." Now what does *that* mean?

My headache has gone, but the hangover has left me feeling tired and irritable so it's hard to motivate myself. Eventually I drag myself from the sofa, splash cold water on my face and head off to the rendezvous.

It's a warm overcast evening, and as I approach the Amsterdam, I see Tom sitting in a window seat.

It has almost the same layout as *Legends* where we first spoke, and it's only a little further down the seafront. But tonight, at least, it's much emptier; only one other table is occupied.

Tom has changed into baggy hip-hop jeans and a blue, seventies tracksuit top. His beard is waxed into pointy perfection, and he looks younger and fresher than this morning. He's looking good.

I offer him a drink but he shakes his head and waves a full glass at me.

When I return with my drink, I sit opposite him, pulling my chair to a respectable distance.

"So what did you get up to?" he asks.

I smile. "Ab-so-lute-ly *nothing*!" I say.

"I went to the gym, but other than that," he rolls his eyes and continues shaking his head, "God, there's these two guys at the gym, they're *so* annoying." He rolls his eyes and then blows through his lips.

"They're just constantly *there*, you know?"

I shrug.

"It's like, whatever machine I'm on, whatever I'm doing, at some point I look up and there they are, either side of me."

I wipe the foam from my lips.

"Maybe they like you," I say. "Maybe they want a threesome?"

Tom nods. "I expect so, but they're just so..." he shakes his head and sips his own drink. "They're actually gorgeous," he says. "I mean they have nice haircuts, lovely bodies, little matching goatee beards, lovely clothes..."

I raise an eyebrow. "I take it there's a but?"

Tom nods. "Yeah. The *but* is the *conversation*! They just constantly talk through me, and it's all BT you know?"

I shrug. "*BT*?"

"Bitch Talk. You know, she's a bitch, and he's a bitch, and I'm a bitch, and you're a bitch and ha, ha, ha, isn't it *fun* being a bitch!"

I laugh. "Maybe you need a walkman?" I suggest.

Tom nods. "I already decided to get one, just so I don't have to listen to it anymore. It's *unbearable!*"

We chat a little about life in Brighton, and inevitably Tom asks me about myself. I tell him that I'm single, that I split up with my ex last December, conveniently dropping Steve from my history. Poor Steve – he didn't deserve that.

I move quickly on by asking Tom about Antonio. It takes mere seconds for me to start to hate the dark swarthy Italian – the time for Tom to produce the photo. And it takes less than a minute for me to hate his Carmen Ghia, his villa, his swimming pool, and his rich publishing magnate parents.

Yet it's funny, because despite Tom's clear respect, his obvious *love* for Antonio, and his eyes do twinkle as he tells me about him, his body language strikes me as confusing.

Maybe it's just the alcohol, we're on our third round already, or maybe it's the music which is getting louder and louder, but he seems to be sitting closer than before, leaning in towards me ever more, and he seems to be missing no opportunity for contact. A poke with a finger here, a slap on the shoulder there, a pinch of the cheek...

"Didn't you say you don't go to Italy so much now?" I ask, as casually as possible.

Tom nods, but his face changes, becoming instantly taut and pale.

"Yeah," he says. "A bad thing happened."

I frown.

"A terrible thing," he says shaking his head. "I haven't been able to go back since. But I will, eventually."

I nod. "A bad thing you don't want to talk about, I take it."

Tom sighs heavily and swallows hard, apparently with some difficulty. "I just can't," he says with another shake of his head. "Sorry."

The bell rings. Last orders.

"OK, so!" I say, purposely moving on. "What now?"

Tom looks up. He forces a smile but his eyes look terribly sad.

"D'you want to go to a club?" he asks.

Revenge seems instantly familiar, so much so that I keep looking around trying to work out where it reminds me of. We order more beer and stand at the edge of the dance-floor watching the carnival crowd dance to the fun-but-tacky music. When I need to go to the toilet I correctly guess where it is, which only emphasises the strange feeling of déjà-vu.

By the time I get back, Tom is on the dance floor, blending into the carnival laughter, the jumping, waving madness of it all, so I go and join him, but someone else has spotted him. She's six foot four inches, has shoulders you could hang a marquee on, legs like Joanna Lumley and is wearing a very tight, *very* short red PVC dress.

I linger behind her looking at Tom, watching him as she pulls on his beard. He catches my eye and breaks into a grin.

"I like this," she says, her deep voice destroying any remaining doubt that she represents the T in LGBT.

Tom runs a hand over her arse and says, "And I *love* your outfit."

As Sophie Ellis Bextor's nasal, *Take Me Home* slips from the speakers, PVC-lady begins to shift her hips and flop her ironed blond hair from side to side.

She raises a finger and chews a cuticle. "Oh this old thing?" she says, running a hand over her dress. "I'd rather you loved *me*."

"And so say all of us," I think.

Tom laughs, flashing white teeth. "That really is a great dress though," he says, imitating her groove.

She laughs madly, runs a hand over his hair, then spins on one heel and heads off across the floor.

Tom steps up to me smiling. "Isn't she great!" he says.

I'm impressed at his reaction. Warm, friendly, amused, unthreatened. Personally, I have always been a little scared of big trannies.

"But shall we go downstairs?" he adds. "I hate fucking Sophie Ellis Bextor."

On the ground floor the atmosphere is much more chilled.

The music is louder; they're playing rhythmic trancy Goa, and the men – for here there are only men – are younger, more masculine, better built.

The feeling of familiarity is even stronger now; in fact if I didn't know better I would swear that I actually *have* been here before. I decide that it must look a little like *Le Klub* in Nice.

The dark dance-floor is packed with sweating steaming male flesh; half of the guys have their T-shirts in their pockets.

We get fresh drinks from the bar and move to a raised side area. We look down at the dancers.

In front of me – I could actually reach out and touch them – a group of muscular bearded boys are dancing badly. Body builders are always so stiff and I wonder briefly why that is. Do their muscles actually prevent them moving properly? Or are they just so body-conscious that they can't let themselves go?

The one nearest me has huge hoops hanging from his nipples, which gyrate and glitter temptingly as he moves rigidly from side to side.

Tom stands to my left and occasionally points someone out, saying, "Wow! Look! He has better tits than the tranny," or "Now that! That is *nice*."

When he speaks, he leans in making my ear vibrate, which, with the beer, the tribal rhythms and the smell of testosterone, is giving me a heady, horny, hard on. I lean on the shelf separating me from the dance floor to conceal it, but it actually makes things worse. Tom now lays an arm across my back as he speaks to me.

"Anything you fancy out there then?" he asks, his lips actually touching my ear lobe.

"*You,*" I think. "How about all of them?" I shout.

A humanoid synthesiser starts to soar above the rhythms and the dancers start to raise their arms. Tom leans in again.

"You should get out there," he says. "You might get lucky."

I shrug.

I realise that if I don't get away soon I will end up kissing him, so I grin, down the third of a pint remaining in my glass, and trippingly descend the stairs into the heaving mass.

A spotlight is sweeping across my face. One guy is dancing behind Mr Pierced Nips, rubbing faded denim to faded denim, whilst another dances in front stroking and playing with the rings.

I look beyond them at Tom and nod at them eliciting a grin. He lifts his T-shirt to indicate that I should take mine off, but I feel a little out-pecked, and anyway, I'm more interested, actually captivated would be the word, by the glimpse of Tom's chest, by the swirling river of hair trickling down his chest, disappearing into his belly button.

The beat speeds and the dancers become more frenetic; the hairs on the back of my neck bristle.

Tom disappears from the raised walkway and surfaces at my side grinning madly. I smile back and we start to move together.

The DJ slowly pulls out components of the music, gradually deconstructing the sound, leaving it ever more desolate, hard-edged, industrial, and then, as the beat reaches its climax, he whacks it all back in. The dance-floor goes wild; Tom pushes out his lips, rips his T-shirt over his head and waves it above him.

The crowd pushes us together and I let it happen. My arms rub against the hairs of his chest. A strobe blinds me and I step back and watch Tom's stuttering disjointed movement beneath the on and off flashing of the light.

After a minute or so the beat fades and then ceases, leaving only a drifting synthesiser. The dancers raise their arms in the air; Tom steps towards me, grinning and, when someone bumps him from behind, he falls forwards.

I catch him, savouring the contact, the warm sweatiness of his body. He smiles and lets me support his weight. Then with mock effort, he finds his feet and stands. I lean in until our faces are mere centimetres apart.

An orange spotlight sweeps across my face and I close my eyes and lean towards him, opening my lips, smiling beatifically.

The synth gets louder, higher, more insistent. The moment of the kiss is upon us, the music shifting and changing, now sounding weirdly sub-aquatic. I can feel the heat of Tom's face only millimetres away. The movement of the lights penetrating my eyelids, the swaying bodies around me, it all makes me feel dizzy, so I open my eyes again and smile salaciously.

But Tom has pulled back. He's stopped dancing and he's frowning at me and shaking his head.

My smile fades and I lower my arms.

Tom shakes his head again.

"What's wrong?" I ask.

"I'm going to go get a drink at the bar," he says.

I nod, and start to follow him.

"You stay!" he orders. "Enjoy!"

Now this feels *really* familiar. This rejection, this dance-floor, this very moment is *so* familiar I could *swear*...

And then it comes to me. I *have* been here before. This *is* the very club I came to seventeen years ago, the club where Dirk, my lanky American obsession refused to kiss me, the *very* room where I learnt that we were, "just friends."

Dazed, I turn and study the room. The décor has changed, sure; but it's definitely the same building.

People are still swaying, their arms in the air.

"This is where Dirk danced," I think. "And over there..."

I see Tom standing at the bar. It's the very spot where I stood watching Dirk.

So this isn't déjà vu. I *have* been here before. I have been *exactly* here before.

The DJ whacks in the bass and people whoop, bursting into dance again. Everyone, that is, except me.

French Pickup

I spend a week pottering around Owen's house.

I receive my forwarded post from Isabelle. Thankfully she has left out the invitation to the remembrance service but it's almost as powerful by its absence. I actually wish she had sent it so that I could read it and bin it once and for all.

I log on to Internet sites and post cheques to pay my French bills hoping that once it's all done France will again fade away. To help it on its way, I think about Tom.

It's obvious that this is a pointless exercise, but it's like a sore tooth, and I can't help but run my tongue over it; the gentle pain of impossibility infinitely preferable to the repetitive mantra of the accident, of Steve's death.

One Thursday morning, I decide to treat myself to breakfast at a café I saw at the end of the cycle path.

It's a sunny optimistic morning, one of those days when everything from the air in my lungs to the smiling joggers to the bouncing, droning jet-skis reeks of better days to come.

By the time I reach the *Meeting Place* I am feeling relaxed and ravenous. I chain Owen's bike to the rusting railings, order a full vegetarian breakfast from the ginger-haired German girl behind the counter, and carry my steaming coffee over to a table at the sea's edge.

I sip the boiling coffee and stare at the sparkling horizon and wonder why some days are good days, and some days are heavy and sad.

The guy next to me is reading a French newspaper – *Libération*. There is so little news about France in the English media. Were it not for the constant menace of those evil Eastern Europeans taking all our jobs, one could forget that continental Europe exists at all. I decide to keep an eye open in case he leaves it behind when he leaves.

I eat my breakfast and watch as a fishing boat cuts a glimmering scar through the smooth surface of the sea, the sound of its engine drifting in and out of earshot.

When, with a conclusive movement the man shuts his *Libération*, I glance over.

He smiles at me. "Bonjour," he says.

I blink in surprise. "Bonjour," I reply.

He laughs. "You don't remember me?"

I shrug and blush. "Sorry, I..."

"I'm a friend of Jean, I saw you the other night... In *Legends*."

I have a vague impression I remember him, but it's hard to be sure.

He nods at the chair opposite me. "May I?" he asks.

I nod. "Sure," I say.

"Benoit," he says, holding out a hand.

I smile and shake it.

"You missed a great party the other day," he says. "You should have come."

I blush slightly.

"John told me you know," he continues.

I frown.

"About your little suspension experiment," Benoit smirks.

I open my mouth in outrage. "Hey, they shouldn't have told you..." I protest.

Benoit shrugs. "You should let them have their fun you know," he says.

I wrinkle my nose. "I guess I'm just not ready," I laugh.

"They're very safe," Benoit says. "And actually very good."

I blush again. "I'm tempted I guess," I say. "But, well, as I say..."

I think again about John and Jean's dungeon, and a brief flash of Benoit strapped up in their harnesses appears in my mind's eye. I feel instantly aroused.

Benoit nods. "Well, never rush yourself," he says. "Chaque chose en son temps." – *Everything in its time.*

"And now it's time for more coffee," I say.

Benoit nods.

"Not here though," he says with a grin.

Pavlov's Terror

Benoit's flat is lovely and not at all what I expected. For some reason – probably his general neatness – I saw him as a Habitat and steel man. But as I look around, it's more junk shop bonanza than industrial chic.

A vast grey sofa occupies one wall, worn comfortable chairs fill every corner, and the wall space is filled with huge photographs.

In the hallway Benoit has a huge trestle desk covered in piles of photographs. I nod appreciatively and look around.

"Great photos," I say.

Benoit looks up from the espresso machine – proper coffee being the official reason we are here – and smiles.

"It's what I do," he says switching between languages. "Je suis photographe."

He finishes setting up the machine, flicks a switch and moves to the window.

"It takes time to get hot," he explains, turning the catch and sliding up the huge sash window. "If you lean right out, you can see the sea," he tells me proudly.

I cross the room, inevitably remembering the last time someone told me to lean out and look at the view. The lean had turned into a kiss, and the kiss had turned into a nightmare.

I grip the windowsill and lean out, glimpsing the café where we just met. When I turn back, sure enough, Benoit is standing so close that I can barely focus on his stubbly chin.

"Can I ask you something?" he asks seriously.

I nod.

"Can I kiss you?" he says, earnestly.

I blush and grin simultaneously. "Um, well, I suppose," I say. "Yeah."

The front of my jeans starts to fill.

Benoit takes the remaining half step towards me, rests a hand on my arse and brushes his lips against mine.

"Good," he says, pausing. "It is what I have been wanting since I saw you."

I half open my mouth and he sucks at my bottom lip, then, slipping an arm behind my head, pushes into my mouth.

We kiss for a moment, rolling our tongues around. It feels warm and welcoming. He tastes sweet.

"Mmm," I say. "Chocolate?"

Benoit pulls away and laughs. "You can taste?"

I nod and pull him to me again. "Tastes good!"

When he leads me through to the bedroom, I am gripped by stress, swamped by memories of less than successful sessions, and specifically, the memory of the debacle that followed the window-kiss in Nice. It was the only other time I can remember being picked up in the street, and it ended, oh-so-unexpectedly when I took my T-shirt off. I think back to that arsehole waiting until I was naked in his lounge to tell me that I was *fat*. My hard-on fades.

Benoit shucks his jeans and underwear, and stands without embarrassment wearing only a grey T-shirt.

His dick hangs heavily between his legs, in perfect proportion with the rest of his chunky body.

He nods at me. "Your turn," he says.

I take a deep breath and pull my sweatshirt and T-shirt over my head, getting momentarily stuck in the darkness.

When Benoit comes back into view he has removed his T-shirt too, revealing velvety swathes of brown body hair, the slightest of tums, and a muscular torso.

He looks at me in an appraising kind of way and I stop breathing.

He bites his lip, and says, "Désolé, mais..." – *Sorry, but...*

I groan. I think, "No! This can't be happening."

My heart skips a beat and I stand stupidly fingering my T-shirt, unable to decide what to do.

"Is the past destined to repeat for ever more?" I wonder. Have I done it all? Does it all just go round and round from now on?

Benoit turns away from me. I glance at his muscular buttocks protruding pertly and feel the blood drain from my face. I start to untangle the T-shirt so that I can put it back on.

When I hear the creak of a door, I look up. Benoit is peering coyly over his shoulder, not the expression I expected at all.

"Sorry," he says again, "but... Would you mind if I put my chaps on?"

I frown at him.

"They're new and I really like them," he says, a childlike grin upon his face.

I start to smile.

He pulls a polished pair of chaps from the wardrobe and turns back to face me, his dick jutting.

I grin broadly. "No problem," I say.

Benoit slides a leg into each tube, then turns and faces the mirror as he fastens the waistband. Peeping out of the soft leather, his buttocks look sumptuous. I move forward and stroke his arse.

"You're right," I say. "They look great."

He looks back at me, one eyebrow raised. "I have another pair, an old pair, if you want."

I hold out a hand and laugh. "Oh, go on then, give 'em here," I say.

Benoit doesn't have a downstairs Disneyland, but he has a well-equipped playground and enough toys to keep us busy on this dull grey Monday afternoon.

Just before six, still wearing his old chaps, and straining against a huge chrome ring, I'm pushing Benoit down over the workbench and scattering his photos.

I glance sideways at the mirror and see myself pumping into him, pulling on his harness, and as I shriek my way into the day's second orgasm, I realise that with a few props, well, I don't look so bad.

Different Truths

Jenny marks the days of the week with her phone calls. She leaves upbeat power-messages urging me to call her back, but as I guess she wants to come and stay again, and as I *don't* want her to, I conveniently *forget* to call back.

I dig out Owen's scales, they are covered in dust at the back of his wardrobe, and I note with horror that I have put on nearly three kilos since March. Exercise is the only solution, so now twice daily – on the way out, and on the way back – I cycle past the end of Benoit's street. Each time I think vaguely about calling in, each time I become vaguely aroused, but each time I refrain. If he had wanted me to call, I figure, he would have given me his number.

Tom on the other hand *has* given me his number, but I don't *dare* use it. The picture his name used to generate in my mind, the wry smile and the cheeky grin, has been replaced with the look of horror he had when I tried to kiss him.

But on Saturday morning, as he runs across Eastern Street to speak to me, it all seems forgotten. He looks thoroughly thrilled.

"Mark!" he pants. "How are you? I've been meaning to call, but I've been busy. Antonio's here." He nods across the street at a man in a black suit and a roll neck sweater.

"Look, I'm sorry about..." I say.

Tom interrupts me. "It doesn't matter. Look, why don't you come for coffee? I'd love for you two to meet."

I open my mouth to say no, but then change my mind. The perfect antidote for my Tom obsession is, I decide, his boyfriend made real.

"Sure," I say with a shrug. "Why not."

As the three of us wander towards the North Laines, Tom tells us about his week, about Antonio's surprise arrival. He is taller and older than I imagined, but overall, I would have to admit that he looks even better in real life than in the photo. He remains staunchly silent though, even trailing a couple of paces behind us.

As we pass in front of *Komedia*, Tom raps a table with his knuckles. "What about here?" he asks. "It's in the sun."

Antonio rattles out some machine-gun speed Italian, but I don't catch a word, and Tom replies, tit for tat. I have no idea what they have said to each other, but Tom instructs me to sit, then heads inside to order.

Antonio reluctantly pulls up a chair.

"Did you want to go somewhere else?" I venture.

He shrugs. "No, here's fine," he says. He speaks without any trace of Italian accent.

I decide with an unhealthy feeling of glee that they must be arguing, but when Tom returns he seems unfazed by Antonio's glaring blue eyes. He slips into the seat and looks at Antonio, then at me.

"She's gonna bring them out," he explains.

Antonio releases another burst of Italian.

Tom frowns. "Speak English," he says with a shake of his head.

I shrug. "It's OK, really."

Antonio looks coldly at me and then does a kind of upward nod in my direction. "Parlo Italiano?" he asks.

I shake my head. "Sorry."

He shrugs.

"Only English and French I'm afraid," I add as if that will mitigate my ignorance.

Antonio chews the inside of his mouth.

"I was just saying that the coffee is dreadful here," he says, again with no trace of Italian accent. If anything he sounds slightly nasal, slightly American.

I wonder at his aggressive manner and wonder if Tom has told him about the attempted kiss.

Tom laughs. "Antonio says the coffee is dreadful *everywhere*."

Antonio nods. "In England," he corrects. "Everywhere in England."

Tom wrinkles his nose at me. "It's just his thing," he says with a little shrug. He says it in the way a parent would tell you about their beloved child's latest amusing quirk.

"You could always drink tea," I suggest.

Antonio looks at me coldly, apparently deciding that the statement isn't worth comment.

"So you speak French?" he asks eventually. "How come?"

"I live in Nice, well, usually," I say. "Not far from you."

Antonio nods. "I know where Nice is," he says.

I restrain a frown but think, *"What's his problem?"*

"Pretty much everyone does," I reply. In an attempt at softening the statement I add, "It's tourist central."

The waitress arrives, providing a welcome interruption.

Tom slides my cappuccino across the table saying, "Antonio used to have a boyfriend in Nice, didn't you."

Antonio shakes his head. "No he was in Grasse, but he moved."

I nod. "How long ago? I used to live in Grasse."

Antonio shrugs and sips at his coffee.

"A long time, at least five years. You wouldn't know him."

I shrug. "I was in Grasse until about four years ago," I say. "Stranger things have happened."

"What was his name again?" Tom asks.

"He wouldn't know him," Antonio answers, then turning to me he adds, "He was straight."

"Straight?" Tom wrinkles his nose. "I kind of doubt that, but anyway...What was his name?"

"Hugo," Antonio says.

I frown. My mouth is full of hot coffee, but I hold it there. There aren't a lot of Hugos in France, there are even less Hugos in Grasse, but *straight*?

"Hugo, that's it," Tom nods. "So how can he be straight if you dated him hon?"

"Exactly," I think.

Antonio shrugs again. "He was straight before, and he went back to his wife after. He just had a thing with me."

Not my Hugo then. My breath returns to normal. I don't think I could have stood sharing the love of my life with Antonio; still, an unexpected blast from the past.

Hugo! I picture the last time I ever saw him, replay him telling me he wanted out, but never explaining why. *"Closure,"* I think. *"That's what they call it; that's what I never got."*

"You had me worried there," I laugh. "I dated a Hugo, quite a big thing really. But mine *definitely* wasn't straight."

Tom looks at me. "I don't get the straight business though," he turns back to Antonio. "If you and he were..." He makes a little fucking mime with his hands then continues, "Surely he was *bi* at least?"

I run my finger around the edge of the cup. "There's a lot of that in France and Italy," I say. "Guys who define themselves as straight but still shag men. Can't be doing with it myself."

Antonio leans forwards. "Most of my exes were straight," he says. "I converted them," he adds proudly. "Who you sleep with doesn't define your sexuality."

The statement strikes me as stupid and vacuous.

Tom apparently thinks so too. "Antonio!" he says. "Who you sleep with *is* your sexuality!"

"Well, he was married before me, and he went back to his wife afterwards. *You* work it out," he replies.

"Must be hard," I say. "To lose your man to a woman."

"Hard for the woman too I suppose," Tom agrees. "They have kids?"

Antonio nods. "Yes, two. In the end that was why we split up. He kept talking about them all the time, wanting me to meet them. I just didn't want to think about his wife and kids you know?"

I nod. "I can see that."

"But when he was touring it was hard because sometimes his wife would come and visit..."

I frown. "When he was *touring*?" I ask. "What did he *do*?"

Antonio licks a finger and smoothes an eyebrow. It's a strange gesture. Out of place.

"He's a dancer," he says.

My world stops. I stare wide-eyed at Antonio. He simply stares back.

"What?" he asks me eventually. "You don't think dancers can be straight? I can tell you that the majority..."

"Hugo *Damiano*?" I say.

Antonio's eyes widen. "How do you know that?" he asks.

I shake my head and blink.

"How do you know that?" he repeats.

I smile in confusion. "I dated him," I say.

Antonio shakes his head. "I don't think so," he says. "He only dated me. He's straight."

90

I shrug. "Well I dated him," I say. "For nine months."

Antonio frowns and shakes his head. "No," he says. "You didn't."

"He had a Ducati motorbike," I say.

Antonio shakes his head. "No," he says again. "It can't be the same…"

"And two cats," I continue. "Garam and Masala."

Antonio frowns and pales a little. "OK, you know him," he says. "But you didn't date him. I don't believe you."

I rub the bridge of my nose. "Antonio. I went out with him for *nine* months."

Antonio shakes his head and shrugs. "I'm sorry," he says.

Tom frowns at me, then at Antonio. "Hey, Antonio. If Mark says he did…"

"But he has a *wife*?" I say. "Is that *true*? Are you *sure*?"

Antonio shakes his head. "It can't be the same guy."

"Did you *see* his wife?"

Antonio nods. "Sure, and his kids. You see; it's not the same person."

I look at Tom. He's biting his bottom lip, looking from one to the other, excited yet perplexed.

"Look. Antonio," I say. "I don't want to get vulgar or anything."

He looks vacantly at me.

"But his dick," I say. "Well, it's big, and it curves to the right. It's really big. And it curves a *lot*," I add.

Antonio stares at me wide eyed. His eyes start to glisten.

We sit in silence for a moment, each trying to reassemble the truth.

Tom speaks first, rubbing Antonio's shoulder. "Why is this so important though?" he asks, a worried tone creeping into his voice.

He looks back at me and stretches his fingers. "Why?"

I can tell that I'm flushing red as my anger mounts. "It's just a bit of a shock," I explain.

Antonio looks up. "Yes," he agrees. "His car was a VW, a Beetle back then, right?"

I nod. "A white one. It never worked."

Antonio nods.

Tom shrugs. "But so what?" he says.

"It's a shock," I say. "To find out someone you loved, someone you spent time with lied." I shake my head still absorbing the truth of it all.

"To learn that anyone can lie *that much*."

Tom nods at me blankly, then looks back at Antonio who has slumped over the table, his forehead resting on his hands.

It's the missing information, without which our break-up could never make any sense, and without that sense, all relationships since have been compromised.

If you learn that someone can get up and walk away from the best relationship you've ever had; if you learn that apparently for no reason, anything, no matter how good it is, can just *end*, well, it makes it hard to believe, hard to trust, hard to truly give yourself over to building anything ever again.

But there *was* a reason, a reason for the mysterious trips with his brother, a reason for the private phone calls, and ultimately a reason why he dumped me.

Hugo had a wife. Hugo had a bloody wife and kids!

I'm confused. I feel both relieved and angry at the same time. Actually I'm feeling *really* angry; I almost feel the desire to punch someone.

"I'd like to go," I say, standing. "Sorry."

Antonio looks up at me. He too has angry tears in the corners of his eyes. He nods coldly.

"Um, I'll catch you two later then," I say.

As I walk away, I hear them start to talk in Italian. It sounds like an argument, but then, to me, Italian always does.

As I walk home, I do a lot of head shaking. This elicits some strange looks from the shoppers, but in the end I neither strike out nor weep. In fact, by the time I get home, a peculiar feeling of amusement has developed.

The whole thing is just so ridiculous, so unbelievable. Could the idea that I dated a man with a wife and children for nine months and never even suspected the truth be anything *other* than a joke?

Back at the house, I sit staring at the wall, and gradually I realise just how many signs there were, how many indications I naively ignored.

The private phone calls "about work" that always had to be made in another room, calls that ceased if for some reason I walked into the room. The trips away with his brother to see their old grandmother;

Jesus! The kids' toys in the cupboard, supposedly left by a friend who used to share the flat with him. It's amazing, but in half an hour, I have gone from pure disbelief to a more satisfactory understanding of our entire relationship than I could have dreamt of.

I'm actually feeling relief that there *was* a reason Hugo left me. It's been so unnerving living with the concept that the guy I loved most left me on a whim, or worse still, was *with* me on a whim.

But then I realise that with my relief comes a kick. Sure, Hugo was straight, so the reason that relationship ended was that he wanted to go back to his wife, to his children, to his old life. But he was also a liar. Someone I loved was capable of consistently, undetectably lying through his teeth every day for the best part of a year. If you can't trust the person you love the most, then can you ever really trust anyone again?

Entrapment

I stare at the wall, obsessively running images of my yearlong relationship with Hugo through my mind, hunting for clues. The reality gap between the Hugo I dated and Hugo, Antonio's ex doesn't, I realise, mean that my version of the truth is the false one.

Perhaps, I reason, there is a third reality, a third version of events able to encompass everything that we both believe to be true, but try as I might, and no matter how many times I sift through the images, no new data comes to light.

The phone rings, and because I am grateful for the interruption, I snatch it from the receiver, but when I hear the voice at the other end I grimace.

"He lives!" Jenny exclaims. "Geez Mark, I've been trying to call you all week."

I silently mouth the word *"fuck"* and swallow, biding for time. "I, um... Did you?" I say unconvincingly.

"You know I did. I left enough messages," she spits.

I wince. "Messages?" I say. "How are you ever going to pull this off?" I wonder.

"Erh, *hello*?" Jenny says sarcastically. "You know, *messages*? On your *answer-phone*?"

An idea starts to form, and I grin at the naughtiness of it.

"Answer-phone?" I repeat, suppressing the smile. "There is no answer-phone, Owen doesn't have one," I say.

"But I left..." Jenny pauses.

"I don't know whose phone you left messages on, but it sure wasn't here," I laugh.

Jenny pauses. "But..." she says. "Really?"

"Really," I say.

"No, hang on," she says. "It has Owen's voice on it, *and* his number in Australia."

I frown, getting into my role. "Really?" I say. "I don't see..."

"Oh, I get it, he must have BT Call-minder. Oh Mark! Didn't you even know?"

"Call-winder?" I say. I bite my lip wondering if I'm overacting.

"Yeah, huh! I suppose you have been in France. Yes, English phones have a built in answer-phone," Jenny explains. "You have to dial one-five-seven-one to access it."

I smile at the conceit of "English phones." My French phone has had voicemail for fifteen years.

Jenny calms down and explains the intricacies of BT Call-minder to me; how to tell if there are messages, how to consult them, delete them. I'm such a good actor I actually write the instructions down on a piece of paper. I'm feeling so pleased with myself that I forget why I didn't want to answer the phone, and so, taken by surprise when she asks me what I have planned for the weekend.

"Nothing," I say.

I mouth another, "*fuck.*"

"Good," Jenny exclaims. "Well, get your party shoes on 'cos Jenny's coming to town."

"Oh good!" I say.

Critical Mass

As we take our seats I glance nervously at Tom and Jenny's faces. I'm having trouble imagining that the evening is going to be a party at all; Jenny looks glassy and hermetic, Tom has a pale flushed air about him, and anticipation of the two together makes me feel stressed and twitchy myself.

"So where's Antonio?" Jenny asks.

Tom shrugs and starts to remove his leather jacket. "He's changed his mind. Tired or something," he says.

Jenny wrinkles her nose. "Or something," she says. "Sounds ominous, did you two..."

Tom gives her an icicle glare, freezing her mid sentence.

She glances towards the bar. "I'll get some drinks then shall I?" she asks, forcing a smile.

"Antonio's not that comfortable around my gay friends," Tom says with a shrug.

"Really?" I say with a grimace. "It's a shame, I wanted to talk about Hugo, to fill in some of the gaps so to speak."

Tom nods. "That's probably half the problem actually. He hasn't wanted to discuss that business at all. Not once."

I nod. "I was pretty angry at first. But then it just started to strike me as funny."

Tom smiles weakly. "Yeah?" he says.

"I suppose that sounds weird," I say.

Tom shrugs. "Hugo sounds weird," he says.

I laugh. "That's the funniest thing. He wasn't weird at all. He seemed perfectly normal, quite loveable really."

Tom nods. "I think it dented Antonio's ego a bit. I think he liked being the only guy ever to have netted him."

Jenny arrives with my pint and returns to the bar for the others.

I nod. "I guess you could feel that way. If you were into the whole hetero thing."

Tom blinks slowly and works his mouth. "I'm jealous actually," he says.

I shrug. "Well don't be. You're worth ten Hugos."

He blushes slightly. "Yeah, but it's like, he was so important because he was *straight*."

"*Supposedly*," I point out.

"Yeah, *supposedly*, and Antonio was so flattered because this straight guy chose him. I guess my being with him means nothing really, me just being a big poof and all."

I nod my head sideways to suggest uneasy agreement. "I think you're overstating it, but I know what you mean. It *is* a bit homophobic."

"You said there's a lot of it in Italy?" Tom asks.

I nod. "I don't know whether it's because they're Catholic, or because the language barrier has cut them off from the whole gay lib movement, but so many French and Italian men have issues with their sexuality."

Tom frowns. "That surprises me," he says.

I shrug. "You deal with it, but it gets to be a bore. Every relationship seems to have this time bomb just waiting to self destruct."

Tom raises an eyebrow. "Yeah?"

"It's complicated," I say. "But there always seems to be a moment when the parents turn up, or the little sister finds out, or some colleagues from work see you out together. There always seems to be some moment when it all goes haywire."

Tom smiles and laughs sardonically. "Or the wife and kids turn up."

I nod. "Exactly," I say.

"Still," Tom forces a smile. "Look on the bright side. Antonio says I look like Hugo at least."

I nod. "Yeah. I thought that too actually. You really do."

He wrinkles his nose.

"That's not a bad thing though," I say. "Believe me."

Jenny sits heavily, plonking the pints on the table. She looks even bigger than during her previous visit. I almost mention it but, watching her drink a third of a pint in one sip, I change my mind, deciding it's really not my business.

"That guy has no idea how to pull a pint," she complains.

I lift mine up. "Looks fine to me," I say, sipping it. "Tastes fine too."

"Yeah, well, you didn't see him do it. It took him forever." She shakes her head and turns to Tom. "So how have you been?" she asks.

Tom nods half-heartedly. "Good," he says. "Antonio came over, which was a nice surprise."

Jenny nods. "Yeah, so I gathered," she says. "He lives in Italy right?"

Tom nods. "Yeah, in Genoa, near the French border. It's quite near Mark's place actually, well, a couple of hours away."

"Must be hard," she says. "Living that far apart."

Tom shrugs. "He comes over every couple of months, and usually, I go over too, so…"

I know I can't ask Tom about it again, so in my mind I *will* Jenny to do it for me, beg her to ask him how often, when he goes, why he hasn't been recently, but she just nods and looks around the pub distractedly.

"Not as busy as the other one, the airport-lounge-place is it," Jenny says.

"Charles Street?" I prompt.

Jenny nods.

"More of a chatting pub this one," Tom says.

Jenny laughs. "An *ugly* pub, more like."

"Hey," I say. "That's not fair."

She shrugs. "OK, an *old* pub then."

Tom frowns. We both look around.

"What about them?" I ask, nodding at a group of cute thirty-somethings in the corner.

Jenny sighs. "OK. But apart from them, well, it's a bit geriatric isn't it? I hope we're going somewhere else later."

"*Why* are you so rude?" Tom asks her.

I purse my lips and breath in, watching Jenny's face for a reaction. She seems unfazed.

"I just preferred the other place, that's all," she says.

Tom drops his jaw in amused outrage. "You *hated* Charles Street," he says.

"You didn't want to meet there," I point out. "You said no."

Jenny shrugs. "Whatever. I just don't see why you limit yourselves to gay places. It's so tired," she says.

"You sound like Antonio," Tom mutters.

"Hey, there's a whole world out there boys," Jenny says.

Tom sips his pint and then places it with precision on the table.

Without looking up he says, "So why don't you stay in Surrey?"

I bite my lip and stifle a smile.

"*What*?" Jenny whistles.

Tom raises his head and looks her straight in the eye. He raises an eyebrow. "If you don't like it here, then why don't you fuck off back to Surrey?"

I wince. I feel like I'm sitting in the dentist's chair; and the dentist has just struck a nerve. A red rash rises from Jenny's blouse, moving up and enveloping her face.

Tom continues, "I mean, you hate the pubs, you don't like the gay scene, you don't like Brighton, the people are ugly. It's just so..." he pauses and stands, stroking his beard. "Boring," he says finally. "It's just so fucking *boring*."

He turns and crosses the bar, disappearing into the toilets.

Jenny stares at the table, then at me.

I run my tongue around my teeth.

"Well?" she asks.

I shrug. I attempt a smile that says, *"Hey girl. Nothing to do with me."*

"What's *that* all about?" she asks. "He's *your* friend."

"That?" I repeat.

"Yeah. I mean it's not about me is it. I assume he's fallen out with Antonio."

I shrug and turn to the window, weighing up, comparing, and choosing. Jenny or Tom, aggression or complicity, confrontation or truth.

I turn back to face her.

"I don't think he put it well," I say.

"Put *what* well?"

"Well, you're actually quite..." I search for the word. "You *are* quite negative," I say.

She grimaces at me.

"It *is* hard work," I say in apologetic tone. "I'm sorry, but it's true." I nod. "It *is* boring."

She pulls her bag towards her and grips it like the grab rail on a roller coaster.

"Maybe I *should* just fuck off then," she says. "If I'm *boring* you."

I shrug. "Couldn't you just..."

She grabs my hand across the table. Her eyes are glistening. "Mark? Do you *want* me to go?" she asks.

"I..." I see Tom standing behind her and pause.

"You *do*, don't you! You actually *want* me to go!"

"Look," Tom says, sitting down.

"Mark here thinks I should fuck off too," Jenny tells him.

"I didn't say..."

Tom shakes his head. "I'm sorry," he says. "I didn't mean that to sound the way it did. It's not just you..."

"No *just* me?" Jenny cries.

Tom pauses and rubs the corner of his eye. "I've had a really bad week," he says. "Antonio's been... Well, he's been awful." His voice trembles a little as he says this.

I frown.

"He's been criticising everything," Tom continues. "Brighton, my clothes, my friends, my furniture. I don't know what's wrong with him."

Jenny gives me a *told-you-so* look.

Tom sees it. He looks at her sadly. "But you're *really* hard work!" he continues. "You're really critical, and it just never stops." He reaches for her hand on the table. She resists for a moment then gives in.

"It's all hard enough, you know?" he says. "Life is hard enough, without us all being bitchy to each other."

Like a slowly cooling thermometer, the colour sinks from Jenny's face until only tiny red blotches remain on her cheeks. She looks as if she's been slapped, which I suppose, verbally, she has been. She smiles at me weakly.

"It's true," she says. "I suppose. A bit." She makes a little noise half way between a laugh and a snort. "I've had a hard week too," she adds.

Tom takes a deep breath. "So can we just all try, for tonight, to be cool? To be nice? To enjoy ourselves?"

Jenny nods. "I suppose..." She pulls her bag towards her again. "Maybe I should just go though," she says, looking up at me inquiringly.

Tom shakes his head. "You know what I'd like," he says.

Jenny looks back at him and shrugs.

Tom grins weakly. "I'd like us all to get absolutely slaughtered," he says.

I smile. It's not what I was expecting.

"Can you? In your condition?" Tom adds, nodding at her stomach.

My eyes widen. I grind my teeth. *"Surely he doesn't think..."*

Jenny stares at him, silent, motionless, and reddening anew.

Under the table, I kick Tom sharply, but Jenny notices and without moving her head in the slightest, swivels her eyes to look at me.

Tom looks from Jenny to me and then back again.

"Sorry, I didn't mean..." he says. "I mean, I thought, after last week, when you were sick, that maybe, you couldn't, you know, get drunk," Tom splutters. "That's all."

Jenny runs her fingers through her hair and smiles sourly. She rubs her stomach and nods slowly.

"You thought I was *pregnant*," she says.

"No... Maybe. I mean I didn't really think at all," Tom says.

Jenny nods. "I see," she says, sitting back in her chair.

She sighs deeply.

"Jesus," I mumble.

There's a pause. No one speaks. I wonder what will happen. Wonder what *can* happen after that.

Jenny finally breaks the silence. "Well I am," she says. "So now you know."

I look from one to the other, my mouth ajar. "But..." I say.

Jenny stares at her hands, slowly turning her glass.

"But I don't see," I stammer. "I mean, why didn't you say?"

Jenny shrugs. "I *think*..."

She pauses a moment before continuing, "Well, I know actually, I just didn't... I just *don't* want to talk about it."

I swallow and look back at Tom. He opens his mouth to speak repeatedly, but says nothing.

"Can we, I mean, *should we* congratulate you?" I ask.

Jenny shrugs. "I don't know," she says. Her face is taut and pink. She looks like an over-ripe fruit about to burst. "It's complicated. That's the thing I can't work out... And until I've worked *that* out, can we just talk about something else?"

Tom and I nod.

"Otherwise, I might just fall apart," she says. Her eyes are watering and her voice is wobbling. "And believe me, we don't want that." Here she forces a thin-lipped smile.

Tom and I stare at each other, then at the table.

"OK," Tom says. "Sorry."

I nod slowly, and then clap my hands with false enthusiasm. "OK… What shall we talk about?" I ask.

Behind Jenny the group of thirty-somethings bursts into a peal of camp laughter. Jenny leans forwards and speaks very quietly.

"Could we *please* talk about going to another pub?" she says.

Boulevard Of Broken Dreams

The Princess Victoria is buzzing, as Tom predicted, with the required mixture of gay and straight clientele.

The strained atmosphere gradually dissolves, fizzling and fading with each pint of beer. There are moments when I even glimpse the old Jenny I used to know, and remember what used to be so funny about her. Her life was always a little tragic; her boyfriends always treated her badly or, in my case, turned out to be gay. But Jenny always managed to exaggerate the narrative to the point where it passed from tragic to funny, even for her. That was her specific thing, turning the awful into the awfully funny. That was not only how she survived, but also how she kept her friends entertained.

"Anyone for another before last orders?" Tom asks.

I notice for the first time that his voice is slurring, and when I answer, even though I only say, "*Sure*," I hear that my voice too is lacking a little precision.

Jenny downs the dregs of her own Smirnoff Ice and bangs the empty bottle on the table.

"Me too," she says.

Tom stands, but pauses. "Are you sure you should be drinking this much... I mean, seeing as you're pregnant?" he asks.

Jenny sits heavily back in her chair and shrugs. She starts to smile.

"I'm not even sure I should be pregnant this much," she sniggers, rubbing her belly. "Seeing as I'm drinking."

Tom looks at me and opens his hands in a *what now?* gesture.

"Get the lady what she wants," I say.

Back at Owen's place, Tom and I help Jenny up the stairs to my room where she sprawls across the bed.

"Best not undress her," Tom laughs. "She'll think she's been raped."

"In her dreams..." I giggle.

Tom gives me an inquiring glance.

"Oh, it's a long story. We went out together years ago. It didn't work out for obvious reasons."

Tom grins at me. "Right," he says.

I throw the edge of the quilt over her.

"This your room then?" he asks, sitting on the edge of the bed and looking around.

"For now, yeah. But I'll sleep in Owen's room while Jenny's here."

Tom nods, perusing the room.

"None of this is my stuff though," I add.

"Oh," he says, losing interest and standing.

Jenny, who I thought was sleeping, lifts her head and looks at me.

"Turn the light out and bugger off," she says.

Downstairs in Owen's lounge I drunkenly put the kettle on for tea, first overfilling it, and then over-emptying it. Finally I get it right and plug it in.

Tom sits on the floor leaning against the sofa. He picks up the remote control and fiddles with it.

I glance at him sitting on Owen's floor. It feels nice. It seems right that he should be there.

"You wanna go to a club?" he asks.

I lean in the archway between the kitchen and the lounge. Everything is a little blurred, but by concentrating I can force my eyes into focus.

"Nah," I say. "Sorry, but I'm up to my tits in beer."

Tom giggles. "Me too." He points the remote at me and pretends to zap me. "Can I put the TV on?"

"Sure," I say. "MTV is on button nine if you want some music."

Tom nods. "MTV. Cool," he says, clicking on the TV, which shimmers and shudders into life with a metallic twang. "I don't have MTV."

I turn and concentrate on pouring the boiling water over the teabags.

"It's good when you're pissed," I say. "Not too demanding."

Tom stretches out on his side to watch.

I glance at the TV. Gwen Stefani has her arms and legs sticking out of a tiny house. She's singing, *What-you waiting for.*

I fish out the teabags, burning my fingers in the process, and then add milk. Concentrating to avoid spillages I carry the two cups to the wooden coffee table.

I sit on the sofa above Tom. "Tea's there," I say, but he doesn't answer.

I lean over and peer at his face. His eyes are closed and I'm momentarily shocked at just how much he looks like Hugo.

I sigh and roll back onto the sofa and watch MTV, and drunkenly I think about Hugo and Tom, and then Tom and Hugo.

The music on MTV changes and I realise that I have closed my eyes. I force them open and see the start of a Green Day video.

My eyes ache from trying to focus on the screen, and with a last glance at Tom to check that he's sleeping I give in and close them again.

I think of Tom and Hugo and then Steve, and in some strange way they morph into one, not only with each other, but also with the music, with me, with the world.

Green Day sing on. *Boulevard of Broken Dreams* is the song.

When I awaken, the colourless first light is half-heartedly drifting over the rooftops and leaking through Owen's windows. The TV is off, and Tom has gone.

Public Offer

It's the first time I have been to *The Meeting Place* on a Sunday, and a queue of maybe twenty people has formed in front of the kiosk, so I join the line and shuffle slowly towards the achingly-slow orders counter. I spend the time peering three people in front at a cute goatee-clone and one behind at a too-young-for-me, but pretty-enough guy with a flat top.

When I am next in line to be served, a voice to my left makes me jump.

"Still not managed to order then?" he says, very loudly.

I turn and see Benoit's smiling face. He winks at me.

"Hello, I..." I pause, slowly realising that he's using me to jump the queue.

I glance nervously behind. The guy with the flat top gives me a hard stare.

"You manage to get seats yet?" I ask, getting into the scenario.

Benoit shakes his head. "No, not yet. It's packed. I'll go back and try again shall I?"

He hands me a ten-pound note and says, "I'm wanting a full breakfast, you remember?"

I nod.

"With black coffee," he adds.

The guy behind takes a step forward; I'm sure he's about to complain.

"I know," I tell Benoit. "You said."

The atmosphere over breakfast is strange, not only on our table but on all of the tables around.

Maybe it's Sunday hangover syndrome, maybe it's the grey sky, but everyone seems to have adopted the same hushed tone.

I alternate between making attempts at conversation with Benoit, and wondering if we'll ever have sex again, maybe even after breakfast. It seems a little trampy I guess, but I can't think of a better way of spending a grey Sunday afternoon. Benoit though, is in the same turgid mood as everyone else; his replies are terse at best.

"What did you do last night?" I attempt.

"Nothing much. Watched TV," he says.

I wait for him to inquire about my own evening, then give up and tell him anyway. "I went out with a friend, Jenny, and Tom – John and Jean's friend – you know him?"

Benoit nods. "The guy with the Italian boyfriend," he says, his mouth full of egg.

I nod.

"Nice," he says, forking half a fried tomato into his mouth.

"What are you doing this afternoon?" I ask.

He shrugs. "I am with JJ," he says.

I raise an eyebrow. "JJ?"

"John and Jean," he explains. "I have to be at their house for three."

I wiggle my brow at him. "Sounds fun. Another party?"

Benoit forks a fried mushroom into his mouth then pauses, staring at me.

"I'm having *tea* with them," he says with a sigh. "You are obsessed, no?"

I shrug. "Maybe," I say. "You may be right."

Benoit swallows his mouthful of food and runs his tongue around the corners of his mouth and pulls a slightly vulgar, very masculine expression as he does so.

"Are you horny or something?" he asks matter-of-factly.

I grin stupidly.

Benoit wipes his lips on a napkin, glances at his watch and swigs the last of his coffee and stands.

"Sorry, I must go now," he says, looking at his watch again.

I look up at him, disappointment registering on my face.

"Don't look so sad," he says, crouching down next to me.

I force a smile.

"Come round tonight, if you're free. About seven?"

I smile and shake my head in disbelief. "As easy as that huh?"

Benoit shrugs, then spins on one heel and starts to walk away. Then he pauses and glances back. A dirty grin spreads across his face.

"Sure," he says loudly. "I would love to have another go with your dick."

I hold my breath as the words sink in. Heads turn first towards Benoit to see where the words came from, then to me, the blushing victim.

"And bring condoms," he says. "I'm all out."

All desire fades in my embarrassment.

I finish my breakfast as fast as I can and, to avoid the accusing glances of my fellow diners, I escape along the seafront towards the pier.

Slowly my embarrassment turns to amusement, flattery even.

When I get back to Owen's, BT tells me I have two messages. The first, from Jenny, simply tells me she's home, not to worry, and not to call. She'll see me, she says, next weekend.

"Next weekend!" I think. "Jesus!"

The second message is from Benoit.

"I'm sorry, but I'll have to cancel for this evening," he says. "I'm going to be tied up with JJ."

I pout in disappointment and think the obvious thought, *"Tied up by JJ is more like it."*

The Devil You Know

As the week drags by, I think sweet thoughts about Tom, and then dirty thoughts about Benoit and then back to Tom again, and then back to Benoit, over and over, round and around.

I try to think of an excuse to call Tom but other than a rather lame, "I wondered if you got home OK," my mind's a blank.

Finally, on Wednesday, after rehearsing the conversation a thousand times I decide I'm ready and dial his number.

The call is answered by his voicemail, a simple, "Tom says leave a message," followed by a beep.

It's a possibility I stupidly failed to imagine, and the message that I leave is so pathetic, so stuttering, so mind numbingly awful that I actually pray to God to wipe it out before he hears it.

Benoit however picks up immediately. He sounds unsurprised by my call, in fact, if anything, he sounds bored.

"Hello," he says. "I'm sorry about the other day."

I can hear the TV playing in the background, peals of recorded laughter filling the air.

"No problem," I say. "I was feeling kind of lazy anyway."

"Yes," Benoit replies. "Me too."

I can tell his mind is half with the TV, half with me.

"You have fun then?" I ask.

I hear Benoit's lighter, and even the crackle of tobacco as he drags on the cigarette. It makes me want to smoke, makes me suddenly, desperately, passionately want to smoke. I haven't smoked since the accident.

"Fun?" he asks.

"At John and Jean's," I say.

Benoit coughs phlegmily; my cigarette desire fades.

"Yes, it was good," he says. I can hear from his voice that he's smiling. "We had tea."

"Yeah?" I wait for him to continue.

"And those things with the holes in them; *crumpets*?"

I smile. "Yeah, and?"

"And then..." he says temptingly. "You are sure you want the details?"

I grin. "Yep. I've been imagining it. Lets see if it holds up."

Benoit drags on his cigarette again. "Well, then..." he pauses and sips a drink. Amazingly I hear the ice cubes tinkling against the side of the glass.

"You are sure you want to know?"

"Oh come on!" I say.

"Well then, and this is the exciting bit..." Benoit coughs on his own laughter.

"Yeah?"

"Well, after that..." Benoit says. "I took them to Gatwick airport."

"Oh," I say. "Is that *it*?" I hear the tinkle of ice cubes again.

"Yes. You sound disappointed. What were you *imagining*?"

I sigh. "Well, lets just say something a little more exciting. You took them to the airport? Where have they gone?"

"Grande Canarie," Benoit replies. He says the name French-style. "You *do* sound disappointed. Were you going to visit them again?"

I laugh. "Maybe," I say.

"Hmm," Benoit says, sensuously. "Now there's a thought. I didn't think you would have the courage," he says.

"Yeah, well," I say. "Hey, are you drinking something with ice?" I ask.

Benoit pauses, then replies, his voice bubbling with amusement. "You are a psychic now, yes?"

"Nah, I can hear the ice," I say. "It's amazing actually, I can hear everything. I can hear you breathing in through your cigarette."

Benoit laughs. "Wait," he says. "So what can you hear now?"

I listen, but hear nothing.

His voice returns, "So?"

"Sorry, nothing," I say.

"Again," he says.

For some reason, I start to get an erection.

"Ah," I say. "I heard it then... A zip?"

Benoit laughs. "Maybe you should come round and check," he says.

By the time I have cycled to Benoit's he has turned the lights low, lit a few candles, and put on his magic chaps. He pulls me through the front door into the apartment and kisses me deeply.

"I'm glad you came," he says. "I was working on these," he points at his computer screen; it's filled with black and white photos.

"They make me very horny," he says.

I lean towards the screen and peer at the pictures. They show a man with a tight muscled body being strapped up in a harness.

"Those taken at JJ's?" I ask.

Benoit nods and looks at the screen with me.

"They're great pictures," I say. "Very beautiful actually. Was that the birthday party?"

Benoit laughs. "No, these are art shots. He's a model. It's for a book I'm contributing to."

I smile at him and look back at the screen. "They're great," I say again.

Benoit nods. "There's something very sensuous about the skin and the leather, the light shining off the chrome... It works especially in black and white. I tried colour first, but black and white is much better."

He rubs a hand over my crotch.

"Humm, they have the same effect on you as on me," he laughs.

I roll my head from side to side. "Erm, how *couldn't* they?"

Benoit shrugs. "Not everyone has the same trips," he says. "You'd be surprised."

He leans over and clicks on the mouse. A second page of photos appears.

In these the model is being strapped onto a cross. His perfectly formed arse juts out, caught in the contrast of light and shadow.

"Wow," I say.

Benoit nods, and slips a hand down the front of my jeans. "It's a shame," he says. "I could have had the keys to the dungeon if I had known."

My heart jumps a little at the thought. The idea of being alone in Disneyland with chunky hairy Benoit is much more exciting than being there with John and Jean.

I look him in the eye. "Now that *is* a shame," I say.

The sex with Benoit is amazing. We roll around in the bed,

rubbing and growling, and laughing. He produces a constant stream of toys from a drawer beneath the bed, and whether he reappears with a dildo, or with nipple clamps, or with a dog collar, I fake outrage, playfully resist, then finally give in, and game by game, inch by inch, my body becomes one huge erogenous zone.

Finally, with more fingers up my arse than I like to admit, a screamingly pinched nipple, and Benoit's tongue teasing and probing and encircling my cock, I break into a screaming, back-arching orgasm. Benoit, whose only pleasure it would seem, is my own, watches me excitedly.

"Yes!" he enthuses.

After the briefest of cuddles and a whisky, I am ejected from Benoit's flat with a simple apology that he has to work, and the order to call, "any time."

As I cycle back along the seafront in the fading light, I wonder why the sex with him is so free, so wild, so satisfying.

Is Benoit is just exceptionally good in bed or have I somehow changed?

Perhaps it's simply the isolation of my sex with Benoit that changes everything, the fact that what we do in bed is disconnected from everything else in my life.

Maybe sex exists more easily in its own space, without the expectation, judgement and disappointment; without the constant interpretation that we apply to every act committed by those we love.

Whatever the reason, not caring what Benoit thinks about me, not worrying about him judging me, not giving a damn what he tries to stick inside me or how loud I end up screaming feels good. It feels *orgasmic*.

Partial Truths

I switch on the kettle, and log onto the Internet to check my French bank account. When I return to the computer with my steaming mug of tea, my mouth drops.

I stare at the screen in disbelief. Sure I was expecting this, but the size of the payment, and the reality of it in my bank account is a shock.

I bite my bottom lip to suppress a greedy smile. Eleven thousand Euros!

I sip my tea and stare at the screen, and watch my mind as the emotion shifts from surprise to joy, and on through to guilt.

I force myself to acknowledge that this money is payment for my injuries, not for the loss of Steve, but the two are somehow impossible to separate and I hover on a knife-edge between relief – for I truly need this money – and sadness.

Finally, as the what-ifs slither down the muddy slope and into my mind, I sink into a numb fug of depression. What if we had stopped at the services? What if I had been driving? What if we had stayed an extra half an hour on the beach?

I so don't want to go down this road.

I glance around the room, desperate for a distraction, any distraction. My eyes settle on the phone.

Jenny says she's bored and would like nothing more than to "crank up the hippy bus" and "chug down the motorway."

It's only Jenny, but hell, I need company and I need to be busy. I actually pace up and down the lounge until I see the orange of her van roll into the street below.

The poor girl barely has time to dump her bag before I rush her back out the door.

The Barley Mow already has a weekend buzz about it even though it's just before seven.

Jenny and I take seats facing the door. I left a message on Tom's mobile in the hope that he'll join us. Our Friday nights together seem almost a ritual now.

"Pub's OK," Jenny says, looking around.

I nod. "It's just Owen's local," I say. "I like it though."

She nods, sips her beer and then licks her lips.

"So tell me about your home life," I prompt. "It all seems very mysterious."

Jenny frowns. "Mysterious?"

I nod. "Yeah, you never seem to mention… Erm…"

"Nick?" she says.

I nod. "Yeah, see. I don't even know his name."

Jenny shrugs. "What about him?"

I puff with exaggerated frustration. "I don't know… How did you meet? How long ago? What does he do?"

Jenny sips her drink and stares into the middle distance, apparently thinking about her reply.

I shake my head. "Look, if you really don't want to ta…"

"We met in the local pub," she interrupts. "Nearly two years ago."

I nod.

"He's a builder."

"A builder?" I repeat. "I didn't imagine…"

"Well, he's more of a manager now really. It's his own company."

"So what's he like?" I ask.

Jenny leans across the table and stares into my eyes. "Generally, or right now?" she says.

I frown at the question. "Both," I say.

"Deep down he's lovely," she says. "Right now, he's a cunt."

I'm unable to think of a suitable reply.

"That's why I'm here so much," Jenny says. "Just to get away from it."

I nod. "And I thought it was just to see *fabulous* me," I say.

I grimace at my failed attempt at humour. It sounded more accusatory than anything else.

Jenny shrugs. "I need these breaks," she says. "Sometimes, I think I'm close to losing my mind."

I nod.

"Anyway," she says, sipping at her beer again.

"So do you want to talk about it or forget it?" I ask.

Jenny wobbles her head from side to side. "Both I suppose. I can't really decide."

Her voice trembles. She scrunches up her eyes as if she is in pain. She clears her throat, and then continues.

"The trouble is, I kind of think, well, if I start... Well I might just..."

She sits very straight and stares past me towards the door.

I reach across the table for her hand. "I know," I say. "I know what you mean."

"The thing is, Nick doesn't want the baby. He doesn't want it at all," she says.

"He doesn't *want* it?" I repeat.

Jenny nods slowly. "We've been arguing so much since I told him."

She turns and stares towards the bar and shakes her head. "I don't know what to do really," she says. "I mean I do love him, but..." She sighs.

"Maybe he'll come round," I venture. "Like Darren and Suzie. Do you remember?"

She nods. "Yeah, that's what I was hoping really, that he'd see the baby and come over all paternal." She stares through me. "I'm not sure we'll even get that far though," she adds, biting her lip.

I wrinkle my nose. "What? Divorce? Surely he's not that bad is he?"

Jenny shrugs. "I don't know," she says. "He's so anti."

"Why though? Does he just *never* want kids?"

Jenny shakes her head. "I don't think he wants chocolaty hands all over his Bang and Olufsen. The poor guy can't imagine anything worse."

I move my head from side to side. "Suggests a certain lack of imagination," I say. "Not being able to imagine anything worse."

Jenny manages a little laugh. "Actually part of me agrees with him. Part of me understands that it will be the end of holidays and skiing and white carpets. Part of me doesn't want kids either. But another part of me wants it passionately, desperately," she says.

"And did you know that Nick didn't want kids when you got pregnant?" I ask.

Jenny nods and blinks slowly.

"You didn't trick him like Suzie did, did you? You didn't stop taking the..."

Jenny shakes her head. "I wasn't on the pill, I couldn't. Anyway. We were using condoms, but we ran out. It was only once."

I nod. "So it's his fault as well; I mean, his responsibility."

Jenny pulls her mouth downwards. "It was weird, special circumstances really. I said I thought we'd be OK. What with the time of the month and everything."

I shake my head. "Why didn't you just go get condoms?"

Jenny laughs mockingly. "We were in a traffic jam."

I bite my lip. "You conceived in a *traffic jam*?"

Jenny nods. "Oh, it's a long story, but we were on holiday and we got stuck..."

She breaks into a smile. At first I think it's at the memory of traffic-jam sex, but then I realise she's looking towards the door, re-composing her face.

"Tom!" she exclaims.

Leap Of Faith

Tom looks suspiciously between us. "Did I interrupt something?" he asks.

Jenny shakes her head slowly. "Nah," she says, standing. "I have to go to the loo."

Tom looks at our glasses. "Better get myself a drink I guess," he says. "You two OK?"

Just as Tom sits down with his drink, Jenny returns, her face washed and re-composed.

"So what were you two discussing?" Tom asks. "You seemed very intense."

Jenny shakes her head. "Nothing really, what's new with you?" she asks brightly. "You look good."

Tom licks his lips and looks at Jenny then back at me, apparently deciding how much to tell.

There seems to be a twinkle in his eyes, but whether it's desire, joy, or simple intrigue, I can't tell.

"Well," he says, lowering his head theatrically. "Antonio and I had some big, *big* discussions last week."

I straighten in my seat and nod.

"I think we kind of worked out where we're at," he says, blushing slightly.

I wrinkle my brow and suck the inside of my mouth.

"So where are you at?" Jenny asks.

Tom nods. "Well, I haven't really told you, but we've been a bit make or break lately..."

My diabolical couple-buster does a silent, secret, jump for joy.

"And we've been kind of thinking, well, *I* have, that we need to either get it together, or, well, split up really."

I nod.

"Sooo..." Tom chews a fingernail and looks cutely at me out of the corner of his eye.

I grin and nod. "Yes?" I say.

"So Antonio is moving to Brighton," he says. "Maybe."

I order my face to maintain the current expression of amused intrigue, at least until I've worked out a more suitable one.

"Gosh!" I say.

Jenny casts me a worried glance. "Wow!" she says. "You must be chuffed."

Tom breaks into the sweetest grin of child-like joy. "We're maybe going to buy a house together," he says. "Possibly."

I decide to emulate Jenny. "Wow!" I say.

"That's great," she says.

"Yes, great!" I repeat.

Tom nods and fingers his little beard. "I mean, nothing's certain yet, and I'm trying not to get too excited because, well, in case..."

Jenny and I nod.

"But Antonio's told me to get my place valued and look for somewhere bigger. His company have offered him a UK post and he reckons he could live here and commute to London."

I nod. "You're selling your flat then?" I ask.

Jenny frowns at me.

Tom nods. "Yeah, well, we couldn't live in my place. We'd kill each other."

"Have you ever lived together before?" I ask.

Jenny glances at Tom and, confident that he won't see, she crosses her eyes at me. I can see her point. My inability to feel happy for them shocks me too.

"No," Tom says. "But I guess you just have to just make that leap of faith at some point don't you."

I nod enthusiastically. "Yes," I say. "I guess you do."

Strategic Decisions

We say goodbye to Tom, who grins, gives us a little wave, and heads off towards *Storm*. The moon is full and bright in a cloudless sky giving an eerie bleached effect.

Jenny links her arm through mine.

"That's a very bad strategy you know," she says.

"Strategy?" I ask.

"Yeah, resenting Antonio," she says.

I laugh lightly. "Who resents Antonio?" I ask.

"Well," Jenny says. "If you want Tom then my advice is to just hang around, be there, and be as perfect as you can. And perfect means not disliking his choice of boyfriend."

We swap over to the other side of the road.

"Jenny, they're moving in together," I say. "They're buying a house together. And anyway, who says I want *Tom*?"

Jenny laughs. "You do. And you'd be stupid not to. You two are perfect together."

I frown. I'm somewhat shocked that she thinks so too.

"Perfect except that he's in love with Antonio," I say.

"Well, my bet is that it won't happen," she says. "I mean; would *you* move here? From *Italy*?"

"Well, maybe," I say. "Plenty of people do," I add, thinking of Benoit. "But even if he doesn't, it still doesn't mean that anything will happen between Tom and I."

"Have you *seen* the way he looks at you?" Jenny asks. "I mean, do you actually notice *anything*?"

I frown again. I smirk lightly. "I thought that was just in my head," I say.

Jenny shakes her head. "It's not. He's falling in love with you."

I snort. "He's *not*!" I laugh. "Anyway, if anything, I think I actually need to see less of him."

"Less?"

Jenny tries to walk on ahead, but I drag her right, into the top of

Owen's street.

"Oh!" she exclaims. "We're here already!"

At the bottom of the road the sea is reflecting the moon. "Wow! Look at that," I say.

"Yeah," she says reverently.

"I don't think it's healthy for me to be spending so much time with him," I explain.

Jenny shakes her head. "Why on earth not?"

"Oh I don't know. I suppose I like him too much really. I don't *want* to be his *mate*. You know what I mean?"

Jenny makes a thoughtful, *Hum* sound.

We walk down the hill towards the sea in silence. Eventually she speaks.

"For what it's worth," she says, "Not seeing someone because you like him doesn't make any sense at all. In fact it sounds stupid as can be."

I nod. "I guess so."

"And while you're being consumed by jealousy, Tom is alone in a club full of men, just waiting to meet whoever will take Antonio's place."

We turn up the short staircase to Owen's and I jiggle the key in the lock.

"I must oil this," I mutter, pushing the door open. "That's a bit cynical don't you think?"

Jenny shrugs. "I'm good at relationship stuff," she laughs. "Well, other people's anyway. And long distance relationships *never* last."

I sigh. "We'll see," I say.

"Actually relationships never last, full-stop," she says.

I throw my jacket over the back of the chair. "Yeah, well... As I say, we'll see," I repeat.

Jenny sighs. "Not unless you're *around* to see you won't," she says.

The strange moonlight in the room produces a surreal two-dimensional effect. I look around in surprise then move to the window.

"That's an amazing moon," I say.

"Get back there," Jenny tells me. "Go dance, have fun. Be enthusiastic about Antonio coming. Show your friend how happy you are for him."

I shake my head. "I don't think I want to be his friend though," I say. "I'm too greedy to make do with part time slots with someone else's boyfriend. I want someone of my own. I don't want to be shagging one guy and talking to another."

Jenny moves to my side and looks out of the window. "Who are you shagging?" she asks. "You never mentioned..."

I shake my head and interrupt. "It's not important, and that's the problem. I want it to be important. I want to be in love; I want to have that full-on mad impossible love thing again," I frown in surprise at myself.

"It's overrated," Jenny says. "That full-on love thing."

I turn from the moon to look at her. "Tell me," I say. I touch her shoulder but she pulls away, spinning on one foot and heading towards the door.

"Tomorrow," she says. "We'll talk tomorrow."

I nod.

"Now you go back and save that boy," she says. "I'm going to bed."

I shrug. "Save him from *what*?"

She smiles. "Who knows?" she laughs. "You won't know unless you go."

"I'm not sleepy at all," I say thoughtfully. "The full moon I guess."

Jenny nods at me. "You see."

I shrug. "I suppose I might as well."

Look-Alike

The seafront is strangely deserted; I guess everyone is either already in a club or safely home.

As I walk I stare at the moon floating above the sea. A single semi-transparent cloud has formed in front, making it look even bigger.

At *Storm*, the bouncer opens the door and utters a simple, "Evening."

I start up the stairs, and then pause. "Oh!" I say. "You're leaving?"

Tom, who is at the halfway landing heading down, grins at me.

"Oh, you're back!" he says.

I climb the stairs until we're face to face. "I wasn't sleepy so..." I nod behind him. "Is it no good in there?"

He waves his head from side to side. "I was bored really, that's all."

He looks sad. His earlier effervescence has faded.

"You OK?" I ask.

He wrinkles his nose and nods. "I hate clubs on my own," he laughs. "Still, seeing as you're back..."

He reaches for my hand and turns and starts to climb the stairs again.

"Lets give it another go," he says.

The club is busy and bouncy. It's difficult to see how anyone could be bored and the thought that Tom was leaving until he saw me leaves me feeling flattered.

The majority of the men are muscle-boys, T-shirts in pockets.

"Wow!" I shout as we push towards the bar. "What a selection!"

When I reach the counter I turn to Tom, squeezing his way through behind me.

"The trouble is," he says looking left and right, "these people all spend more time at the gym than they do reading."

I frown at him and shrug. "So?"

"They're all so fucking ignorant," he says.

I wrinkle my nose at him. "Let me get a drink and you can tell me all about it," I laugh. "Lager?"

Tom nods.

I wave a banknote at the barman and scrutinise the men lined up along the bar.

I catch sight of a guy who seems familiar, and I frown, then realise that he looks exactly like Jimmy Somerville.

I suddenly wish they were playing *Small-town Boy*, or *Tell Me Why* instead of this smooth funky house. I wonder when club music stopped being fun, stopped being music you could whoop and shout and jump to, when the tunes people sang along with, the b52's or even Sylvester finally disappeared from the clubs.

I pay for the drinks and pocket the change, pushing my way back to Tom who has been squeezed away from the bar.

"Thanks," he says, reaching for the drink. "I ran out of cash, so..."

"So what happened?" I ask. "Not like you to be pissy."

He shakes his head. "Oh, some arsehole had a go at me on the dance-floor. He tried it on with me once, and got upset when I refused."

I nod and sip my beer. "What did he say?"

"When? Today?"

I nod.

Tom laughs. "He didn't actually say much. He just pinched my waist and said, *Oh dear, Tom. If you can pinch more than an inch*."

I grimace. "Ouch."

"In the middle of the fucking dance floor."

I pull a face. "That is pretty rude," I say. "Arsehole."

Tom nods. "I know; gay men are the most fat-phobic society on earth."

I shrug. "Except maybe models; anyway, they're only trying to cover how unworthy they feel," I say. "It's not really their fault." I open my eyes wide. "Society *made* them feel that way."

Tom shrugs. "Did society make them arseholes too?" he asks.

I laugh. "No, you're probably right. They did that all themselves."

He sips his drink again then frowns. "Can I ask you something?" he says.

I nod and smile.

"And you'll answer honestly?" he asks intensely.

I nod again, beginning to worry that he might ask me how I feel about him. Jenny hasn't prepared me for that one.

"Do you think I'm fat?" he asks. "I mean... I know I'm not skinny, but do I look fat?"

I laugh. "Absolutely not," I say.

He grabs my free hand and slides it under his T-shirt, placing it on his waist.

"I mean, there's a bit of fat there... But I'm forty, right? That's normal, isn't it?"

The contact with his hand, his waist, his body, is giving me the stirrings of an erection. I laugh, pull my hand away and shake my head.

"Tom, if you didn't have fat, you'd be dead. Your body is perfect."

Tom pulls his T-shirt back down and looks left and right.

"Yeah," he says. "Fuck 'em."

"Tom, really," I say. "You're..." I shrug.

Tom looks at me and frowns. "Go on?" he says.

I decide to make a joke of it. I think of a character from a comedy series, who says everyone is gorgeous.

"You're *gorgeous!*" I laugh.

He breaks into a grin. "Well thanks," he says. "You're pretty lovely too." He stares into my eyes. "I'm glad you came back," he adds.

I swallow and glance towards the bar.

"Did you see that guy?" I ask, changing the subject. "The one that looks like Jimmy Somerville?"

Tom shakes his head. "Nope."

I step back towards the bar and peer through the crowd.

"Still there," I say, nodding towards the end of the bar. "Over in the corner, alone."

Tom follows my gaze, and then breaks into a grin.

"That *is* Jimmy Somerville," he laughs.

I smile and shake my head. "Yeah right," I say. "That's Jimmy Somerville twenty years ago. Think about it."

Tom nods, then peers at the distant figure again.

"No that *is* him," he insists.

I look again at the figure. "If that's Jimmy Somerville I want to know what skin cream he uses!" I laugh.

Tom laughs. "He probably uses fresh sperm," he says.

I open my mouth in mock outrage. "You're getting confused with Marc Almond," I say.

"Well, he *has* aged well, I give you that," Tom says.

"It's *so* not him," I insist.

Tom looks at me coquettishly. "I bet you," he says, his eyes twinkling.

"You bet me what?"

"Dinner!" he says.

I grin and reach forward to shake his hand, then I start to move away.

Tom grabs my shoulder. "Where are you going?" he asks.

I shrug. "To ask him!"

Tom groans.

The Jimmy look-alike is propped in the darkest corner of the bar, and as I approach, I realise that the shadows may be hiding wrinkles, but as I get closer I'm certain that it's not him; the guy looks twenty-five for heaven's sake.

"Excuse me?" I say.

The man glares at me over his beer.

"Are you Jimmy Somerville? Because I betted that you weren't and..."

The man forces a tired grin and nods. "I am," he says with a sigh. His accent is thick, Scottish.

I laugh. "Sorry," I say. "It's just, well, I said you looked too young to be... Erm."

He wrinkles his brow and nods at me to continue.

"Well, to be *you*, really."

He looks at me tiredly and rolls his eyes. I start to realise that he thinks I'm some drawling fan, thinks that I'm simply fawning over him.

"I said you looked like Jimmy Somerville twenty years ago," I add, blushing at the realisation that I'm making it worse.

"Soo," he says with a nod. "Am I supposed to be flattered?" He pronounces supposed, suppoosed.

I realise the awfulness of fame, the impossibility of accepting a simple compliment, and at the same time I start to feel annoyed at his arrogance.

I shrug. "Take it how the fuck you want," I laugh. "But if someone told *me* I looked too young to be me, *I'd* be flattered."

With that, I give him a slap on the shoulder, and spin back through the crowd towards Tom, or rather towards where Tom was.

Fat Fighters

I find Tom on the dance floor, shimmying again with his tranny admirer. Tonight she's wearing a leather mini-skirt and thigh high boots.

He makes a drinking gesture and points to where he has left my pint. I down half of the remaining lager before heading across the dance floor towards them.

"So?" he asks.

I nod. "You're right. I owe you dinner," I shout.

"*This* is *Belinda*!" Tom says, tipping his head to one side.

The tranny dances up and gives me her limp hand. I bow and kiss it.

"Good evening," she shouts.

"We have to stop meeting like this!" I laugh, but when she leans forward indicating that she can't hear I simply shrug to show that it is of no importance.

The music is cheesy house and the dance-floor has divided into two distinct zones. The muscle boys at the far end, and everyone else, the trannies, the girly-boys and the fully clothed on our side, near the bar.

Tom touches my shoulder and leans into my ear. "So?" he asks.

I nod. "I said! You're right."

He shakes his head. "The *skin* cream?" he asks.

I laugh again. "I don't know!" I say. "I forgot."

He pouts petulantly.

"He's a twat though," I say.

Tom nods.

"Disappointing," I add.

I dance half-heartedly and watch Belinda grooving her hips until the DJ fades into a track I know, Late Night Alumni's *Empty Streets*. I start to groove seriously and watch as Tom and Belinda do the same.

When a hand touches my shoulder, I turn. It's Jimmy grinning stupidly at me. I pucker my brow in surprise, unsure how to react.

"Hey," he shouts, addressing me, then Tom. "Is that true?"

Tom dances forwards and smiles at him. "What?" he asks.

"Did this twat bet? Did he bet that I'm not me?" Jimmy says.

Tom laughs and nods his head exaggeratedly, in time with the music.

Jimmy slaps me on the back and laughs. "OK, sorry mate," he says. "I thought you were taking the piss."

I shake my head and smile back.

Jimmy nods. "That's cool," he grins with an exaggerated nod. "That's really cool."

I nod.

"Hey man!" he laughs. "I'm made up," he says. "I'm really made up!"

Still grinning, he grooves through the crowd and takes up position at the shoreline, where the sea of semi-naked muscle-bunnies meets the land of the clothed.

Tom leans towards me and says, "He isn't made up. He's off his fucking head!"

I nod. "Yeah, he seems cool though."

I glance across the dance-floor and Jimmy gives me a grin and a thumbs-up.

The music shifts and speeds. A laser creates a green ceiling of light just above our heads.

Cigarette smoke swirls, caught in the light like clouds in a fast-forward sky. People lift their hands, irresistibly drawn to break the beam.

Belinda grooves ever more seriously and starts to pout. Actually, I realise, she is starting to gurn, starting to produce the strange lip movements that go with ecstasy.

I wipe my brow.

"Fucking hot!" Tom shouts.

"Take your top off!" I say, hopefully thinking of the swirling hair on his chest.

He shakes his head and nods towards the muscle boys. "Too much competition!" he says.

A jet of dry ice fills the air, and momentarily everyone disappears. The green laser ceiling becomes a brilliant swirling mass.

As the fog fades, I see that Belinda has Tom's T-shirt. She's waving it above her head.

Jimmy reappears through the mist, I watch him dance and flashback to the *Small Town Boy* video clip. I realise that he still moves the same way; still makes the tight little digging movements of the eighties.

That song! It defined a new era. An era when an out and out gay record could feasibly become a major hit. What optimism that simple success gave us.

People are moving from the bar to the dance floor, squashing us ever closer. Tom's chest is tantalisingly close. I let my arm brush against his skin.

He moves towards me and lays a hand across my back and shouts, "Stop it!" in my ear.

I'm amazed that he has noticed. I shake my head and decide to bluff. "Stop what?"

Tom steps backwards and starts to dance, starts to do the same little digging movement with his arms.

"That!" he shouts, nodding towards Jimmy. "He'll realise!"

I grin dumbly. It's true. I've reverted to my eighties college dance, the Jimmy Somerville chicken wing. I make an "oops" face and force myself into a different movement; but it's surprisingly hard.

A bare-chested guy pushes towards me from my right and then elbows me out of the way. He inserts himself into the space between Tom and myself.

I feel irritated, but I look at the shape of his arse, the smooth back descending into low cut blue jeans, and decide it's not so bad.

I glance up at Tom, try to catch his eye, but he's not impressed. In fact, he's frowning at him. I see that Belinda is glaring too, and moving forwards.

Then I see the man lean towards Tom, see him start to speak. My antenna is registering trouble, something about the man's stance, the way he's stretching his shoulders, spreading his feet, making himself look bigger, like a cat arching its back.

He reaches out and blocks Belinda's path with his left arm. Tom's face shifts to an expression of outrage; Belinda knocks his hand away and steps forward again. In her boots she's actually a good four inches taller than him.

"Why don't you fuck off to the children's corner," I hear her say.

The man pushes her sideways with his arm. He pushes her hard and she totters and wobbles in her high heels. For a moment it looks as if she has found her feet, and she sways in a circular motion, seemingly finding her centre of gravity. But then she teeters backwards once again and collapses into the crowd.

"I wouldn't fuck you if you begged me," the guy spits. "You fat bastard!"

A clearing is forming around us. Tom shakes his head, his mouth open, apparently lost for words.

Unsure how to react, I move towards Tom's side, but the guy blocks my path with his right arm, knocking *me* backwards.

People have stopped dancing, most are watching the dispute, some look concerned, some amused, excited by the action.

Belinda reappears and she's crimson with anger. She pushes between Tom and his aggressor and points a finger at the man's chest. "Honey," she says. "You *so* need to fuck off."

"Who the fuck are you?" the guy shouts.

"And *perlease*, get a plastic surgeon on those *ears*!" she laughs.

He lurches towards her, but as he raises his arm, as he moves his hand back to punch her, his elbow sweeps an arc only inches from my face, and without thinking, I grab it, spoiling his swing.

He shakes me free and using his left hand instead, places his hand, fingers stretched, across Belinda's face. In an obscene gesture he simply pushes her from the picture.

Tom looks around, and apparently seeing someone he knows, shouts, "Do something! Get the fucking bouncer!"

The guy has now turned to face me. I note he has a scar across his forehead.

"Another one!" he says. "Who the fuck are *you*?"

I get my first glimpse of his blue eyes. They hold a bottomless rage, a deep unhappy drunken madness I've seen somewhere before. And I know that there's no clever answer, no easy way to stop this spiral of violence. He's out of control.

I swallow hard and instinctively pull my glasses from my nose, and slide them into my shirt pocket. But just as I stretch my neck, just as I prepare my body for action, the music stops and the dance floor is drenched in a blinding white light.

Momentarily distracted, the guy glances left and right, then a huge bouncer – with arms the thickness of my waist – pushes me out of the way and grabs him by the shoulder. He looks like Steve, the bouncer from the Jerry Springer show; in fact the whole scene looks pretty much that way.

"Enough!" he shouts.

The guy points at Tom accusingly. "He started it! That fucker there!" he says.

The bouncer nods at a colleague who grabs Tom's shoulder. "OK, you too," he says.

Tom shakes his head. "Me?" he says, looking desperately to me for support.

"He's not..." I start, but the bouncer is ignoring me.

I touch him lightly on the shoulder, something he doesn't like at all. He turns jerkily and glares at me.

"Get your fucking hands off me!" he says.

I lift my hand. "Sorry! I say. "But he didn't start this."

Belinda steps forward. "It's not our problem," she says, "It's the prick with the big ears."

Big Ears lurches towards her again but the bouncer grabs him by both shoulders and pulls him back.

The security staff look at one another, and, seemingly having communicated without words, the first one reaches for my shoulder and the second places a hand behind Belinda, pushing her forwards.

"OK, all four of you then. Out!" the first one says.

"No way José!" Belinda shrieks, prising off his hand, "Fuck you!"

A third guy appears wearing a headset. "What's happening here?" he says.

Tom, Belinda and Big Ears all shout at the same time. The result is an incomprehensible cacophony of shrieking.

I turn to look at the guy with the headset, but he is leaning listening to someone, to Jimmy. He nods as he listens and then glances up, first at Belinda, and then at me.

He leans towards the big bouncer, says something low, something inaudible. Again, the two staff stare at each other, and then in a single movement, they release Tom and Belinda before grabbing Tom's aggressor and bustling him towards the door.

"I'll fucking 'ave you!" the guy shouts, as the two men literally carry him up the stairs.

I catch Jimmy's eye. As he slips back into the crowd, he winks at me.

The lights start to dim again. Tom pulls on his T-shirt. He looks pale and ghost-like.

"Shall we fuck off as well?" he asks.

Belinda who is still red faced, forces a smile. "Hey, come on boys," she says. "We're a team!"

She feigns holding a gun in the air and says, "Charlie's Angels, look out!"

Tom grins weakly.

"Anyway, Tom!" she says. "You don't want to leave yet. Let them get rid of Big Ears first."

The man with the headset steps up to Tom, leans into his ear and says something before readjusting his headset and walking away.

Tom shrugs at me. "Might as well stay," he says.

I reach in my pocket for my glasses and realise my hand is trembling. "Well, actually I could do with a stiff drink," I say, glancing at the bar.

Tom smiles weakly. "Well, that's a happy coincidence," he says. "The owner just offered us a free bar."

Belinda pouts and wiggles her shoulders as she gets back into her role. "Hon," she says. "Never refuse a blow job, and *never* refuse a free drink. Mine's a double Bacardi. With Coke."

Tom sighs and nods at me. "You?"

I shrug. "I'll come with you," I say.

People are moving back onto the floor, but still talking a lot about the incident, still sneaking surreptitious glances at us.

Tom pulls his T-shirt down and we push through to the bar. He glances down at himself and tugs on the T-shirt again.

"You look fine," I say.

He smiles. "I shouldn't let it get to me," he says with a shrug.

"Is he the guy you had trouble with earlier?" I ask.

Tom nods. "I refused to sleep with him. It was ages ago though..."

"Well, you're in a relationship," I say. "It's not even like it's an insult..."

"No," Tom interrupts. "This was even *before* Antonio. I refused him because he's a cunt."

I grimace.

Tom nods. "No he *is*. He's a bare-backing, bug infecting, evil fuck."

I frown. "Another bare-backer?"

Tom nods and laughs angrily. "Yeah, right. And guess who his best mate is?"

I shake my head.

"That evil fuck you were talking to in *Legends*."

I nod. "You already knew that guy then?"

Tom nods agitatedly. "Yeah. Those two fucks wanted to share their *gift* with me."

I shake my head. "That's *crazy*. That whole scene is madness."

"So now, every time I see him he says something insulting, something about how unattractive I'm looking. The tosser."

I rub Tom's shoulder. "Poor Tom," I say.

Tom sighs again. "Yeah, well, as I say. I shouldn't let it get to me."

I shake my head. "Nah," I say. "You really shouldn't. You're the sexiest guy here."

Tom laughs.

I nod. "You *are*."

Tom laughs again. "You're not coming on to me now are you?" he says, the rage in his eyes fading, the twinkle returning.

I give a little laugh. "If you were single I would," I tell him. "If you were single, I think I would do everything I could possibly think of to come on to you."

Tom breaks into a grin, and then turns to the barman and orders.

As we wait for the drinks, he says, "You know what?"

I shake my head and raise an eyebrow. He smiles, stares into my eyes, and blinks very slowly. It's the same expression my cat makes when I speak to her.

"If I was single, I'd let you," he says.

I smile sadly at him. "Yeah," I say. "I know."

Profound Discoveries

When I eventually leave the club, the owner pats me on the back.

"I'm really sorry about before," he says. "I didn't know you were Jimmy's mate."

I nod at him, fraudulently thinking, *I'm not.* I can feel myself swaying slightly and I wish he would just open the door.

"No problem," I say. "And thanks for the drinks," I add.

He pushes the door, forcing against the small crowd gathered outside.

I gasp. Rain is plummeting from the sky. A wall-to-wall sheet of rain.

"Jesus!" I exclaim. "When did *that* happen?"

"That's why we call it *Storm*!" the owner laughs.

A man with a shaved head and bushy eyebrows turns to me and shakes his head. "Dunno where it came from," he says. "But I ain't going anywhere till it stops."

I regretfully glance behind me at the staircase, but the door closes pushing me into the group.

I hesitate for a moment considering my options: return to the club, stand here, get soaked... But then a huge drip lands on my temple.

I steel myself and push through. "Make way!" I shout.

"You're bloody mad mate," laughs the guy with the eyebrows.

It's warm, and for a moment, the rain actually feels pleasant.

The four am streets are deserted and the street is filled with white noise, the hammering, rushing, gushing of rain hitting cars, tarmac and me. Water is sliding down streets, bubbling out of blocked drains, and gushing in glassy sheets over the edges of gutters.

I head to the seafront, skirting along side walls trying to avoid the worst of it, but it's pointless and by the time I get to the end of the tiny street I am already drenched; my shirt is clinging to my torso and my feet are squelching in my trainers, producing foaming squeegee bubbles with every pace.

I run across the road and stare briefly at the pier, ignoring, then actually starting to revel in the rain.

An occasional wind is gusting salt towards me, and the street-lamps are dappled by the halo of falling rain.

I turn my face skywards and open my mouth, then turn and start to walk briskly homeward.

Rain is trickling down my back; it's the only unpleasant sensation it's creating, but it makes me shiver, so I start to walk faster, then break into a jog.

It's a peculiar feeling jogging, and I realise that I haven't run anywhere for years, probably not since my twenties.

As I run, as I watch the rain falling past the sodium street-lamps as I see it rhythmically squelch and squirt away from my feet as they hit the pavement I start to feel high.

I run past a set of traffic lights and see the reflections on the tarmac shift from green to yellow to red. I stare out at the sea and laugh a little madly, a slight note of hysteria entering my voice.

The intensity of the rain increases, and I grin at the thought that it is truly madness to be out in this. It's like standing in a shower cubicle fully clothed. I get lost in the sensations of my feet in their watery housings, at the feeling of the water trickling down my face, over my lips.

A song from the nightclub slips into my mind and I start to hum, then sing the words as I run. "I'm alive, and it's amazing, I'm gonna let my joy shine out..." I sing breathlessly.

Is it the evening with Tom, or the words he said? Is it a chemical phenomenon caused by beer, or adrenaline or endorphins? Could it be atmospheric: the moon, the rain, or positive ions? I don't know where the feeling comes from, but I don't remember *ever* having been happier. My brain is united with my body; I feel thoroughly wholly me, not only present in my mind, but in my hands, my chest, my pounding feet.

I'm grinning madly and my eyes are wet and salty and the world is wet and salty with sea and spray and rain, and together we are one, we are good, and it is wonderful.

I arrive at the house panting madly and stand for a final moment outside the house, wondering again where it appeared from, wondering how the weather can move from a clear moonlit night to a downpour in a couple of hours, then I push in through the door and close it behind me, silencing the madness of it all.

I take off my shoes in the hall. In the lounge I realise that my jeans are still dripping, so I take them off and put them in the kitchen sink.

Halfway up the stairs, I drunkenly pull off my shirt and hang it over the banister.

In the bathroom, I lean against the white tiles and stand beneath the boiling water of the shower for what seems like a few seconds. Only when the water runs cold do I wake up and cut the flow.

As I step from the shower I slip and steady myself by hanging onto the curtain, but it comes away in my hand. I giggle, pull a towel from the rail and drop the curtain on the floor.

I stumble into my room and am about to throw myself on the bed when I see Jenny. She's sleeping on her back and her mouth is wide open and for some reason this strikes me as hilariously funny.

Snorting with repressed laughter I back out of the room and across the corridor where I fall onto Owen's bed.

When I close my eyes the room spins, so I strain, forcing my eyes to focus on the globe lampshade.

I think of Tom and Jimmy and Belinda and I grin to myself as I hum the song again.

"I'm alive, and it's amazing..."

The song goes round and round in my head, round and round go the disco lights, round and round goes the globe above the bed, round and round goes the room.

I jolt awake for a second. I just worked out why the room goes round and round... It's the spinning of the Earth on its axis. Only sober people can't sense it. You have to be drunk to feel the spinning of the Earth.

I close my eyes again, happy with my profound discovery. It's essential that I remember this tomorrow. It's hugely, profoundly important for the entire world, an answer, in some way to the great universal question. It's essential that I tell everyone this as soon as...

Life Goes On

It is just after midday when hunger forces me from my pit. My stomach is screaming for food and my head is pounding for aspirin.

My tongue is coated in some kind of alien slime as if I have been abducted during the night and experimented upon. I steady myself in the doorway and squint at the daylight thrusting through the bathroom window.

Downstairs, Jenny is sitting on the sofa reading an old newspaper. She is wearing men's blue pyjamas and has her feet tucked beneath her. I pick up one of my shoes from the hallway floor and head straight for the kitchen.

"You perform a strip tease or something last night?" she asks, peering over the top of the paper and nodding at the pair of jeans she has hung over the back of a chair.

I click my tongue against the roof of my mouth in preparation for speech, but I manage only a sigh.

Jenny folds the newspaper and stretches out on the sofa, propping herself up on her elbows to better observe me.

"Bad night?" she asks.

I turn on the kettle and slump onto one of the dining chairs.

"Nah, great," I say unconvincingly.

She frowns at me. "Looks like it," she says.

"Hangover," I mumble. "I need aspirin."

Jenny grins. "Don't move," she laughs. "I'll get it."

I rub my forehead. "Got free drinks all night," I say.

Jenny stands and pulls the aspirin from the kitchen drawer, fills a glass of water and places them before me.

"Free drinks?" she says, impressed. "In the club?"

I force a regretful laugh. "Yeah," I say, shaking my head and popping the aspirin. "*God knows* how much I drank."

I pull a face and stretch my legs. "My ankles hurt," I groan.

Jenny smiles. "Too much disco dancing no doubt; is this kettle for tea or coffee?"

"Tea please. No, it's because I ran home. It was raining."

"You ran?" Jenny glances at the window. "It *rained*?" she says incredulously.

I laugh. "Yeah, it pissed down," I say. "And yes, I ran."

She pours the boiling water into the cup and slides into the seat opposite. "Sounds like I missed a wild night," she says.

I look at her and see her breasts peeking from the top of her pyjamas and flash back to twenty years ago; an image of her sitting on top of me, those same breasts, which even then were huge, lolloping around, putting me off, making me lose my oh-so-necessary concentration.

"So is there a reason why the drinks were free?" she asks.

I laugh. "Yeah," I say shaking my head. "What a night!"

We drink tea, and more tea, then coffee and more coffee, and round after round of toast and marmalade and I tell her about the events of the night before.

I tell her about the near-fight, and Belinda and Jimmy Somerville and we somehow digress onto Mark Almond, then Duran Duran, Depeche Mode and our college years.

It's the most relaxed conversation I have had with her so far, and it's only when she sits up in her seat, pushes a hand through her hair and says, "I suppose I should think about getting myself together and getting home," that I remember she has a home – that this isn't her home.

"You don't sound keen," I say.

Jenny nods. "Well, as you know, all's not well at the ranch."

I fiddle with a teaspoon, rocking it from side to side.

"I know," I say. "D'you want to tell me about it?"

Jenny sits back in her seat with a sigh and stares at her mug, running her finger around the edge. The she looks up and stares me straight in the eye.

"Well, you know Nick doesn't want the baby," she says.

I nod. "You said. You conceived in a traffic jam, right?"

Jenny laughs mockingly. "Yeah."

I laugh. "I wondered if I dreamt that bit. How did you actually manage that?"

Jenny smiles sheepishly. "Oh, it's not that hard really. We were on holiday, in the camper van." She shrugs. "We were stuck for like five hours in this *huge* traffic jam. We ended up making tea and snacks and then," she shrugs.

"As I say, I never thought that I'd get pregnant. It was *so* not the right time of the month."

I smile and frown at the same time. "Poor babe; so did you think about, you know…?"

"Aborting?" Jenny nods. "Sure. Wouldn't be the first time either."

"Really?"

"Yeah… Look, lets not go into that eh?" she says. "That's ancient history now."

I nod. "OK. And this time?"

Jenny shrugs. "Well, this time, I'm thirty-nine," she says.

I shrug. "So?"

"So it's getting late in the day…"

I nod. "Oh right, yeah. And by the sounds of it Nick won't come round any day soon."

She nods. "So if I want kids one day," She blows between her lips. "The options aren't good."

I reach across the table for her hand. "What *are* the options?" I ask.

She laughs sourly. "I can stay, and have the baby, and see if he changes his mind, and probably end up a single mother."

I nod thoughtfully.

"I can abort, and leave him, but who says I'll meet someone else anyway?"

I tut. "Of course you'd meet some…"

"In time though?" she interrupts. "In time for me to get pregnant again?" Her voice quivers. "I was single for three years before Nick," she continues. "And the menopause could hit like *that*." She clicks her fingers. "Plus, well, I *do* love him…"

I stroke her hand. "It's a hard call," I say. "Do you think he might come round?"

Jenny shakes her head. "Yeah, of course," she says. "Pigs might fly."

"But does he see how hard this is for you?"

Jenny looks me in the eye again. "You need to understand that Nick is an egotistical arsehole," she says.

"An egotistical arsehole whom you love?" I say.

Jenny nods then pulls her hand away.

"Anyway," she says. "I'd better get going. The arsehole is taking me to dinner tonight."

"How can you though? I mean, how do you manage to just carry on with something that big between you?"

Jenny laughs sourly and strokes her belly. "Something this big?"

I smile. "You know what I mean."

She shrugs. "Life goes on," she says, standing. "Life goes on."

Chasing Rabbits

I leave the house with Jenny, wish her good luck and wave her goodbye as I wander down towards the seafront.

I wonder about her dilemma, wonder what she will do, wonder how the man who loves her could force such a hard choice upon her.

It's a warm sunny, summer afternoon; the air is still and clear, seemingly washed by the night's rain.

The beach is crowded; the first time I've seen it so busy, and people are nestling in the red pebbles, or playing at the water's edge, or swimming, making little ripples in the glassy sea.

I realise that I haven't been swimming since last summer and wonder just how cold the sea in Brighton would be. I spent my whole childhood swimming at Eastbourne, but after fifteen years in the Med I find it hard to imagine.

The atmosphere on the beach is calm. Everyone seems to have their eyes closed, to be simply smiling at the sun. Even the children are playing quietly at the water's edge, piling pebbles here, fishing with nets there.

The breeze is so light and so warm – body temperature – as to be barely perceptible. I stare at the horizon and wonder why some days are slow and calm, others enlivening and yet others filled with treacherous storms and unexpected downpours. It's all to do with weather maps and isobars, but beyond that does even science know why? Can even science tell us where it all originates?

I glance to my left. A group of friends are chatting quietly, occasionally breaking into relaxed Sunday laughter. A young woman with hippy rainbow weaves in her hair smiles at me.

I smile back and notice that one of the couples in the group is male; a man with a ponytail is resting his head on his friend's chest. I watch his head rise and fall as his partner speaks and I'm suddenly overcome with jealousy at their intimacy. It suddenly seems obvious again that this is what I want, that this is what I need. Not dirty sex with Benoit or John and Jean, but someone to cherish me and stroke my hair on a summer's afternoon.

Another different voice pipes up immediately.

It says, "Hey? What about that though? Wouldn't that be cool? Wouldn't that be sexy?" I think of their playroom and start to feel aroused.

I smile at the voices and quietly start to reflect upon and catalogue the different conflicting Mark's within.

Mark who wants to have fun in JJ's world, Mark who wants to marry someone like Tom and live in a cottage somewhere. Mark who could stay in Brighton forever drifting along the seafront as the moon waxes and wanes, as the storms come and go, as one season follows the other. Mark who wants to jump on a plane back to Nice, to see his flat and his cat and walk past the gardens where he last had lunch with Steve, Mark who wants to jump in an orange VW camper van and drive and drive, Mark who likes leather and motorbikes and being an unshaven biker, Mark who feels so grown-up and elegant and *adult* buttoned up in a suit. Mark who wants to run, Mark who wants to swim, Mark who wants to sit and eat Jaffa-Cakes until they need a crane to get me out of the arm-chair.

The older I get, the more of me there seem to be and the more they seem to jostle for position. Sometimes I wonder if it's possible to make a life that's big enough for all of them.

Or maybe as the Bulgarian proverb says, does the man who chases two rabbits end up hungry? Does one have to decide, exclude and specialize or run the risk of ending up with nothing at all?

Beyond the edge of the pier the surface of the sea has a different texture. It is rippled and pocked and I stare at the sparkling strip reaching out towards the horizon. I notice that it is growing, spreading, stretching downwards towards the beach, slowly encroaching on, gradually digesting the smooth glassy zone around the land. It's moving fast, and it's quite amazing to see how definite the edge is, how it moves towards us replacing the calm with its disorder.

I glance left and right to see if anyone else has noticed but people are still calmly smiling towards the sea, still stroking hair, still piling pebbles.

The line sweeps on towards us, the strip of smooth cling-film-covered, rubbery sea now mere yards wide, now mere feet, now...

Gone. A gust of breeze hits the beach as the last inch of

smoothness vanishes blowing hair, forcing through buttons, swirling crisp packets.

It's as if some celestial pause button has been released and everyone on the beach moves and fidgets. People pull on T-shirts, wrap towels around themselves, the kids kick the pebbles over and run giggling along the water's edge and I stand, look around me and head back towards the town.

I wander in a daze, still reflective, still a little hung-over, until I find myself staring at a shop window, staring at a rack of running shoes.

I have never been a runner, never had any *desire* to be a runner, but here I am at forty thinking, *"What a gorgeous pair of trainers."*

I shrug and push in through the door. I was once a smoker. I once didn't like classical music. I once didn't eat mushrooms. What's a new pair of running shoes in that slow breakdown of specialisation, that growing appreciation of everything that marks middle age?

As the salesman approaches I realise that I'm doing this the wrong way around; that getting an opinion about my knee should come before buying running shoes, but the salesman is enthusiastic and cute and I end up leaving the store with a bright *Sports World* bag under my arm.

I have spent more than I have ever spent on any pair of shoes, but what can I say? They were so sumptuously springy I was bouncing around the shop; I bounced all the way to the cash till.

As I close the shop door and mentally plot my route home, I hear someone call my name. I look over and see John and Jean sitting on a wall. Jean is rolling a cigarette, John is grinning at me. I wander over and we kiss hello.

They look healthy and brown and I remember that they have just got back from their holidays.

"So how was Grand Canary?" I ask. "Sunny apparently."

John nods. "Great actually, yes." He frowns. "How did *you* know where we were though?"

I smile. "Benoit told me," I say.

Jean looks up from his cigarette and smirks. "Ah yes," he says. "Benoit told us he saw you. He says you're not so... coincé after all."

"Oh," I say blushing. "Did he?"

"Yes," John says. "He said you're an excellent shag. Gave you an eight actually."

"Oh," I say. "*Did* he now?"

The boys nod. "You should drop by," John says.

"Yes," agrees Jean. "Come try the rest of our equipment," he laughs. "I'd like to see you with that king-size up your arse."

I blink at him and grimace. "That thing wouldn't fit up *anyone's* arse," I say.

Jean laughs. "You'd be surprised," he says, lifting his arm.

He makes a fist and winks at me. "*This* would fit," he says.

I grimace.

"Come round, we'll show you. You could get to like it," he laughs.

John nods at me sincerely. "It's like a drug," he says. "You'd love it; it's amazing."

"I..." I shake my head. "I gotta be going," I say, turning into the crowd.

As I walk away I think about the heroin thing again. Maybe SM really *is* like a drug; maybe John is right, maybe it *would* turn out to be the most incredible, orgasmic, addictive experience I ever had. Maybe I *could* get to like it.

But would I *want* to? That's the question.

I would never try heroin because I know it's abusive – because I know it would destroy me.

Maybe there *are* things in life you simply have to decide you're not going to try. No matter how good they might feel.

Ghosts

I awaken earlier than usual, much earlier. As I lie in bed looking at the first light filtering through the curtains I can feel that there is a reason I'm awake so early – that this is a different kind of day.

I lie in bed, listening to the gulls screaming, to the clanking of a milk float, almost sniffing the air to see what is different.

And I realise that it's going to be *Hot*. The capacity of the day for hotness is palpable. There's a strange quiet stillness, a feeling of early calm to be enjoyed before the heat of the day makes it all unbearable. It's a familiar feeling; back in Nice, every day from June to September starts that way.

I shower quickly, swig down hot coffee and orange juice, and head outside. I consider jogging but my calves and ankles are taut and sore. Today will be walking only, I decide.

At the end of the street I see the postman with his pushbike. He looks like some relic from a fifties movie. I glance at my watch; it's just before eight.

As I walk towards the town a plan forms. I'll get into the shops, buy some sports socks and some shorts, have coffee and be back home before the day begins, before the shoppers and tourists swarm into the city centre.

The air is warm and still, the sea is smoothly undulating, people are out doing early morning stuff: delivering packages, climbing into cars, jogging, walking dogs...

A couple of exceptionally well organised tramps are cooking sausages and eggs on a camping stove beneath the walkway, and simultaneously packing their sleeping bags into a shopping trolley. The chef looks up at me from his frying pan and says, "Good Morning."

I smile at him, but feeling I am violating their privacy I hurry on.

The town centre is quiet; few people walk the streets. Young men in big shirts and shiny ties head to their day's labour behind the tills of Next, Burtons, Nationwide; girls with tied blonde hair wear little black dresses and disappear into French Connection.

I head up past the clock tower and as I cross the broad pavement towards Churchill Square, I wonder if *Sports World* will be open yet.

I glance around for a clock, but something else catches my eye, someone I know. I slow to a stop. I watch him step from the bus, watch as he crosses in front of me.

My heart starts to race. *Steve*!

It's can't be Steve of course. Wrong town. *"Steve is in Nice not Brighton,"* I think. *"Steve is dead."*

But he has Steve's walk, Steve's hair. He's even dressed in the same casual sporty clothes that Steve wears. *"Wore,"* I correct myself.

He disappears into *Dixons*, and I stand, insanely routed to the red pavement, watching people criss-crossing the space before me.

Realising that I am holding my breath, I consciously force myself to inhale. Then I start to follow him, drawn, zombie-like towards the store.

I peer in through the window and see him swipe a package from the shelves – a pack of blank videocassettes. He places these on the sales counter, glances at his watch and nods and smiles in response to the salesman's joke.

A few minutes earlier I would have been hard put to create a coherent mental image of Steve. It's been months since the accident, and it feels like much longer. Even when we *were* together, well, it didn't last long.

But as I watch him smile, I remember. And the memory makes me smile myself.

I watch the gesture as he nervously runs a finger around the collar of his tracksuit top as he talks. Every inch of him, every gesture, *is* Steve.

He laughs again and hands over a banknote. I can hear my own heartbeat. He lifts the bag from the counter and turns slowly towards the exit, towards me.

He vanishes behind a huge red *sale* poster in the window, then reappears only feet away.

I step forward. I have to speak to him. "Excuse me?" I say.

He stops and turns to me, raising an eyebrow. And the instant I look into his eyes I see that it is not him. It is not him at all.

"Yeah?" he asks. His voice is deeper than Steve's. The language is

English. His accent is pure East Sussex.

"Sorry, I... Have you got the time?" I ask.

He glances at my wrist and frowns. I realise that I'm wearing a watch so I lift my wrist and wrinkle my nose.

"It stops all the time," I say.

He nods, unconvinced, and pulls a mobile from his pocket. "Five past nine mate," he says.

I nod. "Thanks," I say, croakily.

The man frowns at me, forces a smile and then hurries away.

I stand in front of *Dixons Biggest Ever Sale* and watch him walk away; watch the man who is exactly like Steve, and yet is nothing like Steve slowly disappear from view.

I feel a sting behind my eyes, a tremble in my hands, in my lips. I push my hands into the pockets of my jeans and force my teeth tighter together and squint and swallow.

I stare silently into the middle distance and slowly my heart slows and I am left feeling stunned and thought-less as if brain function has been momentarily suspended. I take a deep breath and start towards home.

I pass the clock tower again and decide to head right, to head straight down to the sea. A sit on the beach will clear my mind. I can come back and tackle *Sports World* another time.

Red Means No-Go

As I cross the pelican crossing, a horn sounds. I pause momentarily, wondering if I have stepped out at the wrong time but pedestrians continue to cross, flooding either side of me.

I step forwards, but the horn sounds again, so I turn and peer at the car – a red Mini – but a reflection on the windscreen prevents me from seeing inside.

The side window slides down and a head appears, spiky hair jutting into the daylight.

"Mark!" he says.

I half smile, half frown at Tom's eager face.

"Here, jump in!" he orders.

"I…"

"Get in, we can talk. I'll pull over further up," he says.

He leans over and pushes the passenger door open.

The lights change, and without thinking I get into the passenger seat and pull the door closed behind me. Heat is shimmering from the bonnet of the car, but the inside is cool and crisp with air-conditioning.

"But I…"

Tom glances in the rear view mirror and accelerates away. I reach for the dashboard, brace myself in the seat.

"Nothing can happen," I tell myself. "We're in town travelling at…" I glance at the speedometer. "Ten miles an hour."

Tom swings right and parks the car in a loading bay. He pulls on the handbrake.

"That's better," he says, reaching for the keys and switching off the engine.

He turns to me and his smile fades. "What's wrong with you?" he says. "You look like you've seen a ghost."

His keys swing and bump against the plastic.

I snort ironically and raise my hand to rub the bridge of my nose. Tom peers at me enquiringly.

"I have," I say. "Kind of."

He releases his seatbelt and turns his body slightly towards me, squeaking on the leather of the seat.

"You have?" he asks.

"I'm sorry," I say, smiling weakly. "I just saw someone... Someone who looks like someone I know, someone I knew. A friend."

Tom nods slowly.

"A *dead* friend," I explain.

Tom scrunches his eyebrows into a look of concern and strokes my knee. "Oh..." he says. "Poor you."

I nod and give a little shake of my head. "It's nothing, I'm fine really; I just..." I shrug. "He *really* looked like him that's all."

Tom nods.

"Like Steve, my ex."

Tom nods again and blows through his lips. "Your ex," he repeats. "God!"

He glances at his watch. "Look... You fancy a coffee? I have time. Just about."

I glance around looking for coffee bars.

"My place is just round the corner," he says.

I grind my teeth together in hesitation.

"It's *literally* two blocks," he says.

I shrug. "OK," I say. "Sure."

I sit in silence as he drives to the flat. It really is two blocks away but all the same I grip the side of the seat. It's weird sitting on the right, in what should be the driver's seat, but with no steering wheel.

As I get out of the car, I say, "That was OK actually," and Tom frowns at me in amusement.

I shake my head. "Don't listen to me," I say. "I'm just being weird today."

Tom walks to my side and touches my shoulder. "Yeah," he says in a concerned tone. "You're a bit NQR today aren't you."

"NQR?" I raise an eyebrow.

"Not Quite Right," he grins.

I laugh lightly. "Yep. That would pretty much describe it," I say, following him down a flight of steps. "*NQR*," I repeat.

Tom pushes open the door to the basement flat. "It's a mess," he warns. "I've been too busy to clean."

He looks back at me sheepishly. "Actually, I'm *always* too busy to clean," he laughs.

The flat is big, but being underground it's fairly dark. The lounge is filled with an eclectic collection of character-full antiques, a Louis XV meridian covered in purple velvet sits in the window, an ornate carved white armchair opposite.

Along one side of the room an alcove contains a big double bed covered with satiny quilts and cushions providing both bed and seating.

"Sit," he instructs me. "I'll make coffee."

I perch on the edge of the meridian, actually wondering how strong it is, and look up through the window.

A pram passes, followed by a pair of feet in black leather, high-heeled boots.

"Cool flat," I say. "It reminds me of that Almodovar film."

Tom pops his head around the corner. "*High Heels*?" he laughs. "That's what I thought when I moved in. Every time I see a woman walk by, I think of the opening sequence from that film."

"Sorry I was weird," I say.

"Uh?" he shouts from the kitchen.

"I'm sorry I was weird," I say loudly. "I had a funny morning, that's all."

"Sure. You take sugar?" he asks.

"Yeah, two," I say. "I feel OK now."

I stroke my hand along the carved armrest of the meridian. "I love your furniture," I say, running my fingernail around a red sticker.

"Yeah," Tom laughs, his voice getting louder as he returns with the coffees. "Most of it will have to go probably," he says, placing them on a side table.

"Antonio is into minimalism in a big way," he says, sitting opposite me. He nods at the red sticker. "That's what the stickers are for. Red means *no go*."

I frown at him.

"The stuff he hates has red stickers on. The stuff he likes, green ones."

I pull a face. "How strange," I say.

"I suppose if we're going to live together..." Tom shrugs. "It's only stuff."

I nod. "I suppose so, but well, stuff's important isn't it?" I say. I stroke the back of the meridian. "And this is really nice," I add.

Tom nods. "Yeah, well, you can have it when I move if you want."

"But that seems really..." I am about to say, *controlling*, but I hear Jenny's voice in my head, telling me not to be negative. "Strange," I say.

"That's just the way it is I guess." Tom sighs and looks around the room. He strokes the padded arm of his chair. "I covered this myself," he adds.

I nod. "It's lovely."

He laughs. "It's very throne like. Very Queen Victoria."

I smile. "But Antonio is not amused."

Tom shakes his head and taps a sticker on the chair back. "Yellow. Means possibly. If I'm good."

I nod. "How... Organised," I say. I scan the room, playing spot-the-dots. Every piece of furniture truly does have a dot. Most of them are red.

Tom follows my gaze, then sighs, and says, "So do you want to talk about it, or are you OK?"

I frown at a large, black, clasped case in the corner.

"Sorry?" I turn back to face him and shake my head. "Oh, no, I'm fine. What's that in the corner?"

Tom glances over. "The blob lamp?"

I shake my head. "The black..."

"Oh, the sax. It's my saxophone," he says.

"Sax," I say. "Do you... um... play?" I ask. My voice rasps. I try to control my expression and end up pulling a pained, tight-lipped smile.

Tom nods. "Sure," he says, adding with a shrug. "I'm pretty good really. I learnt to play when I was eight, well, clarinet. And sax when I was, oh, about twelve I suppose."

I bite my bottom lip and shake my head and picture Steve's sax sitting in the corner of my flat in Nice. My vision is blurring, wrinkling as water fills my eyes. My throat is swelling making it hard to swallow.

Tom frowns and then moves across the room, dropping to his knees before me.

"You're not OK at all, are you?" he says.

He puts a hand on my knee and looks up at me. I smile and

actually manage a laugh, despite the tears in my eyes.

"I'm being stupid," I say. "I don't know what's wrong with me."

Tom wipes a tear from my cheek with his thumb and smiles sadly. "You really don't like saxophone huh?" he laughs.

I smile and snort at the same time. My nose runs, so I wipe it on my hand. "This is all daft," I say.

Tom nods, encouraging me to continue.

"Steve had a sax," I say. "I have it," I shrug. "At home."

Tom nods. "Steve?"

I nod. "The guy who died, I never heard him play though."

My voice quivers and fails. I sigh and force a smile. "Sorry, I don't know what's going on. It's Steve day today or something," I say.

Tom smiles warmly. His eyes seem to be glistening too. "That's the trouble with the dead," he says. "You never know quite when they'll surface."

I shake my head. "This is all just a bit melodramatic." I manage a little laugh.

Tom pulls me towards him and hugs me, rubbing my back. "It's OK," he says. "My mum died recently, and, well, I know what it's like."

I hear his voice cracking too, and it pushes me over the edge; I snort and release a snotty sob.

Tom rubs my back. "It'll get better," he says. "You just have to know that it'll get easier, and wait."

We remain like this for a couple of minutes. My sadness fades and to my shame, the hug starts to make me feel horny. Embarrassed, I push away and head to the bathroom to wash my face.

When I return, Tom is on his mobile. I watch him for a minute or so. He shrugs an apology at me and moves to the window.

"Yes," he says. "I know."

" ... "

"I'm just going back."

" ... "

I stand and look at his CD collection.

"It's lunch time," he says.

We have a surprising number of identical CD's.

"Well I think he's OK," Tom is saying. "So why shouldn't..."

I run my finger down the spines: Japan, Kid Loco, David Sylvian, Everything But The Girl... I grin. Tom even has Kate Bush.

I glance over at him but he's frowning as he listens. He glances up at me, then says, "Hang on," and lowers the phone to his chest.

"Sorry Mark, I think this is gonna take a while if you know what I mean. Work shit. Could you just see yourself out? Would you mind?"

I nod. "No problem,"

I drink down the last of my coffee, and push out the front door.

As I climb the basement stairs I look regretfully back in through the window at Tom.

"For god's sake," he's shouting.

I make a grimace as I climb the stairs and think, *"Poor Tom!"*

Just as I reach the top, I hear one last phrase.

"He's a friend for fuck's sake. *Uno amico*!" Tom says. "I bumped into him in the street!"

General Stickiness

At two pm when I get back up, I feel revived and normal. My theory of going back to bed in order to start the day over has worked.

A little apprehensive of the monsters lurking in the depths of my mind, I spend the afternoon reading the newspapers, surfing the net, checking my finances, transferring money around, and listening to Radio Four. Anything, in fact to keep my brain occupied.

I'm just noticing the fading daylight, just starting to worry about spending the evening alone when the phone rings. Like a drowning man grabbing at a rope, I swipe it from the base.

"Mark?" says Benoit's voice.

"Hi," I say, trying to remember how I feel about Benoit. It seems as if I last thought about Benoit weeks ago.

"I thought I'd call you," he says. "Check that you are OK."

I look at myself in the mirror as I speak, and rub my chin deciding that I need to shave. I frown.

"Why wouldn't I be?" I say shaking my head and wondering how Benoit could know.

I can hear the TV playing in the background again; sirens and squealing tyres.

"I saw JJ yesterday and they said that they saw you, that you were strange," he says. "So I am calling to verify."

I frown. "Oh, right," I say. "Benoit, do you *ever* switch off your TV?"

He laughs. "It worries you? Hang on..."

The sound of the car chase fades then disappears completely, and Benoit's voice returns. "Better?"

I smile. "Sorry. It didn't worry me, I just wondered," I say.

"Well, it keeps me company, I suppose," Benoit says. "Otherwise I get lonely."

It's a nothing phrase, but strangely it opens a doorway into seeing Benoit differently. Seeing him as a human being. For some reason, I callously hadn't imagined that Benoit could *get* lonely.

163

"So?" Benoit asks.

I cough. "No, look," I say. "To be honest, I was a bit miffed actually."

"Miffed?"

"Yeah, disgruntled," I say.

"Sorry, I..."

"A bit *annoyed*," I explain.

"Oh," says Benoit. "I have annoyed you?"

"Yes," I say. "A bit."

"Oh."

"I just didn't much like the idea of you talking to John and Jean. About us I mean."

"About *us*?" Benoit sounds incredulous.

"Yeah, about the sex we had."

I wait for him to reply, but there is only silence followed by a tone indicating that he has hung up.

I frown at the handset and shrug. "What a twat!" I say.

I wave the phone dismissively in the air and replace it on the base station. I turn to go to the kitchen, but it rings again, calling me back.

"You hang up?" Benoit asks.

I shake my head as if he can see me. "No!" I say. "I thought *you* did."

"Oh," says Benoit.

"So where were we?"

"Well," Benoit sniggers. "You were about to come around and tell me how angry you are, and then we were about to have sex, and I would never tell this to a soul," he says.

I laugh. "Is *that* where we were?" I say. "Really!"

Benoit giggles. "Yes," he says. "I think so."

I frown and look around the apartment, weighing up the options. Stay here alone or cross Brighton again.

"Hey, you don't fancy coming here for a change do you?" I suggest.

"Ah. Yes..." Benoit says. "This would be good, I've been here all day working. I'm bored with my apartment. Though maybe I should come after food. I haven't eaten yet."

"Me neither," I say. "I was going to get fish and chips."

Benoit laughs. "You English. So sophisticated."

I laugh. "Yep," I say. "That's me."

"Maybe I bring you fish and chips then. Maybe we eat them together," he says.

It turns out to be as strange eating with Benoit as it was when we had breakfast together.

We eat in a weird muffled silence with only the sound of our rustling, chewing, breathing. It's only when Benoit points a ketchup-coated chip at me that things ease up.

"Do you want to suck my chip?" he giggles.

I grin and as suggestively as I can I suck the ketchup off, following it with a pickled onion.

Benoit frowns at me. "Share!" he says, leaning forwards.

I crunch the onion in half – the vinegar makes my nose tingle – and then I lean forward to kiss him, passing half across.

A few minutes later we are lying naked on the floor and Benoit is dipping chips into my belly button-come-ketchup-reserve.

I dip my own finger in and draw little red rings around his nipples. "Dirty boy," Benoit laughs, "Now you lick that off."

It's all disgustingly sticky, but at least the stickiness between us has vanished. We roll around in a mess of ketchup and tartar sauce, and kiss and cuddle and rub each other into a frenzy. It's all very low key, very good-natured. The earth doesn't shift on its axis, but by the time we bring each other to orgasm my mood has shifted and I'm feeling thoroughly optimistic.

Afterwards, we shower and dry each other, then we lie on Owen's bed and Benoit smokes.

The after-sex smoking ritual reminds me of home, makes me feel homesick even, and I start to speak to Benoit in French instead.

The conversation drifts easily as the last of the light fades and the curtains blow in and then out on the evening sea breeze.

Benoit tells me he's from Tours, tells me his family are farmers, that he came here for a holiday five years ago and never went back. He says he has no desire to go home, but that his financial situation might force him to.

I make a mental note to give him the cash for the fish and chips in the morning and tell him how I ended up in Nice and then about my job, about my time in New York.

Benoit moves onto his side and slowly draws rings around my

nipple as I speak, telling him about Hugo and the fact that Antonio dated him, then about meeting Steve, about the car accident, about Owen bringing me here.

Eventually I realise that Benoit's finger has stopped moving, and I gently raise myself so that I can see his face and see that he is sleeping. I wonder how long he has been absent. His mouth is open and he has the slightest of smiles on his lips.

Moving slowly, I reach over, remove the ashtray, and switch out the light. It's barely ten pm so sleep doesn't come quickly.

I lie and listen to the sound of the curtains dragging across the floor, and the distant sound of the waves, and the in and out of Benoit's breathing.

I think how long it has been since I listened to someone sleeping, think how simple, yet ecstatic it is feeling his body heat beside me, feeling the raising and lowering of his chest next to me, simply being here in this bed right now with a fellow human being.

The sound of the wind and Benoit's breathing mixes with the white heaving of the sea, and slowly the tide edges its way up the beach, surrounding then washing over us, submerging the day in a brilliant white foam of sleep.

Lost In Action

I awaken to the screaming of seagulls. I lie on my side trying to differentiate the whooshing of the cars on the distant main road from the sound of the waves, so present at night.

Suddenly I remember Benoit, and roll towards him. Empty space.

I sit up, rub my eyes and look around the room in surprise. I hold my breath for a moment, listening for sounds of movement in the house. No Benoit. Then I sigh, and roll out of the bed.

Downstairs I make coffee and sit watching the steam rise and thinking about the previous evening. The memory of his ketchup games makes me smile, and I realise that it's the first time we have spent the night together. I wonder if this means something; I wonder if Benoit is becoming something other than occasional shag.

I tip my head to one side, considering the possibility. It would seem ironic that I should travel a thousand miles from Nice back to England to meet a Frenchman from Tours.

I sip my coffee and frown. In fact, I realise, I don't know if he stayed the night at all. I turn the cup and stare at my distorted face reflected in the china, then I reach for the phone.

Benoit answers immediately with a gruff, "Yes?"

I grin at the deep cigaretty French-ness of his voice.

"Morning sexy," I say.

Benoit sighs. "Morning," he says.

"Just thought I'd check…"

"Check what?" Benoit interrupts aggressively.

I frown at the phone and start again.

"Just thought I'd check that you exist. That I didn't dream you up."

Benoit exhales sharply. "No," he says. "I'm real."

"So why did you sneak off like that?" I ask, forcing, with difficulty, a warm tone into my voice. "I was looking forward to…"

"I didn't have my stuff, so I had to come back. I never intended to stay the night. That's all," he says gruffly.

I grimace. "OK, no problem, I just wondered," I say. "What time did you leave?" I force a laugh. "I didn't hear anything. Amazing!"

"About two," Benoit replies coldly.

"And what stuff?"

"Stuff?"

"Yeah, what stuff did you need to sleep till seven instead of two?" I ask, wincing at the vague tetchiness entering my voice.

Benoit coughs. "I fell asleep with my lenses. I didn't have the stuff for my lenses, and I didn't have my meds. That's all."

I nod. "OK," I say, slowly processing the sentence.

"Meds," I think.

"And now I'm working," Benoit adds.

"Meds," I think again.

I wrinkle my brow. "OK, well, have a good..."

But Benoit has hung up.

I remember last time, and stand over the phone for a few seconds in case he's going to call back again, but it remains silent.

"Fuck him," I say quietly.

As I shower, my mind runs through the conversation. Of course there are a hundred possible reasons why Benoit might be taking meds, but slowly, like lichen climbing a tree, the idea that Benoit has HIV seems inescapable.

HIV is back again. That wearing, tiring, boring, terrifying disease is back in my life. I sigh heavily again and step out of the shower.

I stare at myself in the mirror. And *contact lenses*? I didn't know Benoit wore contact lenses. I'm realising that, of course, I know very little about Benoit.

I run through every sexual act he and I have performed, and even though it has all been safe; even though I don't even know if my supposition is true, I start to feel angry that he never warned me.

AIDS. Again. Will it ever end?

As I towel myself dry, I consider phoning him again, but it's clearly not the moment.

Instead I dress quickly and head downstairs. I pull on a denim jacket and swipe my keys from the table. Patting my pockets to check I have everything, I head towards the door. *Sports World* awaits.

But as I pat my rear pocket, I frown. No wallet.

I leave the front door ajar and run back upstairs to the bedroom. I swipe my jeans from the bed and frown. No wallet there either.

I stare at the ceiling for a moment, remembering. The combat trousers I'm wearing *are* the trousers I wore yesterday. I glance around the room and head back downstairs to the lounge.

These are the trousers. This is where I lay when Benoit undid them. I crouch on all fours and look beneath the sofa.

I stand and run my hand behind the cushions.

I check the kitchen surfaces.

I frown. I run back upstairs and check under the bed. I tidy the pile of jumpers on the dresser. I sigh.

I go back downstairs. I check under the sofa again, pointlessly.

Then I angrily remove my jacket, close the front door and put my keys back on the kitchen counter.

I sit at the kitchen table and run my hand across the top of my head.

"Fuck it!" I mutter.

I sit with my head in my hands and retrace my steps. *Sports World,* Tom's, place, here...

I rub my chin and realise that I have no money, realise that I don't even have any way of *getting* money without my Visa card.

Only then, only after checking the entire house over and over and over again; only after phoning *Sports World* and then phoning Tom; only when Tom has crouched on all fours and checked under his own sofa, and declared that, "There's a lot of dust, but no wallet," does the terrible dark thought cross my mind for the first time. Maybe Benoit picked it up by accident? Or maybe Benoit *stole* it.

I detest myself for even imagining such a scenario. I order my mind to discount the thought *immediately*.

But he *was* very strange on the phone this morning. He was *very* jumpy.

"*Fuck!*" I know I have to phone Benoit again.

Benoit's *Allo*, is even shorter, even sharper than the last time.

I take a deep breath. I try French.

"Benoit," I say. "Mark encore. Désolé."

But Benoit replies in English. "Mark, I have work to do, I cannot..."

"Benoit, I know, I'm sorry. It's just I can't find my wallet anywhere?" I say.

Silence.

"And I wondered if you had picked it up, by accident or something," I say.

There is a long pause, before Benoit says, "Your wallet?"

"Yeah," I say, as lightly as I can manage.

"You think I have your *wallet*?" Benoit repeats incredulously.

"Yeah, I mean, it might look like yours or something," I say.

Another pause.

"Or something?" Benoit repeats.

"Hell, Benoit, I don't know. But I've lost it so I thought I'd give you a call and..."

"Mark, I don't have your wallet. I didn't take anything else from your house," Benoit says. "Now goodbye."

"OK, sorry..." But Benoit has hung up again.

In an act of fury, I throw the telephone across the room. So that it doesn't break I aim for the sofa.

"Fuck, fuck, FUCK!" I say.

To calm my nerves, and because anything else I might do requires cash, I go for a jog along the seafront. As I leave, the sun is still out, but a wall of grey is approaching from the east.

By the time I get back, the sky is black and ominous, and the first drops of rain are falling.

As the rain trickles down the windows, I assemble the various piles of coins from around the house. I have the princely sum of six pounds and twenty-two pence.

I phone my bank. They tell me that it will be "up to ten days" before my new Visa-card arrives, that is, before it arrives at my *French* address! Six pounds clearly will not suffice.

After considering all the options, I call Jenny. She can afford a *Smeg*, I figure, she can lend me some cash.

It rains all week. Constantly. Endlessly.

Some days it drizzles, and some days it pours, and some days it *excitingly* drifts from one to the other, but at no point does it stop.

I sit and stare outside. Then I stare at the contents of the freezer and concoct previously unimaginable meals from the limited contents.

I phone Tom twice, but get the answer-phone both times. He doesn't call back.

I toy with the idea of calling Benoit; imagine the conversation, testing various techniques in my mind. Apologising, accusing, phoning for a neutral chat... But in my dry runs they all end in disaster. I may be wrong about the wallet. And I may be wrong about his HIV status. But somehow, it just doesn't seem that likely I am wrong about both. I feel hard and cynical about it, but I just can't face trying to sort any of it out.

On Friday evening when I hear the sixties' chugging of Jenny's twenty grand camper-van, I am desperate, not only for company and conversation but for cash.

The freezer contains three fish fingers and I have twenty pence left.

A Difficult Client

Jenny pulls her coat from her head. "Jesus! The rain!" she exclaims.

"I know," I say closing the door. "It hasn't stopped all week."

I smile at her, and then break into a frown. Jenny pauses, mimicking my expression.

"You look weird," I say. "Your makeup or something?"

Jenny shrugs. "Thanks," she says.

"Sorry," I say. But as I lean in to kiss her cheek she pulls away.

"No, it's me," she says. "I bashed my cheek. I covered it up, but..."

I stand back and look at her cheek. I can see it is swollen, and it has a vague blue tint, peeking through the caked foundation.

"Geez," I say. "How did you do that?"

Jenny rolls her eyes, and turns into the lounge. "It's too dumb for words," she says. "I walked into the clothes line."

Wrinkling my nose, I follow her into the lounge. "The clothes line?" I repeat doubtfully.

Jenny slumps heavily in a chair. "Well, the pole actually. We've got one of those rotary ones?"

I nod.

"It span around in the wind," she says. "And whacked me."

I make a face. "Ouch," I say. "Strange but true."

Jenny nods and makes a twilight zone sound. "My life. Where fact is stranger than fiction," she says. "Does it look *that* bad?"

I shrug. "Nah, it shows, but..."

"I look a bit like coco the clown, right?" she asks.

I shrug. "You just look a bit... Overdone, I guess."

Jenny sighs. "Oh well, so, do I get a cup of tea or not?" she asks.

I grimace. "If you've got some cash for milk you do," I laugh.

"Oh yeah! I almost forgot," Jenny grins. She grimaces and touches her cheek. "It hurts when I smile," she says. "

She reaches into her jean pocket and produces a wad of banknotes.

"I got two hundred. Will that be enough? To tide you over?"

I take the money. "Thanks," I say. "I'm really sorry."

Jenny shakes her head. "Don't be. Nick thinks you're my gigolo now, but," she shrugs. "Frankly, who *gives* a damn?"

I stuff the money into a vase and keep a single ten-pound note.

"Now," Jenny says. "Tea please. With milk."

On Jenny's advice, I reluctantly phone Tom again, but again I get his voicemail. "See," I tell her, waving the phone. "He doesn't talk to me anymore."

Jenny frowns and sips her tea. "But I wanted to see him," she says.

"Me too," I laugh. "I think Antonio's told him to stay away from me."

Jenny bites a fingernail. "Why would he do that?"

I roll my eyes. "Um... *Hello*?" I say.

She nods. "Yeah, you're right," she says. "But I don't think Tom's the type to be bossed around. Do you?"

I shrug.

"He'd be right though," she says.

"Who? Antonio?"

Jenny nods. "Yeah. I mean; this won't work at all if you can't get to see him?"

I smile at her. "*What* won't work?"

Jenny raises her eyebrows and nods. "Our strategy," she says.

I cross my eyes. "*Your* strategy," I say.

Jenny nods. "OK. My strategy," she says. "But it won't work." She sips her tea again and stares out at the rain then she takes a deep breath.

"OK," she says, pulling her phone from her pocket. "Time to play dirty."

I frown at her.

"He's being difficult," she says. "Playing hard to get. Gimme the number," she says.

I frown.

Jenny nods earnestly. "Give me Tom's number."

"But, why?" I ask.

"Give!" she insists.

Tom answers *Jenny's* call immediately. I rest my chin on one hand and listen in annoyance.

"Tom!" Jenny says. "Jenny here. Mark's friend."

"..."

"Yes, that's right. In Brighton."

"..."

"I'm at Mark's, that's right."

"..."

"Yeah, I know, he's opposite. I expect he's wondering why you take *my* calls and not his."

I bite my lip and smile.

"..."

Jenny laughs. "Only joking, I *know* you were going to call him back." She winks at me.

"..."

"Yes, he's taking us both to dinner tonight," she says.

"..."

"Yes, that's right. Me too."

"..."

"Well, I think he *tried* to tell you."

"..."

"Yes Tom. I'll be there as well."

"..."

"I don't know, hang on." Jenny holds the phone to her chest and shrugs. "Where are you taking us?" she asks me.

I open my hand and shrug. "What do *I* know?" I say.

She lifts the phone to her ear. "Did you hear that?"

"..."

"Yeah, Mark doesn't know. You're the local boy after all," she says. "*Food For Friends*?" she raises an eyebrow at me.

I nod.

"Seven pm?"

I nod again.

"OK, great. See you later," she says.

Jenny clicks her phone shut. "See," she says. "Easy."

I laugh. "Very clever," I say. "No one could deny your efficiency."

Jenny laughs. "We use it at work a lot. Swapping phones to get in touch with difficult clients."

I nod. "But it doesn't answer the real question though," I say. "Why he didn't answer *my* calls."

Jenny nods in agreement. "He made sure I was going to be there. He asked, like, three times."

I nod. "Yeah, I heard."

"So, either he's in love with *me*," she says. "It is *possible*, after all..."

I wrinkle my nose and shake my head.

"But unlikely I agree," she says.

"Unlikely," I repeat.

"Or he's scared of being alone with *you*." She nods melodramatically.

I snort. "Me being so scary and all," I say.

Jenny pushes out her lips, and looks at me craftily from the corner of her eye.

"But if you ask me," she says thoughtfully, closing one eye. "The most *likely* explanation..."

I nod.

"Is that he's scared of himself."

I wrinkle my brow.

Jenny nods again. "He's scared of what he might do if he's *alone* with you."

I laugh and shake my head. "You're too much," I say.

Jenny shrugs. "Why?"

"Oh, you just overestimate my powers of seduction."

Jenny shakes her head. "Nah," she says. "I don't think you have any powers of seduction at all."

"Oh," I laugh. "Thanks."

"But for some reason, Tom does," she says. "There's no accounting for taste."

Food For Friends

Food for friends is all stripped pine and born-again-vegan smiles. But it does what it says on the box, and the atmosphere – of the restaurant at least – is relaxed and friendly.

Tom is already seated by the time we arrive and as we enter, we actually catch him fiddling with his hair, using a black and white framed photograph beside him as a mirror. He turns and blushes slightly. "I'm having a bad hair day I think," he says.

We pull out chairs and sit.

"Wow!" Tom says, frowning at Jenny's cheek. "What happened to you?"

Jenny touches her jaw gently and turns to me. "Is it looking worse?" she asks. "Do I need to redo my makeup?"

I glare at Tom, mockingly rebuking him. "Nah," I say. "It's fine."

Jenny turns back to Tom. "I bumped my cheek," she says. "At home."

Tom purses his lips and nods. "Walk into a door again?" he says earnestly. "Shall we call you Luka?"

I pick up the Suzanne Vega reference, but Jenny just frowns at him.

"Look, if he's been slapping you, you can tell me," Tom says with mock concern.

Jenny gives a little shake of her head as if to shake off an insect. "He hasn't!" she says. "I told you. I bumped it."

Tom raises his hands. "Just joking," he says. "It's just, with Mark's reputation for domestic violence," he laughs.

Jenny bites her lip and exhales. "Sorry," she says. "I though you were insinuating that... Never mind."

Tom shakes his head and grimaces. "Nah, never mind," he says. "So! Other than your cheek, how are you?"

Jenny smiles thinly. "Fine Tom," she says. "How are you?"

I chew the inside of my mouth and frown at them both.

Tom shrugs. "Me? I'm OK I guess," he says. "Missing Antonio a bit more than I'd like."

Jenny nods. "So when do you next see him?" she asks.

Tom shrugs. "Beginning of August, over a month."

Jenny nods. "And do you ever go *there*?" she asks. "I *love* Italy. Nick and I drove to Tuscany at Easter. It was great."

Tom nods. "Yeah, It's nice," he says. "I used to go quite a lot, but I haven't been back since March."

"So why don't you go?" Jenny asks. "Can't you just get a cheap flight and go? I mean, if you miss him."

Tom nods his head from side to side. "I could I suppose," he shrugs. "It's just, well, I haven't wanted to go much lately."

We both frown at him, so he coughs and continues.

"I've been too upset really," he says. "Since my mother died."

Jenny frowns. "Gosh, I'm sorry," she says. "I didn't know."

Tom nods. "It was kind of my fault," he says, his voice dry and quiet. "I haven't been able to face going back since."

Jenny nods and puts a hand on his shoulder. "God, she was with you when..." she says.

Tom nods solemnly and coughs. "Anyway," he says. "Can we talk about something else?"

I nod warmly at him. "Sure," I say.

"Oh!" Tom exclaims, turning to me. "Did you find your wallet by the way?"

I shake my head.

"Bummer!" he says. "I actually cleaned the *whole hous*e looking for it."

I shrug. "It's a mystery. Anyway, I cancelled my cards, ordered a new driving licence."

Tom grimaces. "That's the worst bit really, isn't it? All that paperwork."

I nod.

"Well, that and the housework!" he laughs.

A waitress with an orange flattop and dungarees appears.

"Hello," she says smiling beatifically and handing us menus. "I'll come back and take your order in a minute, OK?"

Though Tom insists that it is usually fabulous, the food is mediocre and the conversation is false and forced giving the evening a strange, strained feeling.

Listening to Jenny and Tom is like following a poor play with bad actors and dreadful dialogue. It may just be in my own brain, but each sentence seems a slightly inappropriate response to whatever went before.

When I myself speak to either of them, it's like talking to someone who's watching TV. They either ask me to repeat myself, or reply inappropriately. A couple of times they both ignore me completely.

In the end, we all seem to just give up and eat our food in silence.

Just after nine-thirty, Tom makes his excuses and scurries off into the wet darkness. As we head back across town, Jenny links her arm through mine and we squash together beneath her small umbrella.

"That was nice," she says.

I laugh. "Was it?" I say. "Can't say as I noticed."

Jenny huffs. "Yeah, you're right actually," she says. "It was dreadful. Tom seemed strange, distracted... You know?"

I laugh. "You both seemed weird to me," I say.

We run across the road in the path of an advancing bus. As it swishes past it sends water from the gutter onto the pavement, narrowly missing my feet.

Jenny pulls my arm tighter. "Sorry," she says. "Actually my jaw was hurting. It was really hard to eat. I was wishing I had ordered soup."

"Your jaw?" I repeat.

Jenny nods. "Humm," she says. "The pain seems to be moving down. I was wondering why it was getting worse."

"Did you see a doctor?" I ask.

Jenny shrugs. "No. I'll go Monday if it's not better," she says. "And what on earth happened to Tom's *mother*?" she asks. "Did you know about that?"

I shake my head. "I knew he didn't want to go back to Italy. But I didn't know why," I say.

Jenny yawns. "God, I'm knackered," she says. "And, he said it was his fault too," she continues. "Imagine that. Feeling responsible for the death of a parent."

I glance regretfully into the *Bulldog* as we walk past.

"Maybe that's why he was weird," I say. "Maybe we shouldn't have mentioned it."

We cross the path of a group of girls in their late teens walking down the hill. They are wearing school uniform, but have tied knots in their white blouses to reveal their belly buttons. They are soaked with rain, and drunkenly laughing.

"God!" I say when they are past. "You don't get that in France."

Jenny frowns. "What?"

"Those sort of dolly-dog teenagers," I say. "Drunk with their tits hanging out."

Jenny laughs. "Blame Britney Spears," she says. "Everyone else does."

We walk for a while in silence. I listen to the sound of our feet on the pavement and to the whooshing of cars driving past on the wet road.

I think about Tom. "People often blame themselves though," I say.

Jenny glances sideways at me. "Uh?" she says.

"I mean Tom, you know... saying it's his fault. People often say that sort of thing when someone dies," I explain.

Jenny sighs. "Yeah. You mean like, if only I had called her to see if she was OK, she might not have killed herself sort of thing."

I nod.

"If only I hadn't left three hundred Paracetamol in the bathroom, she might not have swallowed them all."

"Yeah," I say, frowning at her.

"If only we hadn't left the rope in the garage, she couldn't have hung herself."

I jerk Jenny's arm. "Enough!" I say.

As I glance sideways at her, a car approaches lighting us up with its headlights. In the white light, Jenny's face looks swollen and pale. *Ghoulish* would be the word. I pull her arm a little tighter.

"Are you OK?" I ask. "I mean, is everything gonna be OK with you?"

Jenny laughs and shrugs. "I don't even know what OK is really," she says. "I can't even imagine what an OK outcome might look like," she says. "Do you know what I mean?"

I sigh and nod. "It will though," I say, turning right into Owen's street. "You know that, right?"

Jenny sighs.

"In the end, things always do sort themselves out," I say. "One way or another."

Keyhole Truths

I wake up just after eight, and lie in bed listening to the sounds of the morning. Something has changed, and after a few sleepy minutes, I realise what it is. The rain has stopped.

I doze a little longer, and then roll out of bed and glance out of the window. Puffy clouds are moving steadily through a clear sky; the trees and bushes in the gardens are swaying gently from side to side.

I squint at the light and glance again at the alarm clock. I'm astonished to see that it is now ten fifteen.

I pull on a pair of jogging trousers and a sweatshirt and head downstairs. As I reach the ground floor, I pause, my hand on the end of the banister. Jenny's voice is leaking around the lounge door, which is ajar. She is clearly on the phone, and she sounds agitated.

I turn to return upstairs, but overcome by curiosity, I pause a moment and listen.

"For god's sake mother," she is saying. "Just trust me for once in your life, I'm nearly forty."

I grimace and start to quietly climb the stairs.

"I don't care what he says, OK? Just don't tell him," Jenny says.

I frown and pause again.

"I know mum," she says. "I will explain, but for now, please just don't tell him where I am, and don't give him the phone number."

I pull a face and creep up the remaining stairs.

I shower and shave, then dress and head back down. As I reach the bottom stair, I hear her voice again. Only this time she is speaking softly, sweetly.

"You know I love you," she is saying.

I vaguely consider returning upstairs, but it seems a little ridiculous, so rather than walk in on her I decide to nip over to Mr Patel's for a newspaper and milk. That way she'll hear me and realise that she only has a few minutes remaining privacy.

"You know I'd never let anyone hurt you," she says.

I open the front door and head out into the gusty street. As I descend the front steps, I glance back at the lounge.

Through the bay window I see Jenny and the sight makes me pause and then frown. Her face is tear streaked, and she is still speaking. But she's not holding a phone at all. Instead her arms are wrapped around her own body, encircling her belly. She catches sight of me and turns back into the room.

I pause and stare at the window, slowly working it out.

By the time I return, Jenny has washed and recomposed her face into an expression of sarcastic indifference.

"So you finally got up," she says as I drop *The Guardian* into her lap.

I nod. "It was weird, I awoke at eight, and then I slept for what seemed like five minutes and, *tad-a!* It was ten," I say.

Jenny unfolds the newspaper crisply. "So what's happening in the world?" she asks.

I fill the kettle and take a seat opposite her.

"So what's happening in *your* world?" I say.

Jenny shrugs disinterestedly. "God, they're still going on about school dinners... I mean; it's like such a shock. No one *knew* they were shite?"

I frown at her.

"Did these people never *go* to school? Did they never *have* boiled cabbage and semolina pudding?"

In an attempt to enter her field of vision I lean low over the table.

"Jenny," I say solemnly.

Without moving the angle of her head, she swivels her eyes and looks up at me. "Mark," she says.

"Are you OK?" I ask.

She says nothing. She looks back at the newspaper.

"What's happening?" I say. "I saw you in the window. You looked upset."

Jenny sighs and folds the newspaper. Then she sits back in her chair and stares at me.

"I'm good," she says.

I say nothing. I simply wait for her to continue.

"I've got a lot on my plate," she continues. "But I'm good," she forces a weak smile, and then lifts her eyes to meet mine. "Really," she says. Her eyes glisten. "Thanks though," she adds.

I rub my chin and nod.

"I've made decisions today," she says. "I've decided to keep the baby. I don't care what Nick does, or says. I'm having it."

I reach across the table and touch her wrist.

"And what *will* Nick say?" I ask.

Jenny laughs. "I think I need to leave Nick behind on this one," she says.

I nod gravely.

She swallows hard. "I *do* love him," she says. "But he's a shit."

Jenny thinks about this and then nods in apparent agreement with herself.

"Do you want tea?" I ask.

Jenny gives a little laugh. "Yep," she says. "See how decisive I am today?"

We eat a hearty cooked breakfast and then head out to the van.

"Thanks Mark," she says as we hug. "I did mean to stay longer, but I suddenly want to go back and sort all this out," she says. "Before I lose my resolve."

She climbs up into the driver's seat, and opens the window.

"See you next weekend maybe?" she asks.

I smile. "You're welcome anytime, you know that," I say.

She swings the orange VW out towards the street, then winks at me unconvincingly and accelerates towards the seafront.

I try and relax with the newspaper, but my mind keeps trawling over my limited understanding of Jenny's situation, of her options. I wish I had asked more questions.

After an hour of staring at the page I am feeling almost sick with stress, so I pull on my running shoes and head down towards the pier.

The clouds have thinned and are blowing rapidly across the sky, casting dark shadows over the sea. One could almost imagine that the dark forms are monsters or submarines lurking beneath the surface.

I jog to the pier, walk to the end and back, and then jog back home, but even after exercising, even after showering, Jenny is still on my mind.

I slump onto the sofa and finger the telephone, then shrug, and saying, "Oh, what the hell," I dial her mobile.

"Huh!" she says, answering almost immediately. "I'm not even home yet and you're missing me already,"

"Something like that," I say.

"Did I leave something behind?" she asks.

"No," I say. "Look... I'm worried about you. Are you sure you're going to be OK?"

"Huh!" Jenny laughs. "Of course I am. Now, I'd love to chat to you about my life Mark, but I'm driving along the M25 and it's totally illegal."

"Sorry," I say. "Can you call me, when you get back?"

"Mark, I'm sorry, but I doubt that that would be a good idea. Nick gets jealous and I really don't want, shit Mark, there's a police car. Gotta go."

I sit in silence fingering the telephone. Her relationship with Nick strikes me as incomprehensible as ever. She can spend every weekend here, but she can't phone me. I don't get it.

I spin the telephone around on the table, and then cast it aside.

"Nothing I can do," I say out loud. "You're on your own girl."

Nightmare Reality

Though the weather improves day by day, the week drags by depressingly slowly so I try and set projects to occupy myself.

On Tuesday I cycle to Newhaven and picnic at the end of the sombre stone jetty, but it's windy and as soon as I take my sandwich from the lunchbox it blows away and drops into the sea.

On Wednesday I actually try and swim. There are enough kids thrashing around in the shallows for it to seem feasible, but within minutes my extremities are numb, and within half an hour I am at home shivering beneath a hot shower.

On Thursday morning I phone Tom to see if he's going to be around this weekend, but he pointedly tells me he's waiting for a call from Antonio, and promises, then fails, to call me back.

Suddenly, I am hating being in Brighton. I seem to have lost Benoit, and I am realising that I never really *had* Tom. I don't even dare call Jenny for fear of upsetting her jealous arsehole husband, and though her situation is dreadful, I feel powerless to help.

It all seems to have gone frustratingly wrong, and Thursday evening, as I take my pint and move to one of the Amsterdam's window seats, I realise that I'm sitting here not to survey the cute guys arriving, but in order to be forewarned in case Benoit or for that matter the Nazi skinhead turn up.

Yes, I'm sitting here in case one of the few people I actually know in this town turns up, so that I can slip out the back door *before* they see me. The thought sends me over the edge.

I sip my beer and look around the bar and think of Nice in July. I'd be eating a pizza on a terrace somewhere right now. The temperature would be nearing thirty degrees. The sea would be in the twenties.

I sip my beer and nod to myself. *"Maybe,"* I think, with a nod. *"Maybe the time has come."*

I awaken early on Friday morning, and am lying in bed, sleepily trying to find a reason to get up when the phone rings. Unable to find the upstairs handset, I bound, naked, downstairs. I swipe the phone from the base.

"Oh... Mark," Jenny says. She sounds disappointed. "I thought it was going to be the answer-phone," she says. "I thought you'd still be in bed."

I stifle a yawn. "I was," I say, "but awake... Couldn't find the phone."

"Look, Mark," she says, speaking softly. "I'm not going to be able to come actually. This weekend that is." Her voice is very faint, almost a whisper.

"Oh," I say, disappointed. "Why? What's up?"

Jenny clears her throat. "Well, Nick's got the weekend off, so I thought I'd stay. We have a lot to work through."

I realise that she actually *is* whispering. I frown.

"Are you still splitting up?" I say.

Jenny clears her throat again. "Nah," she says. "I don't think so. I think we're going to be OK."

"Why are you whispering?" I ask. "Are you sure you're all right?"

Jenny gives a quiet laugh. "Of course I am. Nick's fast asleep. I just don't want to wake him."

I open my mouth to speak, then pause and start again. "So is he OK now? About the baby and stuff?"

Jenny sighs. "Look Mark, I can't really talk now, so..."

I hear a distant voice call her name.

"Shit," she mutters.

"Jenny, Are you sure...."

"JENNY!" the voice bellows.

"Gotta go," she says. *Click.*

I rub my forehead and sink onto the sofa. For a while I stare at the long shadows on the facade opposite, then I worriedly shake my head and return upstairs to bed.

I am walking along the seafront. It is a perfect bank holiday Monday, and the promenade is sparklingly clean, filled with smiling, almost grotesquely happy heterosexual families.

Children hold their parents' hands and skip in blue shorts and pink dresses, or contentedly lick candy-floss or toffee apples on sticks.

I feel different to these people, alone and separate in this peculiar

Stepford heaven.

I walk east. The summer sun beating down scorches the right hand side of my face. The concrete shimmers in the heat. Literally everyone is smiling broadly.

Families are walking four abreast, holding hands in contented nuclear family formation, seemingly unaware of my presence. They all seem to be heading towards the pier, and irritatingly I have to zigzag left and right as I struggle to walk against the tide.

On my left the buildings end and are replaced with grassy sand dunes, and I notice, for the first time, a windmill behind them, a modern, gleaming structure slicing through the wind, shining against the blue sky.

I scramble up the beach and head across the dunes towards the structure, but as I approach, I realise that it isn't actually a wind turbine, but a rotary clothes drier.

As I continue towards it I rise and fall in and out of the hollows, catching ever clearer glimpses of the structure, and as I near the top of the final hill, I see a man with mad blue eyes standing beside it, spinning it and laughing.

To my right the hollows between the peaks are no longer sandy, but muddy and brown, and I notice a series of pulleys emanating from the clothes-drier, stretching across the peaks.

I carefully make my way around the mud-pools, following the system to its destination, a huge iron mechanism pumping a stream of gushing, spluttering mud.

At the bottom of the hollow I'm surprised to see Jenny on her back, the mud lapping around her. I wave to her but she merely raises her head and shakes it from side to side.

I slip and slide down the wet bank to her side, but the nearer I get, the harder it seems to make progress. My feet are sinking into the mud.

The mud is still gushing from the pulley-driven pump, the level still rising around her, and I realise for the first time that she is in danger.

I pull a leg from the swamp and move forward onto the other foot, sinking deep into the mud. As I move, now almost in slow motion, I glance behind at the clothes-drier to see if there is any way to stop it.

By the time I reach Jenny, only her face and her swollen belly are still protruding from the mud.

I kneel beside her and stare into her eyes. They are wide and brown and full of terror.

"Keep it off the baby," she says, nodding at her stomach. "Keep it away from the baby."

I frown at her, unsure what to do. The pipe behind me gushes and gurgles as the level rises. I begin to push the mud away from her face – it's touching her nostrils now – but inevitably it flows around my fingers.

I try to form a tube with my fingers to enable her to breathe, but the mud comes faster and faster and as her eyes disappear beneath the brown sludge it starts to flow over my fingers. I can see it falling into her mouth. I can see her pink tongue gagging and swallowing as it enters her body.

I start to cry, still desperately casting around for help. I see the man on the hill, still spinning the drier.

"Stop!" I plead. "Please?" But he just laughs demonically.

When I look back, my hands have disappeared beneath the mud. I lay my head on Jenny's belly and weep as the level continues to rise.

When it starts to touch my chin, my grief is replaced by fear for my own safety, and I try to stand, but slip and fall again and again. My feet knock against something solid beneath the mud – Jenny's stomach.

Finally the weight pressing against my shoulders is too much, and I give up and lie back, slowly sinking into the mud. As it touches my lips, I realise that it tastes like the black pudding from my school dinners.

It isn't mud at all. It's blood.

I sit and gag and gasp for breath. I look madly around the bedroom, and then exhale deeply.

"Shit!" I say.

I swallow, and lie back, raising one hand to cover my mouth. Then I wipe the tears from my cheek and sigh heavily.

"Wow!" I say.

It takes a few cups of coffee before I start to feel present in the late-morning here and now of Owen's kitchen.

As soon as I feel able to speak, I dial Jenny's mobile, but she's already in conversation or it is switched off, so I leave a message on her voicemail.

In the shower, I realise that she used the house phone to call home, so I rinse myself quickly and head back downstairs.

The last number list contains a single unrecognisable number, so I shrug and hit redial. It rings endlessly and I am just about to give up when a breathless voice answers.

"Hello?"

"Jenny?" I say, relieved that I have the right number.

"No," the voice says.

I frown.

"Oh."

"Who is this please?" she asks.

"Sorry, I think I have the wrong number," I say. *"Weird,"* I think. *"It sounds like Jenny."*

"Jenny who?" the woman asks.

"Jenny Holmes," I say.

There is a pause.

"This is *Mrs* Holmes, Jenny's mother. Who is this?"

"Ah," I say. "Great, I'm, um, sorry to disturb you. It's Mark, Jenny's friend. Could you give me…?"

"Mark," she interrupts. "It doesn't surprise me that you forgot she's married."

I bite my lip. "I'm sorry?"

"She's called Gregory now. Jenny Gregory. She's married you know."

"Yes, sorry, that's what I meant," I say. "Can you give me her number?"

Another pause.

"Please leave her alone," she says. "Don't you think it might be better if you just left her alone?"

"I'm sorry, I…"

"Don't you think you've done enough damage?"

I make a silent, *"Eh?"* sound. "I'm sorry, Mrs Holmes, but I don't really understand," I say.

"He wasn't like this before. Not till you came on the scene."

I shake my head. "I don't… *Who* wasn't like *what,* Mrs Holmes?"

"Nick. They were OK before. Please, just leave her alone, can't you?"

"Well, um, I'd like to, but, I'm not sure I can Mrs Holmes," I say. "I'm, well… I'm her *friend*."

Mrs Holmes makes an exasperated gasp.

"No, I'm sorry, but I'm not going to give you her number," she says. "And I'm going to hang up now."

"But I…"

"So please just leave them to sort their marriage out. Before something dreadful happens."

"Mr Holmes? Please can you ex…"

But Mrs Holmes has hung up.

I drop the telephone heavily onto the base.

"That was worse than the dream," I say shaking my head.

The Only One

I wander solemnly down to the marina and order coffee and a croissant at a quayside café. It's sunny again, the breeze is warm, and the reflections of the water shimmer against the boats as the cables gently clank against the masts. It feels almost Mediterranean.

The terraces are still calm before the lunchtime rush, so I stare at the swaying boats and sip my coffee and rake through my mind for missed information about Jenny, for a clue about what to do, how to act.

I've been warned to stay away by her mother, warned that I am the problem. But what if I am the ally. What if she has it all wrong?

I sigh and bite into the croissant. It's a poor bready copy of the real thing, so I spread it thickly with the butter and jam provided.

A tiny wind-turbine spins on the top of a mast, inevitably producing images of the dream and making me shudder. *Could Jenny really be drowning? Could she really need saving?*

I need to discuss this with someone else who knows her. I have been resisting calling Tom, but he's the only one I can talk to about this. Plus it's the perfect excuse.

I decide to phone him as soon as I get back.

As I climb the stairs to Kemptown, I see a cute guy heading down. It's John.

"Hi Mark!" he exclaims. "Long time no see."

I laugh and pause at the landing. "Not that long," I say.

"So how's things?" he asks.

I nod. "OK really," I shrug. "Fine."

"Seen Benoit recently?" he asks.

I scrunch my nose. "Nah," I say, trying to calculate as I speak just how much to reveal. "I think I upset him," I say.

John raises an intrigued eyebrow. "Yeah?" he says.

"Yeah, I lost something, and well, I phoned him up in case he's taken it by accident, and he kind of went mad," I say. "He thought I was accusing him."

I hear the lie, but calculate that it might just smooth things over with Benoit. *"But then,"* I think. *"Is that what I want?"*

John nods. "Benoit's in a bad phase at the moment, so I wouldn't worry too much."

"A bad phase?" I say.

John nods. "Yeah, you know," he says glancing at his watch. "Anyway, I've got to go. I'm meeting my other half for lunch." He leans forward and we kiss on the cheek.

"Come round," he says, already skipping down the stairs. "We've got some new toys."

I laugh. "Yeah," I say, with a little wave. "Thanks, I can imagine."

Within seconds I'm regretting not pressing him for more information about Benoit, but I'm more worried about Jenny, so I hurry home.

I leave a message on Tom's voicemail telling him I need to speak to him, that it's urgent and serious. He phones back immediately, bless him.

"I'll be driving past the end of your street in about half an hour actually," he says. "You can make me a cuppa."

The sight of Tom on the doorstep stuns me.

Sure, I've never considered Tom anything but attractive, but today he's wearing a black suit, crisp white shirt, and a bottle green tie. The transformation is stunning.

"Wow!" I say, looking at the sleek shimmer of his impeccable clothes. "Look at you!"

Tom grins sheepishly. "I had a meeting with the directors," he explains. "So, you know..."

I stand aside, ushering him into the lounge. "Your lordship," I say.

Tom blushes and heads through to the dining room.

"I never really imagined you in a suit," I say. "Not with the hair and everything."

Tom shrugs. "Doesn't happen often," he says.

I nod at a seat, indicating that he should sit and switch on the kettle.

"It works though," I say. "That suit is stunning."

Tom shrugs and smoothes his lapel. "Yeah," he says sheepishly.

"Cost too much really," he laughs. "But, I thought, well, I only have the one, so..."

I pull two cups from the cupboard and put a teabag in each.

"Tea I presume," I say.

"Yeah," Tom nods. "So what's happening? You sounded serious."

I sigh and lean on the counter top.

"Yes," I say. "Well, I wanted to talk to you about Jenny. I need your advice."

Tom raises an eyebrow and nods.

"Hey, where's your piercing?" I say.

Tom shrugs and rubs his eyebrow. "Didn't go with the suit," he says. "I'll put it back in tonight. So what's up with Mrs Stroppy?"

I smile. "I'm worried about her," I say.

Tom nods. "So he *is* hitting her?"

I frown. I stop breathing for a moment and stare at him.

"Nick, I mean," Tom says with a nod.

It's obvious and amazingly clear and it has never crossed my mind. But the second Tom says it, I know that it's true. At some deep level, it is as if I have always known.

"I think he is," I say. "Yes, I think he probably is."

I tell Tom about Jenny's decision to leave Nick, her decision to keep the baby, and the phone call to her mother. Tom nods and listens and sips his tea.

Finally I shrug. "So what do *you* think?" I say.

Tom nods soberly. "Well if he *is* slapping her around I think we should talk to her, don't you?" he says.

I nod. "I know," I say. "But we don't know that, and even if he is, well, she doesn't seem to *want* to talk."

"Maybe we should go see her," he says. "Maybe we should just turn up. Surrey's not that far, and I've got fuck-all on this afternoon."

I nod half-heartedly. "I suppose we could. Except that I don't know where they live."

Tom shrugs. "Directory enquiries?" he says.

I shake my head. "I don't know Nick's surna..." I stare at the ceiling an instant before correcting myself.

"Actually I do," I say. "Her mother said it. It's *Gregory*. Nick Gregory."

Tom winks at me and pulls his mobile from his top pocket. "It's worth a try," he says.

On the motorway, I try looking out of the side window but it doesn't help. I try closing my eyes and feigning sleep, but that's worse. In the end it's no good. I have to ask Tom to slow down.

He glances at the speedometer. "I'm only doing eighty-five," he says petulantly.

I nod. "I'm sorry Tom, but since the accident..."

He frowns.

"I was in a really bad accident. My friend died," I remind him.

Tom reaches across and touches my leg. "Sorry," he says, dropping his speed to seventy. "Is that better?" he asks, glancing sideways at me.

I wrinkle my nose and grin falsely. He glances in the rear-view mirror and moves into the slow lane.

"Sixty!", he says with a laugh.

I grimace at him and nod. "Sorry," I say. "Thanks."

Tom shrugs, squeezes my leg and returns his hand to the steering wheel. "If it creeps up then just remind me," he says.

"I am sorry about all this," I say. "I mean, I may be imagining it all."

Tom shrugs and glances at me. "I quite like the adventure really," he says. "Surrey! Imagine!" he laughs.

"She couldn't even live somewhere interesting," I say nodding.

"No, but seriously, I'm quite intrigued to see this Nick guy," Tom says. "And if there's no problem, then, well, our dropping in won't be a problem either, will it."

I turn slightly in my seat and glance at Tom from the corner of my vision.

There's something about the largesse of formal clothes, the rigid whiteness of the shirt, the silky plummeting of the suit trousers that hides, yet emphasises the presence of his body within. The desire to reach over and feel his thigh through the fabric is almost overpowering. I'm getting an erection, so I turn and look out of the side window at the countryside spinning by.

Tom reaches out and pushes a button on the CD player. Van Morrison starts to sing.

"Van the Man," I say absently.

"Motorway music," Tom replies.

I slump back in my seat and smile at how good it feels to be here, doing this; how right it feels to be just the two of us on our way to check up on our friend.

"I wonder what will happen when we get there," I say.

Tom glances in the mirror and clicks on an indicator. "Probably nothing," he says. "Probably nothing at all."

What Needs
To Be Done

Just before three pm, we pull into Churchill Close. "Geez!" Tom exclaims. "*Posh houses!*"

I look at the detached properties gliding by. "Yeah," I agree. "Horrible though; I mean, imagine living here!"

"Must cost a couple of million each though," Tom says. "What does this Nick guy actually do?"

"Builder," I say. "He has a building business." Tom nods.

"Jenny works too, normally," I add. "In advertising."

Tom pulls up in front of number seventeen. The house is surrounded by an immaculate, almost plastic looking lawn. In the middle is a pond and a statue, pissing. "Very chic," Tom says with a laugh. "I don't think."

"Jenny's van's there though," I say, nodding at the orange VW. As I climb from the car I see Jenny appear at the lounge window. Before Tom has shut his own door, Jenny has flung the front door open and is trotting towards us.

"She looks keen," Tom says.

"Hiya," Jenny says frowning. "What the *fuck* are you two doing here?" She glances down the street as if to see where we have come from. She looks flustered, pale and blotchy. And she doesn't look keen at all.

"And what's with the monkey suit?" she adds, raising an eyebrow at Tom.

Tom smiles at her and cocks his head to one side. "I thought I'd Surrey it up a little," he laughs, then straightening his tie and putting on a posh accent, he adds, "We've come for *tea*."

Jenny glances down the street again, a nervous gesture I now realise. She's keeping lookout. "You expecting someone?" I ask.

She nods. "Yeah, and it's *not* you! Nick's down the pub. He'll be back in a bit. I'm afraid you can't stay."

I glance at Tom, but his expression is blank, so I turn back to Jenny.

"Oh come on," I push. "We've come all the way from Brighton. Give us a cuppa ma'am?"

She glances at the entrance to the close again, and then looks me in the eye.

"It's really not a good time," she says with a shake of her head. "I'm *really* sorry... You should have phoned."

"Jenny," I say, stepping forwards.

But as I move, she takes a step back.

"I'm sorry Mark," she says again. "But you have to go."

I glance at Tom. He shrugs and rolls his eyes.

"Can I at least use the loo?" he asks, raising an eyebrow.

Jenny stares at the ground, then looks up at me. "Please?" she says. "You have to understand. Don't make this hard on me. I feel bad enough."

I shrug and nod slowly. "OK," I say with a sigh. "I know when I'm not wanted."

I open my arms to hug her and she moves forward. Over her shoulder I see the curtains next door twitching, then as I hug her I notice something is wrong with her hair. It's matted and stuck to the side of her head. When I raise a hand to touch it however, she pulls away.

"What happened to your hair?" I ask, frowning and glancing back at Tom.

Jenny raises a hand and gently touches the side of her head. It reminds me of the gesture she made when she hurt her cheek.

"Oh that," she says. "I, um, got it caught in something. Ripped a bit out. It really hurt!" she laughs falsely.

Tom steps forward. "Show me," he says, his voice suspicious.

"I really don't have time for this," Jenny protests. "Nick will be back any minute."

Tom's lips thin, his expression becomes deadly serious. He looks soulfully at Jenny, then glances at me and raises an eyebrow, asking me for permission to go ahead. I nod.

Tom places a hand on Jenny's back. "And what happens when Nick gets home?" he asks.

Jenny raises a hand to her mouth and chews a fingernail. I notice that her hand is trembling.

"He... He just has a temper," she says. "And he's jealous, and he's been drinking. It's not a good combination."

She steps sideways, but Tom and I move with her.

I lift her chin and look into her eyes.

"Does he hurt you?" I say. "Because if he's hurting you, you must say. You must tell us."

Jenny opens her mouth to speak but says nothing. She stares into my eyes and chews her bottom lip. Her eyes are watery.

"No," she says finally, her voice hard, almost metallic. "He doesn't."

Then she raises both hands and pushes me away. "Now go," she says.

I sigh and look at Tom who shrugs.

"Come on," I say shaking my head. "Let's fuck off."

Tom looks flushed. His neck above the collar is turning pink. He swallows hard. "OK," he says.

We turn towards the Mini, but the sound of a car entering the close makes us pause. Jenny places one hand on each of our backs and gives us a little push. "Go!" she says urgently. Then she turns and trots back down the path towards the house.

I glance at Tom, who winks sadly at me. We move towards the car.

As Tom climbs in, I glance regretfully back at Jenny, but she is already inside, already closing the door behind her.

As I pull open my door, a grey BMW swings into view, driving quickly towards us. I pause, my hand on the top of the open door.

It slows as it approaches, then starts to swing behind the Mini and into the driveway. I peer in through the window, intrigued to at least catch a glimpse of Nick, if that's who this is.

The driver looks up at me, then brakes, tyres crunching on the gravel as the car slides to a stop.

The window opens. His eyes are blue and bright. His long blond hair is pulled into a ponytail. His face is flushed and pink, good looking, if slightly swollen features.

He looks up at me. "So what are you looking at?" he asks.

Tom leans across the passenger seat and peers up at me. "Get in," he says.

"Nothing," I tell the man. "I'm just going."

The guy nods. "Good, 'cos you're parked in front of my house," he says. He isn't slurring, but his voice is a touch too loud, a little too crude. It lacks a certain precision. He's been drinking all right.

I turn to get into the Mini, but something makes me stall. My legs fail to obey. I turn back and frown at the man.

Tom pulls on the pocket of my jeans. "Mark, just *get in*," he says.

"Hang on," I snap. "Something's not right."

As I turn back to Nick, Tom, behind me mutters, *"Something's not right..."*

"If we're parked in front of your house that's probably just because we're leaving your house," I say with a false smile. "I wouldn't worry about it."

The man nods and wipes a hand across his chin. It's an aggressive open-mouthed gesture.

"*Is* it now?" he says, sarcastically. "Is *that* the reason? Well, I won't worry then."

Tom pulls on my rear pocket again. "Mark, will you leave it?" he says.

"Wait!" I tell him. I'm not sure what I'm doing, but I'm sure it needs to be done.

"So, tell me, friend," the man says. "Who the fuck *are* you, anyway?"

"A friend, of Jenny's," I say. "Mark."

I hold out my hand. Nick stares at it with distaste, as if it is some alien object. Then he looks back up at me.

"The poof?" he says. "From Brighton?"

I nod. "Yep!" I say perkily. "That'll be me. The poof. From Brighton."

I hear Tom behind me. *"Shit!"* he mutters.

"So you're the cunt who's been keeping my wife so busy," Nick says.

I run a hand across my head. I hear a click as Tom releases his seatbelt.

"Yep," I say. "You've got me all worked out. I'm the cunt from Brighton."

I glance over at the window. Beneath the sunny reflection on the pane, I can make out the silhouette of Jenny standing as before, chewing a fingernail.

Nick nods. "Good. I'm glad that's sorted. Now you can fuck off back to Queer-Town then," he snarls.

The Paths Separate

I nod slowly. I am frozen at the point between two destinies. It's not as if I'm trying to decide what will happen, it truly is a question of destiny. I'm waiting to see what will happen. This is where the paths split. And someone has to choose.

"And you and your queer friends can stay away from my missus," Nick says.

I nod again. For a moment no one speaks. I feel a vague, unspecified heat. A burning, rising, pulsing heat is spreading through my body, up towards my forehead. The edges of my vision are blurring slightly. I can feel blood pulsing through my temple. It seems to me that in some strange way, Nick has chosen.

"Well, I'm glad I met you," I hear myself say. "I thought you were probably a cunt, and, well, now I know. You are."

I hear Tom say, *"Oh fuck."*

As Nick reaches for his door-handle, I hear a clunk indicating that Tom has done the same behind me.

Nick's nostrils flare. He flexes his shoulders as he rises from the car. He's wearing jeans and a denim jacket. He looks solid and muscular, but shorter than me, one metre seventy-five max.

As I look down at him, flexing his muscles, pumping himself up, I have a sudden desire to laugh at his size. I resist, but smirk all the same.

He pushes out his front teeth and lowers them to his bottom lip, then spits a drawn out, "Fuck, off," at me.

The front door opens and Jenny appears, advancing slowly, her arms crossed across her stomach.

"Mark!" Tom shouts behind me.

I turn to look at him. He's standing one foot in the car, peering over the top of the Mini at me.

"Listen to me; we really need to..." But he stops mid phrase. His mouth drops.

I hear Jenny scream behind me, but as I spin to see whatever they are seeing, Nick's fist meets the left side of my head, just in front of my ear.

The pain of his knuckles smashing into my cheek is gut wrenching. The shock of the blow winds me. The force of his arm behind the fist sends me crashing into the door of the Mini.

I crash and crumple against the car door, then miss my footing and slide to the floor, turning as I fall to look at my assailant.

Jenny has now reached Nick. "Leave him!" she shouts, latching onto his arm.

"Please!" she pleads. She glances at Tom, "Please just *go*?" she begs.

Jenny is hanging on to Nick's right arm, but his left hand is free. He swings at Jenny and the flat of his hand slaps her hard across the cheek. The sheer sound of the slap makes me wince. She stumbles backwards onto the lawn, still, incredibly hanging onto Nick's right arm.

He leans over her and slaps her again, this time on the side of her head. She crumples backwards onto the lawn just in front of the fountain.

Tom starts to move towards them. He's shaking his head. He's saying, "No, no, no, no..." His voice is peculiar and flat. He sounds oddly unemotional.

I struggle to stand; my legs feel rubbery and uncoordinated.

Nick is shaking his arm violently in an attempt to dislodge Jenny, but she is white knuckled, gripping the denim of his jacket.

I pull myself up by the door handle, and manage to balance unsteadily on my two feet.

"Nick, you can't..." Tom is saying. His voice is still strangely calm.

"Fucking get off me!" Nick shouts.

Just as he says "off," he swings his leg and kicks Jenny hard in the ribs. She shrieks in pain, and releasing his arm, she rolls away, her arms wrapped around her belly.

At the instant of the kick, everything shifts speed.

Tom runs and dives onto Nick's back, knocking him to the ground. Memories of the nightmare are pulsing through my mind, so I run to Jenny, desperate to insert myself between her and Nick.

The two men roll around in an indistinguishable mass, until Tom manages to plant the sole of his foot against Nick's stomach and push him hard away. Tom moves onto all fours and starts to scramble towards the BMW.

Nick grabs for the tail of Tom's jacket, but he scrabbles away, standing as he runs, finally dodging behind Nick's car.

As the two men face off over the roof I yank Jenny to her feet and glance back at Tom.

"Nick!" he is saying. His voice is breathless but still spookily toneless. "Just stop..."

Tom's eyes flick towards the Mini and I realise he wants me to get in, he has a plan, and he wants us to be ready to go.

"You can't behave this way. We don't have to fight," he's shouting.

Nick is darting right then left, but Tom, on the other side of the BMW, mirrors every movement.

"This is family," Nick is shouting. "It's none of your *fucking* business."

"But you can't behave like that," Tom says. "And you can't win. There are *three* of us." There's almost a hint of laughter in his voice.

Tom's eyes flick towards the car again, so I grab Jenny's arm and start to manhandle her towards the door.

"Now let's just slow things down..." Tom says.

Nick jerks right, leaping over the bonnet of his car, but Tom is as fast and skips sideways so the end result is the same. They have simply swapped sides, only Tom now has his back to the Mini.

"Slow things down," he says again breathlessly. There is definitely a note of sarcasm in his voice. As if he finds this all slightly amusing.

I push Jenny into the back seat of the Mini. Tears are rolling down her cheeks, but she seemingly resigns herself to leaving.

I look back at Tom who, behind his back, is making a screwdriver gesture. I edge towards the driver's door, and glance inside but can see no tools, nothing resembling a weapon whatsoever.

I glance back at Tom and see Nick's eyes swivel towards me. I see him realise what's happening.

"Jenny, get *out* of the car!" he shouts. "JENNY! GET OUT OF THE FUCKING CAR!"

Tom glances behind to see where we're at, but as he does, Nick lurches towards him, higher than I would have imagined possible, and reaching across the top of the BMW, he manages to swipe and grasp the end of Tom's tie.

"Ha!" he laughs madly. "Fucker!"

Tom struggles against the side of the car but Nick has him in a noose. He drags him sideways, then, down over the bonnet. Finally he winches him in.

Tom glances back at me. His eyes look terrified, but as I start to move back towards him, he says, "Will you *please*, just start the fucking engine?"

I freeze. I could almost cry at my stupidity. The screwdriver gesture was an ignition key. I get in the driver's seat. *Could Tom really have a plan? Could there really be a way for him to get out of this unscathed?*

I turn the key, over-revving the engine as it starts, then check the gears, feel for the pedals, and lean across the passenger seat to survey the two men.

Jenny is peering from the back window.

She says, "Mark. He'll kill him; do something. Really, he'll kill him."

Nick swaps his grip on Tom's tie from the right to the left hand.

Tom glances back at me, nodding maniacally. "Be ready," he says.

I shake my head in disbelief. I'm trembling and tears of rage are pushing from the corners of my eyes.

"How the fuck?" I say. I push on the accelerator and rev the engine again.

Tom turns back to Nick, who is now holding him mere inches from his own face.

"Nick! Listen," Tom says.

Nick's right hand collides with the side of his face. Not a punch, but a heavy slap, clearly the first of many. Nick has decided to enjoy himself.

Tom stumbles sideways, but Nick pulls him back up by the tie, winding it further around his hand.

"Nick, you're making me *really* fucking angry," Tom says.

Whack! Nick's hand slaps Tom's head sideways.

Jenny starts to sit forward, but I push the front seat down locking her in place.

"He'll hurt him!" she says, dissolving into sobs. "He'll really..."

"I'm OK!" Tom shouts.

Nick laughs. "Are you?" he says, slapping him again. "*Are you*?"

I shake my head. "This is *bullshit*," I say, starting to stand.

But Tom raises a hand towards me. It's as clear as can be – a stop sign.

"I give in," Tom tells Nick. "You win. Listen..."

As he says this Tom steps backwards and Nick follows. Tom's back is only a few meters away from the rear of the Mini.

Tom raises his hands to Nick's chest, and grips his lapels. And suddenly I know what is about to happen. Suddenly I know what Tom is about to do. I've seen this before. I've been here before.

I slide back into the driver's seat, test the pedals, and glance nervously down the close. Then I lean over and look back up at Tom.

Tom gives a huge grunt, and, with all his might, he pushes Nick away.

Nick's arms extend, leaving a meter between the two men, but he maintains his grasp on Tom's tie and even laughs.

"Oh no you don't," he grunts.

Jenny is fumbling for the lever to release the seat, so I push her back again.

As I glance back up, I see Tom give a final groaning push against Nick's chest.

"Here it comes," I think, starting to grin, starting to will him on.

I see his head withdraw; I see him lower his forehead. He aims it at Nick like a bull about to charge.

"Yes!" I think. I look on with admiration, willing him to success.

At the perfect moment, Tom stops pushing against Nick's chest and simultaneously places a leg behind and throws himself forwards. Nick is pulling as hard as he can on Tom's tie, his own force combining with Tom's forward lurch.

Tom's head moves forward so fast, it blurs. As it meets Nick's nose there is a gruesome crunch. Blood spurts forth. I gasp.

Nick reels backwards, using Tom's tie to steady himself, but then he releases his grip, totters backwards and collapses like a toddler onto the ground. He raises a hand to his face, to the blood gushing from his nose.

He stares madly at his red hand, then up at us, then back at his hand. He looks astonished, cross-eyed, stunned.

Tom spins towards the car but his city shoes slip on the grass and he loses his balance, one leg shooting out at a mad angle across the lawn.

"Tom!" I scream, "Come on!" My voice is hoarse with terror. For

Nick is already moving onto all fours, already staggering to his feet.

As Tom scrabbles towards the open door, I push Jenny back into her seat again.

"Fucking sit still!" I shout at her.

I put the car into first and glance in front, to check the way is still clear.

Jenny turns nervously and peers through the back window again. "No!" she wails. "Tom!"

As Tom reaches the car, just as he starts to fold into the seat, Nick, now standing reaches inside his denim jacket and starts to pull something out.

He lurches towards the car, and in a single swinging movement removes an iron bar – a wheel-nut wrench I realise – from inside his jacket.

Tom is almost in the car, but just as he throws a leg inside, just as he tips sideways to drop into the seat, his head dips left and moves into the arc of the swinging wrench. It barely seems to touch him.

"GO!" Tom screams.

I rev the poor engine to death, and jerkily drop the clutch, and at the very instant Tom gets his other leg inside we lurch off across the close.

Jenny is screaming, so I glance in the rear-view mirror expecting to see Nick running after us, but he is just standing in the middle of the street clutching his nose.

As we swing around the bend, I glance left just in time to see him sink to his knees.

Struggling to see – my vision seems blurred – and trembling with fear, I drive a few hundred yards to the end of the close, then pull out onto the open road.

"Mark!" Tom shouts. "Change gear!"

Suddenly aware of the screaming engine, I change into second. "Sorry," I say.

A little way up the road, I pull into a bus stop. I put the handbrake on and look around the car, speechless.

With the exception of her cheeks, Jenny is white as a sheet; her face glistens with tears.

"Christ!" I say. Is everyone OK?" I ask.

"I'm so sorry," Jenny gasps.

I look at Tom. "And you, Tom?" I say. "Are you OK?"

Tom shakes his head then laughs. "Geez!" he says. "I think so."

I exhale heavily and raise a hand to my mouth. Tom places his left hand on the dashboard. It glistens with blood, thick and dark.

"Tom! Your hand!" I say.

Tom frowns at me, and then slowly lifts his hand and stares at it uncomprehendingly, slowly turning it from side to side.

He raises his hand again and touches the side of his head. When he brings it back into view it is darker still. The blood is dripping off it onto his lap.

"Shit!" he says. "He got me. That arsehole got me!"

I lean over and grasp his chin, turning his head towards me. The blood is flowing fast and free, a widening river, glistening black and sliding down his neck forming an obscene stain reaching from his collar to his shoulder.

"I'll be OK," Tom says. "Drive on."

I shake my head. "Tom, it's..." I swallow hard. "It's bad," I say.

Tom frowns at me then glances down at his shoulder. When he turns back to me he looks visibly paler, tinged with green.

"Mark?" he says, his voice wobbling. "I need you to... I don't feel quite... I think I'm going to..." His head slumps.

"Tom!" Jenny cries.

Only his seatbelt is holding him upright. My mouth drops. I stare at him.

"Tom," I say touching his leg and leaning over. "*Tom*?"

"What's wrong with him?" Jenny says.

I shake my head.

"What's wrong with Tom?" Jenny asks again.

"I don't know," I say.

"Think," I say.

Jenny grabs Tom's shoulder and shakes him. "Tom?" she weeps.

"We need a hospital," I say.

Jenny shakes Tom's shoulder again.

"JENNY!" I scream. "LEAVE HIM. Just tell me where the *fucking* hospital is."

Jenny stares blankly at me, and then, as if someone has clicked a switch, as if she has suddenly changed modes, she leans down between the two seats, and peers out through the windscreen, getting her bearings.

"Do a u-turn," she says quietly, almost mechanically. "Go down to the lights and turn right. It's at the end of the road."

What Friends Are For

I sip hot chocolate from the vending machine and nervously watch the door. It has crossed my mind that there is probably no more likely place to bump into Nick than the local casualty ward, and the idea of facing him alone terrifies me.

My left ear is swollen and painful where Nick boxed me, and my right ear hurts too with a different kind of throbbing sting. I apparently bashed it when I fell against the Mini.

"At least I'll be symmetrical," I think.

Jenny is the first to reappear, advancing along the corridor like a fragile old lady. As she reaches me I stand and open my arms.

"Jenny," I say.

We hug perfunctorily, and she stands back and smiles weakly.

"Nothing broken," she says. "Just bruises."

"And the baby?" I ask.

Jenny nods. "The baby's fine. Apparently she's a tough little critter."

"She?" I repeat. It's the first time Jenny has mentioned the baby's sex.

Jenny nods. "I forgot to tell the nurse not to tell me..." she shrugs. "So now we know."

I hug her again. "I'm so glad," I say.

"Tom's fine too," Jenny adds.

I push her away and look at her face. Against my will, tears slide from my eyes.

"Oh!" I gasp. "I was so worried," I say. "I haven't had any news at all."

Jenny smiles and bites her lip. "I saw him on the way out. Insulting the nurse."

I frown. "Really?"

Jenny nods. "They're stitching his head. Apparently it hurts like fuck."

I laugh tearfully. "Poor Tom."

Jenny nods. Her eyes are shining too.

"He was amazing!" I say.

Jenny nods, soberly. "Yeah," she says, "he was. *Truly* amazing."

At the sound of the sliding doors we turn to see a policeman enter. Jenny frowns, first at him, then at me.

I shrug. "The nurse said she would have to notify the police," I say.

Jenny crosses her eyes and sighs. "Shit," she says.

"You better think about whether you want to press charges," I say.

Jenny shakes her head. "I *so* don't want to go there," she says. "But I guess it's not only for me to decide."

It's six pm by the time we leave the police station.

Jenny and Tom have negotiated a compromise. They have made an official complaint in the *Daybook*, without actually pressing charges. It means that Nick doesn't need to find out, yet a record of the event exists, just in case.

Jenny requests, then demands that I take her to her mother's house. She even tries shouting into my ear from the rear seat, but I ignore her and head towards home.

Eventually it is Tom who silences her. "Jenny, do you have *any* idea how much that hurts my head?" he says. "Now shut it."

Jenny glares at me in the rear-view mirror.

By the time we hit the M25 Jenny has slumped out of sight on the rear seat, and Tom's head is starting to loll

I feel utterly shattered myself; it's hard to raise the level of concentration required to drive Tom's car down the correct side of the road to Brighton, but, well, someone has to do it.

I lower the volume, and turn on the CD player.

Tom awakens just long enough to hit the CD changer button.

Van Morrison fades away to be replaced by *Everything But The Girl*. The album is *Idlewild*, my favourite.

I smile at Tom, but he has already closed his eyes.

I fidget in my seat and settle in for the drive.

As we turn onto the M23 the light is fading. I fiddle and find the headlights. The clocks on the dashboard produce a warm orange glow.

I glance behind to check on Jenny and smile at the sight of her asleep with her mouth open.

It's a cold greeny-grey colour outside, but we're all safe and sound and heading home. I'm taking my friends home.

I glance over at Tom. His poor bandaged head is rolling from side to side as I drive.

A wave of love for my two sleeping passengers washes over me, making me scrunch up my eyes against the pressure of tears.

As the road bends left, Tom's leg falls against mine.

I glance down at it, making out the shape of his leg beneath the muddy suit material. *"Poor Tom in his expensive suit,"* I think.

His hand sits on top, smooth and white, sprouting from a bloodstained cuff. I glance up at his face to check he's asleep, and lay my hand on top of his.

I'm not sure if he's truly asleep or not, but he sighs and spreads his fingers, and my own fingers fall into the gaps.

I swallow hard.

Back at Owen's, I pull Jenny from the rear of the car and Tom moves to the driving seat.

Jenny yawns, then walks around and crouches beside Tom to hug him.

"Thanks Tom," she says, patting his back. "And, I'm really sorry."

Tom shakes his head gently. "I won't say it was a pleasure, but well, that's what friends are for," he says.

I peer in over Jenny's shoulder at him.

"Are you sure you're gonna be OK?" I say. "I really think you should stay here, or at least let me drive you home."

Tom shakes his head. "I'm fine," he says. "I just want to go home and sleep in my own bed," he says.

"You won't faint again?" I ask.

Jenny releases Tom and stands. He shakes his head.

"No, I'll be fine, really," he says. "It's less than a mile."

Jenny steps back and I shrug and slam the door.

"Maybe see you tomorrow?" I ask.

Tom nods, and starts the engine.

"Oh, Tom," Jenny says. "Don't forget your wallet. It's on the back seat."

Tom nods and then frowns and shakes his head. He slips a hand beneath him and wriggles, pulling a wallet from his pocket. He waves it at Jenny.

Jenny frowns, then crouches beside him. "Hang on," she says, reaching in through the window to the seat behind.

She pulls a second wallet from the rear of the car.

"That's mine!" I say.

Jenny shrugs. "It was on the floor in the back," she says.

I exhale sharply and take it in my hands. I stare at the wallet and shake my head.

"No shit," I say.

Perspective Lines

I sleep badly, waking every time the pillow touches my right ear.

Feeling grumpy and irritable, I finally drag myself from the bed just before twelve. Jenny is in the lounge watching TV.

"Hi," I say, heading through to the kitchen. "Tea?"

Jenny nods, and pulls Owen's dressing gown tighter across her chest. I realise sleepily that she has no spare clothes.

I hand Jenny her tea and sit opposite, folding my legs beneath me on the big armchair.

"Jesus! Look at your ear!" Jenny says. "It's blue."

I shrug. "The same blue as your cheek, I imagine," I say.

Jenny raises a hand and covers her cheek tenderly.

"I suppose we have to take you shopping," I say.

Jenny frowns at me. "Shopping," she laughs. "With this face?"

"Yeah," I say. "Clothes, toothbrush, that kind of stuff?"

Jenny shrugs. "I thought I'd laze around watching TV and wash and dry the stuff from yesterday," she says.

I sip my tea. "Well, I suppose... There's a tumble dryer. But you can't do that indefinitely," I say. "Sooner or later you'll need..."

"But I can't stay here indefinitely anyway," Jenny says. "I don't have anything with me, I don't even have my purse, my money..." She shrugs and shakes her head.

"Well, you can stay here for now," I say. "And you can't go back, that's clear at least."

Jenny shakes her head slowly. "He's not as bad as you think," she says quietly.

I grimace at her. "What do you *mean* he's not as bad as I think?" I say

"I just mean that yesterday was, well, *extreme*," Jenny says.

I nod. "Yep," I say. "Extreme does it."

"But he's not like that usually," she says.

I stare at her. For a moment I am speechless. I sip my tea.

"So what you mean is," I say. "That when he's not slapping you, or pulling your hair, or kicking you in the ribs, or punching your friends, or pulling an iron..."

"I knew you'd be like this," Jenny interrupts. "I just so knew you'd..."

"Well it's not unexpected is it?" I say. "My ear hurts, your cheek is blue, and Tom is at home with stitches in his head."

"That's why I wanted to go to Mum's," Jenny continues. "I knew you wouldn't understand."

I glare at her; then I turn and stare at the silent image on the TV screen for a moment. "So your mother *understands* that your husband slaps you around?" I say flatly. "And that's *good*."

Jenny glares at me and starts to stand.

"Don't walk away!" I spit. "If it's defendable, then defend. If it's understandable, then explain!"

"But you don't even *want* to understand," Jenny says, looking me in the eye. "You just want to argue."

I sigh and sit back in my chair. "Sorry," I say with a little shake of my head. "I don't, you know. Go on; explain. I'm all ears."

"It's just that you saw the worst side of Nick yesterday," Jenny says.

I restrain a snort, and keep my teeth firmly clenched.

"He's not a *bad person*, that's all I mean," Jenny says.

I shake my head. "I... I'm sorry," I say. "But I don't get it. I mean how does he have to behave to be a *bad person*? Would he have to *kill* someone?"

Jenny rolls her eyes at me.

"It's not that far-fetched Jenny," I cry. "He went for Tom with an *iron bar*!"

Jenny sighs and nods. "You did provoke him," she says.

"Verbally," I say. "But... Hang on. Does your mother actually know then?"

Jenny nods and shrugs. "She knows we argue."

"Does she know he hits you?"

"*Slaps*," Jenny corrects.

I feel my face start to redden again.

"OK," I say, "Does she know he *slaps* you?"

Jenny shrugs. "She's old enough to know that relationships go through bad patches," she says.

"Bad patches," I repeat in a whisper.

"She and dad went through plenty of rough times. But you have to take the good with the bad."

"But he didn't *hit* her, did he," I point out. "Your father didn't actually slap your mother around."

Jenny stares at me expressionlessly, one eyebrow almost imperceptibly raised.

"Well *did he*?" I ask.

Jenny blinks slowly.

"Your father used to *hit* your *mother*?"

"They fought sometimes," she says with a shrug.

"And sometimes he hit her, when they fought?"

Jenny shrugs.

"Great!" I say, rubbing my forehead. "Jesus!"

"It's not that unusual!" Jenny says. "For god's sake Mark, people fight and people lash out. It's human nature. Stop being so... So *righteous.*"

I shake my head. "It's not normal though Jenny," I say. "I mean, I can see why you think that it might be, but it's not."

Jenny laughs. "It may not be in gay society," she says, "but let me tell you..."

"John never hit you," I say. "Did he?"

Jenny shakes her head. "John catches flies in a cup and puts them out the window," Jenny says. "Of course he didn't."

"And Giles. Did Giles ever hit you?"

Jenny tips her head sideways and bites her top lip.

"Jesus Jenny!" I say. "Why do you stay with these people? I mean if anyone ever hit me, like even once, well, I'd be gone so quick..."

Jenny stares at the ceiling. "You're not listening Mark and you're not trying to understand. If you leave people every time you have a fight..."

"If people hit you, yes!" I say. "If people are physically violent to you," I say.

"But they are," Jenny cries. "It's reality."

"It's *your* reality," I say. "No one's *ever* hit me, well, except for *Nick.*"

Jenny tips her chin at me. "What about your *parents*?" she says.

I swallow. I half shrug. "My mother slapped me from time to time," I say.

"And your father?"

I shake my head.

"OK, so your mother slapped you. And you considered it normal?"

I shake my head. "Jesus Jenny. No! Why do you think I don't get on with the woman?"

"Well so did mine," Jenny says. "And so did my father. And it's not abnormal," she adds.

"It was a different era," I say, "But that doesn't mean it was *right*."

"You can't just cut everyone out of your life because they..."

"Because they *hit you*?" I say incredulously. "*Yes*! You can. And you *have* to," I say. "To survive."

Jenny stares at me. Her eyes are glistening as the tears well up.

"I knew you wouldn't understand," she says with a little shake of her head.

She stands and wipes the tears angrily on the back of her hand as she crosses the room.

"I'm getting showered," she says.

As she walks past, I reach out to grab her arm.

"Jenny," I plead, but she pulls away and continues into the hall.

I sit and stare at the female presenter on the TV screen, and shake my head. Then I sigh and shake it again.

For the first time I understand how sarcastic, ballsy Jenny can be where she is. Suddenly I see the perspective lines of her life disappearing into the past like a pair of train tracks bringing her to this very point.

"Shit!" I think. "This isn't going to be easy."

Limits

Tom stares at me wide-eyed, then turns and takes his change from the cashier. As he follows me to the big sofa in the window, he says, "But that's madness!"

We squat opposite ends of the sofa, half turning our bodies so that we face each other.

"I know," I say with a doleful sigh. "But she's in this sort of... I don't know. *Victim mode*?"

Tom nods. "I used to work with a woman called Kerry. Every guy she ever dated used her as a punching ball. You ended up wondering if it wasn't in some way her fault."

I grimace to show that I'm uncomfortable with the logic.

Tom shrugs. "She chose those men, she stayed with them..."

"Well, yeah. That's the thing with Jenny," I say. "She thinks it's normal. She says her ex Giles used to slap her as well. Even her parents slapped each other, apparently."

Tom shakes his head. "Stupid bitch," he says. "I tell you, if she goes back to that arsehole, I'll take an iron bar to *her* head."

I shrug. "I expect she'd consider that quite acceptable."

Tom shakes his head. "Silly cow," he says.

I grimace. "I know what you mean Tom," I say. "But in a way, well, it's not her fault if she's ended up here is it?"

Tom shrugs and sips at his cappuccino. "If someone slapped me, I'd be gone."

I shake my head. "You'd nut him I expect," I say with a grin.

Tom grimaces and raises a hand to his forehead. "You know my forehead still hurts?"

I smile. "*Violent* child," I say.

Tom raises his hands in a surrender gesture. "Hey," he says. "He did that all himself."

I nod. "Yeah, I know," I say.

Tom shakes his head. "No I mean it," he says. "He actually did it himself. He was pulling so hard on my tie, all I did was lower my forehead and stop pushing against him."

I bite my lip. "Tough little fucker though," I say. "How is your head? I see you got the bandages off."

Tom blinks exaggeratedly. "Yeah, the bleeding stopped," he says. "But I'm a bit dizzy. It's weird, I'm kind of having trouble focusing. Like my eyes are too close together, you know?"

I frown and peer at him. "Now you mention it..." I say with a laugh.

Tom pulls a face. "If it carries on till Monday, I'm gonna go see the doctor and get a week off work," he says. "I've got two weeks holiday coming up anyway, so it'd be kind of cool to run it all together."

I nod gently. "You deserve it," I say. "Anything planned, superhero?"

Tom nods and raises an eyebrow. "I've decided to face my demons and go see Antonio in Genoa."

My good mood evaporates at the mention of Antonio's name. Amazingly I had forgotten he existed.

"He's still *umming* and *ahhring* about the move, so I thought it would be good for us to spend some time together," Tom continues. He sips his tea and then looks up at me. "What's up?" he frowns.

I shake my head. "Nothing," I say. "I was counting on you to help me with Jenny, that's all."

A chubby bear with a full beard and a leather waistcoat slumps into the armchair to Tom's right. "All right?" he says as he sits.

I nod and smile.

Tom glances at the guy then looks back at me. "Sorry," he says. "I've done my bit. She's all yours now."

I laugh sardonically. "Cheers," I say.

"Where is she anyway?" he asks.

I shrug. "At home, watching TV."

Tom frowns.

"She had no clean clothes to come out," I say.

"You're not worried she'll piss off?" Tom asks.

I shake my head. "Her clothes are in the washing machine. And she has no cash, so..."

Tom nudges me and leans in. "What do you think about our new neighbour?" he asks, nodding towards the chub.

I'm looking at the pile of magazines on the table. The cover of

People says, "Kylie's Undeclared Love Revealed."

I glance at the guy and then snort and turn to Tom.

"Not really my type," I say quietly.

Tom shrugs. "I quite like the big ones," he says. "In a funny sort of way."

"Tom," I say. "Can I tell you something?"

Tom shifts in his seat. "Sure," he says with a nod.

"I..." I shrug and sigh.

Tom grins at me. "Go on," he says. He is blushing a little.

"I just wish you weren't with Antonio," I say.

Tom stares into my eyes, emotionless, unreadable.

"It's selfish," I say. "But I wish you were single."

Tom rubs his chin and then twizzles his beard.

"Thanks," he says.

I shrug.

"You know what?" he adds.

I shake my head slowly.

"Sometimes, so do I," he says with a little laugh.

I frown at him.

"But, you know, you have to take the good with the bad," he says with a thoughtful nod. "And you have to resist. Otherwise nothing lasts."

I smile. "That's what Jenny says," I say.

Tom snorts. "Well, *within reason*," he says. "There have to be limits."

I nod.

"And what about the baby?" he asks.

I frown at him.

"Nick wanted her to get rid of it didn't he?" he says.

I nod. "Yeah," I say. "I don't know where they are on that one."

"Well, that'll be the decider I expect," he says, chewing the inside of his mouth.

I wrinkle my brow at him.

He shrugs and continues. "She may be happy to be slapped around a bit," he says. "But we all have our limits."

I nod.

"The decider," Tom continues, nodding gravely. "Will be whether she's prepared to kill her baby."

I stare at him and then nod slowly.

"If that's the choice he's forcing on her," he adds.

"Yep," I agree. "I suppose it will."

I stop in at Superdrug and pick up a toothbrush and a flannel for Jenny. I expect that a woman away from home needs infinitely more kit than this, but in the end, I just don't have the faintest idea what it might be.

I stop at the cash-point and withdraw the two hundred pounds I owe her, then wander thoughtfully up St James' Street.

By the time I reach the house I have a plan.

Cold-Blooded Manipulation

As we cross the main road towards the sea Jenny says, "I phoned my mum. Nick's been on the phone to her twice already. He wanted her to give him my address, well, your address."

I wide-eye her. "She didn't give it to him I hope?"

Jenny shakes her head. "Relax," she says. "She doesn't even have it."

I nod. "Well, good. You be careful, because she could get it from the phone number if she wanted," I say.

Jenny shakes her head. "She doesn't know that though," she says. "She's not that devious."

"Well good," I say. "Because I don't think I'd want to take Nick on again."

Jenny glares at me, so I drop the subject. We turn towards the pier.

"I'll need to call him though," Jenny says. "No matter what you think of him, he will be worried," she says.

I nod. "Well, leave it till tomorrow, OK?" I say. "It'll do him good to sweat a bit if nothing else," I say.

We walk in silence as far as the pier, then turn and start to return along the lower promenade.

"I'm sorry about before," Jenny says. "I don't want to argue, not with you."

I squeeze her arm. "I know," I say.

"It's just. Well, he isn't a bad person, you know? He doesn't mean to be like that."

I nod. "I guess," I say.

"When he's sober, he's lovely," she says. "He has a really good sense of humour, you'd like him."

I laugh lightly. "Yeah, well," I say. "I guess things are never all black and white."

Ahead I can see the goal, coming into view.

"No," Jenny says. "It's all shades of grey."

I nod. As the first shrieks from the children's play area reach our ears, I take a deep breath. I feel bad about this. It's so obviously manipulative. But then, it's so obviously *needed*.

"But as far as the safety of your daughter is concerned," I say. "It seems pretty black and white, you know?"

Jenny shoots me a sideways glance. Despite my best efforts she has realised what I'm doing. But she says nothing. We continue walking towards the colourful play area. I feel like I'm playing chess with someone else's life.

The shrieks of laughter are warming, and I start to feel better. Kids are running madly, swinging from frames like monkeys, spinning on roundabouts. A little boy is carrying his toddler sister from one ride to another, her feet passively dragging along the ground.

I sit on the wall overlooking the area, and though Jenny glances at me suspiciously, she takes her place beside me.

The cloud that has been hanging in front of the sun finally moves away. "Thank God for that," I say. "I was feeling chilly."

A beautiful little boy with olive skin and jet black hair, peers at us from inside the enclosure, then pushes his little fingers through the fence. He hangs there staring at us.

"I never looked like that," I say. "Lucky bugger."

Jenny smiles. "I bet you did," she says.

I shake my head. "I was the skinny blond one with the thick glasses," I say.

Jenny wrinkles her nose. "I was the fat one with freckles," she says.

I glance sideways at her. "What happened to the freckles?" I laugh.

She shrugs. "They went the same way as your thick glasses I guess," she says. "It's a shame the fat remains."

The little boy sticks his tongue out at us, and screaming engine noises, roars off around the perimeter of the playground.

I laugh. "You wouldn't want that one around for long," I say.

Jenny shrugs.

We sit in silence for a while. A beautiful father comes and picks up a baby who is crawling recklessly towards the roundabout.

"Cute dads," I say.

Jenny laughs. "Yeah," she says. "Did you never want kids?"

I look at her and frown, then sigh.

"I guess I did, once," I say with a shrug.

"Yeah?" Jenny sounds surprised.

"Maybe *wanted* isn't the right word," I say. "I guess I thought I would end up with kids. Before I sorted out my sexuality. I once imagined that it was inevitable," I say.

Jenny nods. "And now?" she says.

I shrug exaggeratedly. "It's kind of like asking if I would have wanted to be an astronaut," I say. "Or an Olympic runner."

Jenny frowns. "You mean just alien?"

I nod my head from side to side. "Just not an option really," I say. "I'm quite good at tailoring my desires to fit what's possible."

Jenny nods. "I guess we all do that," she says. "But you *could*... I mean, gay couples *do*," she says.

I wrinkle my nose. "I know," I say. "I guess."

Jenny sighs thoughtfully.

"I suppose it would just seem, sort of set up," I say. "I mean; it's not like it can just happen, naturally."

Jenny shrugs. "So?"

"So I guess I don't want kids enough to falsify the whole procedure. To force it all to happen," I say.

She nods.

"But when I've had the chance to be involved with friends' kids," I say, turning and smiling at her warmly. "Well, I really like it."

Jenny nods.

"I'm not good at it, but I really like it," I say. "And anyway, most of the gay relationships I see don't last long enough to organise buying goldfish," I laugh. "Let alone having children."

Jenny unzips her cardigan. "It's so much warmer when the sun's out, isn't it?" she says. "So you think children need stable environments?"

I laugh. "I think they need love," I say. "My childhood was fairly stable, in the bricks and mortar sense. But, well, no one would have complained if the love had been a little more visible."

Jenny raises an eyebrow and nods. "I know what you mean," she says.

"And I guess the nicest thing about having children must be trying to do it better. Trying to give them the things you would have liked to have for yourself."

Jenny nods.

"I mean, not the material things, but the unconditional love, the acceptance."

"Yeah," Jenny says.

"And you?" I ask. "Why do you want to have this baby?"

Jenny shrugs. "Do I?" she says quietly. "Want to have this baby?"

"OK," I say. "Then why *did* you want to have this baby?"

Jenny lowers her arms, crossing them around her stomach. "It's just..." she glances sideways at me. "I don't know, biological I suppose," she says. "Instinctive."

She nods and tips her head to one side. "My body wants it to happen," she says. "Every cell is *screaming* for it to happen."

I nod slowly.

"Does that make any sense?"

I laugh. "Yeah," I say. "I guess it makes a lot of sense."

Jenny clears her throat. "I have an appointment you know," she says. "On Wednesday, in Farnham."

I swallow. "Check-up?"

Jenny runs her tongue across her lips. "Abortion actually," she breathes. "In a private clinic."

We sit side by side. The sound of children fills the air, rising to a crescendo. It's as if the volume has momentarily been turned up.

I search my brain for a phrase, something intelligent, something clever, something ultimately convincing. But now we are here at the exact point I imagined, my mind is a blank.

I squeeze Jenny's arm and turn towards her. My eyes are watering and I can see that Jenny's are doing the same. She moves in her seat, half turning towards me.

She looks flushed; her face is taut with the mixed emotion of tears and an unexpected smile.

She gives a little laugh. "But I guess I'm not going am I?" she says.

I exhale heavily and lean over, hugging her with difficulty. "I think that's for the best," I say. "I really do."

Improbability Drive

We walk back in silence. Only as we near the house does Jenny speak. "I'm really sorry you know," she says. "I mean; I do see how stupid this all is."

"I just want you to be safe," I say. "And it seems really clear to me that you want this baby," I add.

Jenny sighs. "It's strange," she says. "It's like there's two different people in my head. I guess that sounds weird."

I shake my head and smile. "My head often seems to contain a whole crowd," I say.

"But it's not like I'm confused," Jenny says. "I just keep alternating one way and another. When Nick's not around, well, it seems obvious." She shakes her head.

I swing on the railing and mount the first step towards Owen's front door. "And when he *is* around?" I say.

Jenny shrugs. "It's like he has some power over me," she says. "I can't explain really, I don't understand myself."

I wrinkle my nose and step aside, ushering her in.

"It's like," Jenny explains. "Nick will say – you know you don't want a baby now. You know it's not a good time."

I nod.

"And I hear myself saying, *yeah, you're right*."

"I guess I know what you mean," I say. "Kind of."

"And then I'm suddenly not sure what I want at all." Jenny pauses thoughtfully in the hallway, then shrugs. "Yeah, I really don't get it," she says.

I throw my jacket over the banister and follow her into the lounge.

"Well, you know what I think," I say.

Jenny laughs. "I can guess," she says.

"I think you should stay here, maybe right up until you have the baby."

Jenny snorts with amusement.

"What?" I ask.

She shakes her head. "Oh, nothing. I just knew you'd say that, that's all."

I follow her through to the lounge. "Probably because you know it makes sense," I say.

Jenny shakes her head. "I don't know," she says. "Honestly, I just don't know."

I look at her sadly.

""Maybe we could ask Owen anyway," she says brightly. "Just in case."

I smile at her, relieved. "He won't mind," I say. "But I'll call him. When's the bugger due anyway?"

"The baby?" Jenny shrugs. "Twenty-first of December, give or take," she says.

"A Christmas baby then?"

Jenny nods. "Babies conceived at Easter are born at Christmas," she says. "You can't get much more Christian than that."

I nod. "Wow, that's a long time though," I say.

Jenny laughs. "Yeah, nine months," she says. "A full nine months after the twenty-first of March equals the twenty-first of December."

I stare at her, my smile fading.

"What's up?" Jenny asks.

I furrow my brow.

"What?" she insists.

I swallow hard and lower myself onto the edge of the sofa.

Jenny crouches before me. "Mark, you look like shit," she says. "Are you OK?"

"The twenty-first of March?" I ask.

Jenny nods.

"That traffic jam wasn't in Italy at all, was it," I say.

Jenny frowns and shakes her head. "What? I don't know what..."

"You said Italy," I say.

Jenny nods. "We were coming home from Italy. Yes. So?"

"But the traffic jam was in France, right?"

Jenny nods. "Yes, but..."

"In fact, it was just after Fréjus," I say.

Jenny shrugs. "We were stuck just after Cannes," she says. "I remember because we wished we had turned off."

I laugh and shake my head with a snort. "How amazing is that," I say.

Jenny frowns. "You're not saying…"

I nod. "While you were shagging in your camper van, a few miles up the road, they were cutting me out of the wreckage."

Jenny sinks to her knees and takes my hand.

"And your friend died," she says flatly.

I nod.

She reaches behind my shoulder and pulls me towards her. "God, I'm sorry," she says.

I sigh.

Jenny shakes her head. "That's crazy, though," she says. "Isn't that crazy?"

A strong sea breeze is whipping the white tops of the waves.

I sit on the pebbles and stare into the deep sludgy green of the sea and think about the shocking coincidence.

"Surely it must mean something," I think. "Surely something that profound, that unlikely must mean something."

But what *can* it mean?

"Thousands of people were caught in that traffic jam," I tell myself. Hundreds were injured; tens actually lost their lives. But how many conceived? More to the point, how many of my *ex-girlfriends* conceived?

The most shocking thing is a recurrent mental image, which I struggle to push from my mind.

I was unconscious, so it's something I never actually saw; but I have imagined it hundreds of times. Steve, dead, trapped next to me in the wreckage; the *pompiers*, sawing through the metal of the car to free my legs. And now, it has the addition of Jenny and Nick, a few miles down the carriageway, shagging.

I sit and stare at the sea until the sun starts to fade.

Then I shrug. There doesn't seem to be a lot else I can do.

By the time I return, Jenny is up from her afternoon snooze.

"Here," I say thrusting a sugary bag towards her. "I got you two, one each."

Jenny's eyes widen. "Doughnuts," she says. "For my diet."

"Well," I say, reaching out. "If you don't want…"

Jenny snatches at the bag. "I do," she says. "Oh, and the phone rang by the way."

I nod.

"I didn't pick up," she says.

I throw myself on the sofa and lift the phone. I punch one-five-seven-one and lift it to my ear then wince. Benoit's shrieking is so loud it hurts.

"I saw JJ today," he spits. "Je suis vraiment dégouté!"

I grimace.

"That you think evil thoughts about me is one thing..."

His voice is strident, on the edge of a scream.

I pull a face.

"But that you go telling the whole of Brighton I stole your wallet, it's, it's, it's, *c'est inimaginable*!"

Jenny looks concernedly at me. "Bad news?" she says.

I nod.

"So you phone them you *prick*. You phone JJ and you tell them that you are a liar!"

I wrinkle my brow and blow through my lips.

"But don't call me," he finishes. "Don't you *dare* call me ever again."

I slump back on the sofa and stare at the ceiling.

"Serious?" Jenny says.

I shake my head woefully and sigh.

"I've upset someone," I say. "I've *really* upset someone."

Dogs And Babies

The next day Jenny and I go shopping. The excursion has a strange feel to it, as though something isn't quite right, something that I can't quite put my finger on. I ponder that it's simply shopping with a woman, entering clothes shops, looking at make up... But that's not it.

It's only when we enter *Top Shop* and the security guard at the door says, "Hi there," that I realise what's happening. People are being nice, *overly* nice.

As I traipse along behind Jenny, buying exfoliating skin washes from the *Body Shop*, and jeans from the *Levis Store*, I confirm my suspicion.

Wandering the streets with a pregnant woman, the world is an uncannily friendly place. The only time I can ever remember having been smiled at this much was when I carried a friend's baby across town.

I linger near the cash-till of *Top Shop* with the other men while Jenny fingers lacy lingerie in the far corner of the store. I remember another occasion when the world felt this good – the week I looked after a friend's bulldog.

Apparently dogs, babies and pregnant women give you bonus points in this game called charm. It's too weird for words.

Shopping with Jenny has another advantage too. The bored men that the women drag around the stores are, without exception, incredibly cute and amazingly friendly. As the men show their joint solidarity before the momentous chore that is a shopping trip with the wife, winks and eye-rolls abound.

I glance to my left as a biker in black one-piece leathers puts his crash helmet on the floor and leans back against the railings. He has a shaved head, a goatee beard and big motocross boots.

"When did straight men start wearing boots with chromed heels?" I wonder.

He catches my eye and winks at me. "Fun huh?" he says, offering me a chewing gum.

I gasp and stutter, "Um, no thanks..."

Jenny appears to save me. "Come on darling," she says, linking her arm through mine. "Time to move on."

The guy shrugs at me and gives me a smile so cute I could swear...

"When did straight men start to dress like that?" I ask, as we push out into the street.

"Straight?" Jenny laughs, handing me a bag to carry. "He looked like one of the Village People to me."

"So you agree!" I laugh. "Straight men should not be wearing black leather SM outfits."

Jenny laughs. "If he's straight then I'm..." She shrugs. "Anyway, he looked like he was hitting on you."

I shrug. "I wish," I say. "But last time I heard, *Top Shop* wasn't on the list of Brighton's main cruising zones, well, not the lingerie department anyway."

Back at the house, Jenny disappears to change while I make my pizza base. Having left it to rise, I sit and ponder the Benoit conundrum.

I clearly owe him an apology, and Jenny, who I explained the situation to over coffee, says I definitely need to let him know what I really said to John. But I'm actually afraid of his anger.

"I was thinking," Jenny says entering the room behind me. "Maybe you could write him a letter."

I nod. "Yeah, coward's way out. I thought that too."

She shrugs. "Could be quite touching if you do it properly," she says.

I nod. "Except I don't have his address," I say. "So I'd have to go round there."

"I could deliver it for you," Jenny says.

I nod. "Hey you look fresh," I say. She's wearing a white men's-style shirt and new blue jeans.

"Yeah, it feels good," she says. "I was so sick of those clothes." She sticks a thumb into the waistband and pulls. "A bit big though, but I thought, well, I won't be getting smaller any time soon."

I smile warmly at her. "I'm glad to hear it," I say.

"You fancy some wine with this pizza?" Jenny asks. "I thought I might nip round to *Threshers* and get a bottle or two."

I smile. "Yeah," I say. "That would be great."

A sense of relief has settled over the house.

I feel optimistic, as if in some way things are sorting themselves out.

Jenny apparently feels the same. As well as the bottle of red she went for, she returns with a bottle of champagne.

"I don't know why," she says. "But I just felt like celebrating."

Pizza Picnic

The pizza is sublimely successful. Owen's oven is apparently very hot, and within a few minutes the crust has risen to a series of crispy domes; the cheese is bubbling deliciously.

Jenny pops the champagne and giggles as it foams into the glasses. "God I haven't had champagne since... God knows when," she says.

I place the pizza in the middle of the table and raise my glass.

Jenny shakes her head in amazement. "God it looks like a cookbook pizza," she says. "It's a shame Tom isn't here to see it. You could have impressed him."

I shrug. "I did call him, but his mobile's off."

Jenny smiles and raises her glass. "Well, his loss. All the more for us," she says, clinking her glass against mine.

I sip the champagne; it tastes horrible. In truth I've never liked the stuff, but I smile my appreciation anyway and cut into the steaming pizza.

"Despite the circumstances," I say. "I'm really glad you're here."

Jenny smiles and nods at me. "It was nice today, wasn't it?" she says, screwing up her eyes a little.

I smile. "Better than the day before yesterday anyway," I say.

"Shut up and cut the pizza," Jenny says. "I think the cheese is about to spell Pizza Hut."

I frown at her and cut through the pastry. "Humm, crispy," I say. "Pizza Hut?"

Jenny shrugs. "It was an ad campaign we ran a long time ago. The stringy cheese spelt Pizza Hut."

"Fair enough," I say, putting the slice onto her plate.

I slide the knife under a second slice, but just as I start to raise my hand the phone rings.

"Tom maybe?" Jenny says hopefully.

I wink at her and grab the phone. "Hello?"

"Mark?" The voice is unrecognisable. I frown.

"Yeah?" I say suspiciously.

"I wanna speak to Jenny," he says.

I let go of the knife, and lower the phone to my chest.

"It's for you," I say with a grimace. "Someone pissed."

Jenny's smile vanishes. She shakes her head and sighs. Then rolling her eyes, she says, "Oh, give it here."

In order to leave her in peace, I go upstairs to the toilet. I sit on the closed toilet lid and listen to Jenny's voice floating up the stairs, at first, calm, then upset, then finally angry.

When all is quiet, I flush the toilet, just for effect, and return downstairs. Jenny is ashen faced. The phone is still in her hand.

"So?" I say.

She stares at me blankly.

"Well?" I prompt.

She blinks slowly and exhales hard. For some reason I shiver.

"Nick," I say.

Jenny nods.

"Your mum gave him the number?"

Jenny nods again. "He says he's coming," she says. "I'm sorry..."

I frown. "But he doesn't have the address, you said your mum didn't have..."

Jenny interrupts. "Apparently he does," she says. "*He* must have got it from the number."

I slump in my chair and rest my head on my hands.

"He's on a bender," she says nodding slowly.

"What, a piss up?"

Jenny nods.

I shrug. "Then he can't drive from Farnham to Brighton, can he?"

Jenny laughs. "Honestly? I don't think he gives a damn."

"About you?"

Jenny snorts. "About driving here pissed."

I reach across the table for her hand, but she pulls away.

"Maybe I should leave," she says. "You've had enough..."

I shake my head and interrupt her. "There's no way Jenny," I say.

"I could stay in a hotel. Just tonight."

I nod. "And I'll just say, sorry Nick, she's not here, and he'll, like, just go away?"

Jenny wrinkles her brow. "We could *both* stay in a hotel?" she offers.

I nod and briefly consider it. "And tomorrow?" I say.

Jenny shrugs. I glance at my watch. Seven-twenty pm.

"How long does it take?" I ask. "From Farnham."

Jenny shrugs. "In the van it took me two hours."

I nod.

"The speed Nick drives? Maybe an hour and a half, maybe less."

I scratch my chin and taking a deep breath I stand. I walk over and stare out at the evening light.

"I'm really sorry Mark," Jenny says.

I nod. "I know," I say. It's not reasonable, but I actually feel furious with her for bringing this disorder to my life. I close my eyes and blow through my lips in an attempt to calm myself.

"Jenny," I say, turning towards her. "Is there *any* chance that this will be, well, peaceful?"

Jenny has her hands clasped across her nose. She peers up at me and shrugs. But her eyes say it all.

"So he's gonna be crazy again," I say.

Jenny shrugs. "He's been drinking," she says. "That's the problem."

I nod. "So I'm right to be feeling scared here," I say.

Jenny shrugs.

"Are you?" I ask.

Jenny shrugs again, then nods dolefully.

I raise a hand to my forehead. "Great!" I exclaim. "Excellent."

We remain like this for a few minutes, maybe five.

Jenny is white and motionless at the table. I alternate between looking out at the street, and back at Jenny. I'm trying to hide my anger at being forced into this situation, but I'm sure it shows through. Jenny looks afraid of *me*.

"OK," I finally say, moving into disaster limitation mode. "We have to call the police."

Jenny shrugs. "And tell them what?"

I shake my head. "I don't know," I say. "That your mad, violent, metal bar carrying husband is on his way here and that we're scared?" I suggest.

Jenny shakes her head. "I don't think that's a good idea," she says.

I wrinkle my nose at her and cross the room. I swipe the phone from the table. "Maybe I don't care," I say.

It takes an incredible ten minutes to get through to the local police station, and another ten to explain our predicament to the officer on the other end of the line.

He listens sympathetically, and I'm hopeful that he's going to find a way to help us, hopeful, that is, until he sums up.

"So if I've got this right," he says. "You have another bloke's pregnant wife staying with you, and you're scared he's coming to take her home."

I frown at the phone. "No officer," I say, a sarcastic tone entering my voice. "What I'm scared of is that he's going to kick down my front door and drag her back by her hair."

"Yes," says the man. "I understand that."

It sounds more like he understands Nick's desire to drag Jenny home than the fact that I'm about to be beaten up.

"So there's nothing you can do?" I say.

The policeman coughs. "I'm sorry sir, I mean, what we have here is a non present – he's not actually there is he? The husband?"

"No," I say.

"So we have a non-present person, who you suspect might be on his way, to theoretically take his wife home."

"Oh forget it," I say.

"I'm sorry, I just don't see what you expect..."

I click the phone off and drop it onto the coffee table.

Jenny looks at me. "No joy then?" she says.

I shake my head.

"They're always useless," she says. "I phoned them once, and they didn't want to send anyone; said it was a domestic dispute."

I scratch my head. The phone call has doubled my anger. I can feel the blood pulsing through my veins.

Jenny stares at me silently.

I rub my hand across my mouth and glance at my watch. Ten past eight.

"He could be here any minute," I say.

Jenny nods. "Maybe I *should* go," she says.

I shake my head. "No, that doesn't solve anything."

"Maybe we could turn out the lights and pretend we're not in?" she says desperately.

I shake my head. "Nah," I say.

I frown and glance out at the street, then nod slowly. "OK," I say with a shrug. "Lets do that."

We switch off all the lights, tidy the things from the dining room table, and retreat upstairs to the front bedroom.

I figure we can see Nick's arrival better from upstairs, and in some ludicrous way, it seems safer, the furthest point from the front door.

We crouch in the window and nibble at the pizza as we peer at the street.

"Tastes good cold too," Jenny says.

The light starts to fade, the streetlights come on one by one and we sit nervously in the eerie glow, sipping the now-so-inappropriate champagne.

I glance at my watch. Eight forty-two pm. "Maybe he won't come after all," I say.

Jenny shakes her head slowly. "He'll come," she says.

I sigh and shiver, remembering the iron bar, remembering the blood trickling from Tom's head.

"Hang on," I say, jumping up. "Keep lookout, I'll be right back."

I skip down the dark stairs, and on down into Owen's cellar.

When I return Jenny turns and wide-eyes the cricket bat in my hand. I prop it up behind the door. "Just in case," I say.

Jenny says nothing but shakes her head slowly.

I shrug. "Hey, I'm not the one who goes around with a wheel wrench down my jacket."

Jenny nods slowly at me. "I know," she says. "It's just…"

The sound of squealing tyres makes Jenny turn. I run across and slide to my knees beside her.

As the car is thrashed through the gears, it gets louder, until finally it comes into view.

A Golf with go-faster stripes and chrome wheel hubs. We sigh with relief.

I look at my watch again. Eight-fifty.

"He was on the phone an hour and a half ago," I say. "Maybe he really won't come. Maybe he's too pissed to drive."

Jenny shakes her head. "Nick's never too pissed to drive," she says.

"Maybe he fell asleep," I say hopefully.

"Unless he's had an accident he'll be here."

I shake my head and peer out at the street.

"God I hope he doesn't crash," Jenny says.

I shake my head at her. "You're a crazy bitch," I say. "You know that right?"

Jenny nods solemnly. "I know."

Desperate Plans

Another car drives past and we both swallow and swivel our heads, but it's just a Mini – like Tom's only black.

"I'm glad Tom isn't here," I say.

Jenny nods. "Poor Tom," she says. "Though he *is* good in a fight."

I snort. "Yeah."

"I heard a woman on the radio," Jenny says. "On radio four. Her husband used to drink and drive all the time, and..."

"Nick drinks and drives *all the time*?" I say.

Jenny nods and raises the palm of her hand. "*Don't*!" she admonishes.

I shrug.

"Anyway, this woman was so worried, she turned him in. Her husband that is."

I frown.

"Can you imagine that? Turning your own husband in."

I shrug. "I suppose if you were worried enough, if he was dangerous enough. But what do you mean she turned him in? She told the police *what* exactly?"

"She phoned the police and told them that he'd be leaving pub X, and that he'd be over the limit and that he does it all the time..."

My eyes widen. "And?"

Jenny shrugs. "They picked him up and breathalysed him. They had a big debate on the radio about the morality of reporting your own friends to the police for drink driving."

I nod. "Yeah," I say, breaking into a mad smile. "That'll do it."

Jenny frowns at me. Her eyes widen. "Mark, what? I couldn't, I mean..."

I nod. "*I* could though," I say, reaching for the phone beside me.

Jenny frowns.

"I take it you have no objections," I say.

Jenny opens her mouth to speak, but remains silent.

"I take it you wouldn't rather Nick dragged you off by your hair, or that I hit him with that cricket bat?" I nod behind me.

Jenny shakes her head. "No, of course not, but, do you think it'll work? Do you think we have time?"

"I don't know," I say, hitting redial. "But I'm gonna give it a go."

This time a woman answers.

"Hi there," I say. "I spoke to one of your colleagues before..."

"Oh," says the woman. "Would you like me to..."

"No," I say. "Actually, it doesn't matter. There isn't much time."

"Much time?" the woman repeats. She sounds young.

"I'm phoning you because I'm very concerned," I say. "A friend, well, a friend of a friend actually, is driving to my house from Surrey," I say. "As we speak."

"Yes?" the woman says. Her tone is shifting from boredom to excitement as she wakes up from her late shift blues.

"And he's drunk," I say. "Like, *really* drunk."

"And he's *driving*?" she asks, incredulously.

"Yes," I say. "He's *really* drunk. *Well* over the limit."

"Oh," the woman says. "It's an unusual situation, hold on."

Jenny nods at me. "So?" she says, her arms around her knees. The shadow from the window-frame moves across her face as she rocks nervously.

I shrug. "She's asking someone else," I say. "She says it's an unusual..."

Jenny grabs my elbow. "He's on a ban," she says with a nervous nod.

I frown.

"Hello?" says the woman. "The thing is, it's obviously a difficult situation, but..."

"Nick's on a ban," Jenny repeats.

"Hold on a second, please," I say. "Someone's giving me some more information here."

I hold the phone to my chest.

"What do you mean he's on a ban?"

"He's already been banned. He got a two-year ban in April. For drink-driving."

My mouth drops. I move the phone back to my ear.

"I'm sorry," I say, collecting myself. "Yes, the driver, he's already been banned as well," I say.

"Oh," says the woman. "That's very serious then. Hold on please."

I shrug at Jenny again. "On hold again. Says it's serious."

Jenny peers nervously into the street, then reaches out and pulls my watch towards her.

"Hello?" says a new voice. I recognise it as the man I spoke to before.

I hand the phone to Jenny. "You do it," I whisper.

"Erm, hello?" she says. She shrugs at me. "*What*?" she mouths.

"Give him the details," I say.

"Yes, I'd like to report a crime about to be committed," she says.

I nod, impressed.

Jenny covers the mouthpiece. "It's what the woman said on the radio," she says.

"Yes, drink driving, that's right."

" … "

"Yes, by a banned driver."

" … "

"Yes, well, not yet. He'll be arriving here soon."

" … "

"Here? Here is Seven Weston Square," Jenny says. "Yes, Brighton. It's up towards Kemptown."

Jenny has to dictate the registration number, Nick's name, address, date of birth, the date of his driving ban... The details seem endless. I'm actually starting to tremble a little as I wait for her to finish.

Finally Jenny nods at me, indicating closure. "Yes, and you'll need to hurry," she says assertively. "He'll be here at any moment."

She winks at me. "Thank you officer," she says, handing me the phone.

I press it against my ear and then hang up.

"That is such a brilliant idea," Jenny says.

I nod.

"I feel a bit evil though," Jenny says. "It's a bit big brother."

I frown at her. "Big brother?"

Jenny nods. "Turning your relatives into the authorities and all."

I shrug and glance at the cricket bat beside the door. "I just hope they get here before Nick does," I say.

Bad Karma

We sit on our knees peering at the road for fifteen minutes, then move back so that we can lean against the bed.

"No police," Jenny says grimly.

"No Nick either though," I point out. "As long as it's both or neither we're OK."

Jenny frowns at me.

"If we get Nick and no police, or the police and no Nick, we're in the shit," I say.

"Yeah," Jenny says vaguely. "It's warm I think," she says. "But I feel cold."

I nod. "Me too," I say.

I reach behind and pull on the quilt so that it drapes over our shoulders.

"Nerves, I guess," I say.

"So have you *really* never been hit?" Jenny asks.

I frown at her then shake my head. "With the exception of when I was a kid and Nick of course. I learnt to run quite fast," I say.

Jenny nods. "You're lucky," she says.

A lightweight motorbike buzzes down the street.

"It's not really luck though," I say.

Jenny frowns at me.

"The not-being-hit thing," I explain.

Jenny snorts. "Well, you're a bloke," she says. "That helps."

I nod. "But I've walked away from a lot of conflict," I say. "Or I've run away. Violence really scares me. In a way what scares me most is what *I* might do. If I lost it, you know?"

Jenny nods. "I see what you're saying," she says. "But you don't always have a choice."

I peer out at the street. A man in a suit is getting into a Smart car below.

"I guess I think you do," I say, listening to the engine start. "Almost always. There's usually a moment when you can walk... Hey, look.

Policeman." I nod towards the other side of the street.

Jenny moves onto her knees and strains her neck. "That's just a beat bobby isn't it?" she says.

I push my lips out and shake my head. "I don't know," I say. "He's looking this way though."

"And walking on," Jenny adds.

I sigh.

"God this is awful," Jenny says. "This waiting!"

I nod in agreement.

"I almost wish..." Jenny says.

"Shh," I interrupt, raising a finger. I can hear a car door opening.

I lean forward and sure enough in the space where the Smart was parked is a BMW. It's too big to fit, so it's parked diagonally, the front left wheel upon the pavement. The two doors are opening.

"Shit, they're here," I say, moving back from the window.

Jenny sneaks a look and then slides back beside me. Her eyes widen, her face pales. "*They*," she says.

She leans forward again, but then jumps back out of the way. "Shit," she says. "Nigel drove him. He looked up at me."

"Nigel?" I frown.

"One of Nick's builders, a dodgy bugger. I don't like him."

"Fuck," I say. "Dodgy? How?"

Jenny nods. "He's always bringing knock-off stuff to our house. DVD players, shit like that."

I shake my head. "So he didn't drive," I say. "Crafty."

A thud against the front door makes us jump.

"What the..." I say. It sounds as if Nick is trying to knock the door down.

There is a moment's silence, and then the letterbox creaks. "Jenny!" Nick shouts. "JENNY!"

She glances sideways at me. "He *is* drunk," she says quietly. "I can hear it."

I nod and lean forwards again to check out the street. Nigel has the same stocky build as Nick, only with the addition of a beer gut. He's wearing a faded blue polo and chinos. He's standing on the other side of the street staring straight at me.

I freeze and somewhat pointlessly hold my breath.

He reaches inside his trouser pocket and pulls out a Marlborough packet, then pulls a cigarette from the box with his mouth.

"They're not in," he says, lighting the cigarette. It wobbles up and down as he speaks.

I sit back.

"Is the policeman still there?" Jenny asks.

I shake my head. "Not that I can..."

Nick raps on the door again making me start. "Shit!" I say.

"Nick, let's go get a pint and come back later," Nigel whines.

I snort. "A pint," I say. "That'll help."

Nick raps on the door again. "JENNY! MARK!" he shouts.

This time, I too can hear the slur of his voice.

Jenny nods outside. "Look," she says.

Other than the fact that Nigel has moved out of sight I can see nothing. And then I do notice something, a strange flickering on the building opposite, a pulsing blue light.

The police car glides silently into view and pulls up beside the jutting rear of Nick's BMW.

The whole terrace throbs with the light from its blue strobe. Nick rattles the front door heavily, apparently unaware of the police car behind him.

"Getting interesting," I say, crawling forward and lying on my stomach.

The window of the police car slides down. "Is this your car sir?" the policeman asks.

Nick spins on the step, swaying slightly then putting a hand on the railing to steady himself.

"Oh *bollocks*," he says.

I glance at Jenny, and nod for her to come watch. She too crawls forward on all fours.

The policeman opens the car door and stands.

"Sir? Is this your car?" he repeats. His fluorescent yellow jacket glows in the darkness of the street. I lean over and look down at Nick. I can see a bald patch on the top of his head.

"What if it is?" he says aggressively.

I glance sideways at Jenny. She bites her bottom lip.

The policeman peers in at his mate, nods, and then turns back and squeezes through the gap between the BMW and the car parked next to it.

"Not a very well parked car, is it sir?" he says.

Nick mumbles something. Jenny nudges me.

I shrug. "Didn't hear," I whisper.

"Sorry sir?" the policeman says. "I didn't quite catch that."

The policeman's voice is so perfect, so official, so policeman. *"Where do they learn to speak like that?"* I wonder.

Nick stumbles down a step and sways towards his car. "I said," he says laboriously, "Why don't you fuck off and do something useful."

The policeman touches his nose thoughtfully and glances back at his driver.

"You seem a little worse for wear, sir. Been drinking have we?" he asks.

Nick sways. "Yeah. 'Snot a crime is it?" he says.

The policeman licks his lips. "No sir. Though driving under the influence..."

"I didn't drive," Nick spits. "Nigel drove."

The policeman nods and looks left then right theatrically.

"And where might *Nigel* be?" he asks.

Jenny and I ape the policeman, scanning right and left. "He's fucked off," Jenny says. "Brilliant."

Nick shrugs exaggeratedly. "I don't fucking know do I," he tells the policeman.

The policeman scratches his head and turns back to the police-car.

"Yeah," Nick leers. "Fuck off."

I nod, mentally egging him on. "Yep," I say. "Go for it."

I glance at Jenny. She has her eyes closed. She's wearing a pained expression as if she has stomach ache and I remember that this is her husband.

The policeman leans in consulting with his colleague, then stands, straightens himself, and returns to the pavement.

"Well, I'm afraid the car can't stay here," the policeman says. "I'm going to have to call for a tow truck."

Nick sways gently like a tree in the breeze. "All right, all right," he says. "I'll move it, I'll move the fucker..."

I frown and press my nose against the window. The policeman's expression is changing. Just the start of a smile, a well-restrained smirk is appearing on his lips.

"It's karma," I whisper. "They're setting him up."

Jenny frowns at me. "Eh?" she says.

"The car, Nick's going to drive it right in front of them."

The police car rolls backwards and quietly moves behind the BMW, blocking it in.

Nick wrenches open his driver's door and slides into the seat. "Fucking pigs," he says.

"Sir, If you persist in using insulting..." the policeman says.

Nick gesticulates wildly at him. "I'm moving it, OK? I'm moving the fucking car."

As he reaches and starts the engine, the policeman grins. I see it clearly, a fully-fledged smile. Sheer job satisfaction.

He leans on the top of the car, only inches from Nick's face. "Hand me those keys will you sir?" he says.

Nick looks at him and shakes his head. "I'm *moving* it!" he says. "What more do you want? *Jesus*!"

"I suspect you of having consumed alcohol over the legal..." the policeman starts to say. But as he says this, the BMW lurches backwards.

We both gasp. There is a deep crumpling sound as the rear of Nick's car crunches into the door of the white police Rover.

"No-oh," Jenny breathes.

The BMW's engine has stalled. The policeman has stepped back up to the window.

"What the fuck..." Nick starts to say.

In a calm movement, the policeman swipes his baton from its holster and thrusts it against Nick's throat, pushing him back against the seat.

Then he calmly reaches in and pulls the keys from the ignition. "I'll have those I think sir," he says.

He withdraws his baton and straightens up. "Thank you sir," he says. "Now step out of the car please."

Morning Clarity

I open one eye and peer blurrily at Jenny who is sitting on the edge of my bed. "I made you some tea," she says.

My eyes are caked over with a sticky, sleepy film, and though, by straining, I can see the alarm clock, I can't make out the figures.

"What time is it?" I ask.

"It's only nine," Jenny says, "but..."

"*Nine*!" I groan, rolling away from her. "I didn't get to sleep till nearly six!"

"I know," Jenny says. "I only got to sleep half an hour ago, but my mobile woke me."

I groan again, and blinkingly look over at her. She rubs my shoulder affectionately.

"I need your advice," she says. "Sorry."

I sigh and click my tongue against the roof of my mouth, then pull myself up and push a pillow behind me for support.

Jenny smiles weakly and hands me the tea.

"Nick phoned," she says. "He asked me to get his wallet, his passport and his cheque-book; he says he'll be needing them for bail."

I sip my tea and frown at her. "You spoke to *Nick*?"

Jenny purses her lips and shakes her head. "I didn't answer," she says. "He left a message."

I yawn. I feel as though I have simply dozed off for a few minutes, as if we watched the tow-truck take the BMW away only half an hour ago, an impression exacerbated by the nightmarish dreams I had all night; dreams precisely of handcuffs, police cars and tow trucks.

I blink hard in an attempt to clear my vision, and then smile tightly at Jenny.

"Let me drink this and I'll get up," I say. "We'll decide what to do."

I almost fall asleep again; I actually slop tea on the bed as my arm slumps, but in the end, with a deep groan I drag myself to the shower.

When I get downstairs Jenny is standing in the kitchen blowing smoke out of the window.

"*Geez,* that stinks!" I say.

Jenny pulls a face and stubs the cigarette out in the sink. "Sorry," she says.

"And since when did you *smoke*?" I ask.

Jenny shrugs. "I only gave up three months ago," she says. "When I realised I was pregnant." She nods at the packet. "I only bought ten," she says.

I pour a cup of coffee, and then stretching my stiff neck, I move to the table.

"OK, well, bin those please and come over here," I say.

Jenny mockingly pokes her tongue at me and drops the cigarette pack into the bin. I make a mental note to pour water on them later.

As if she has read my mind, she says, "They're all gone anyway."

I shake my head. "So where *is* Nick?" I ask. "Do we know?"

Jenny nods gravely. "Brighton police station. In a holding cell."

I nod. "Right, so if... *when* he gets out," I correct myself, "he'll be straight back here."

Jenny shrugs and nods. "He's got no money, his car's been impounded. He's on a ban. He doesn't have a lot of options."

I shrug. "He can call someone else to sort him out though," I say.

Jenny nods dubiously. "But if he knows I'm here, he'll come here, won't he?" she says.

I roll my eyes and nod. "And if you go get his cheque book for him, he'll definitely know you're here," I say.

Jenny nods. "He kind of knows anyway," she says.

"It's a shame you never pressed charges," I say. "We could have requested that he stay away... As a condition of bail I mean."

Jenny nods slowly. "Yeah, I hadn't thought of that," she says glumly.

I lick my front teeth thoughtfully.

Jenny shakes her head. "This has just made everything worse really, hasn't it?" she says.

I shrug. "Worse than *what*?"

"I mean..."

"I know," I interrupt. "But it's not worse than me killing Nick with a cricket bat is it?" I say.

Jenny smiles thinly.

"Or him kicking shit out of you?" I volunteer.

Jenny shrugs. "I guess not," she says.

I frown at her and sip my coffee. "He phoned you on your mobile you say?"

Jenny blinks slowly at me and almost imperceptibly nods.

I shrug. "You could say you didn't get the message. Stranger things have happened."

"He *knows* I got the message," she says.

I shrug again. "You might be out of batteries," I say. "Or maybe the signal broke up and you couldn't hear."

Jenny scrunches up her face and stares at the ceiling. She taps her hand nervously on the table. "I just don't want to deal with *any* of this," she says. "You *know*?" Her voice trembles slightly.

I reach across the table and touch her arm. "I know," I say.

"Plus, I'm so *tired*," she says. "I can't think straight."

I nod. "I know," I say.

"Oh," Jenny says. She pushes the house phone towards me across the table. "I think he phoned here too, while you were in the shower."

I roll my eyes miserably and pick up the phone, blinking slowly at Jenny as I listen to the message.

"Nah," I say, finally hanging up. "It was Tom."

Jenny frowns. "*Tom*?"

"Yeah," I laugh sardonically. "Says he's fucking off to Italy."

Jenny snorts. "Lucky Tom," she says.

"So," I say, placing the phone back in the middle of the table. "Say you didn't get the message, say you were somewhere else, and..."

I pause, lips parted and stare at Jenny as the idea materialises.

She breaks into a frown. "Mark?" she says.

I narrow my eyes and bite my bottom lip as I compute the possibilities.

Jenny leans towards me. "*Mark*?" she repeats.

I start to smile wryly. "Say you were on a plane," I say with a shrug.

Jenny frowns at me.

"Say you were on a plane to... *Nice*," I say, now grinning broadly.

Jenny sighs and rolls her eyes. "What are you on about?" she says. "I'm not on a plane, *am* I?"

I shrug. "You could be," I say. "Don't you fancy a few weeks in the sun, far, far away from all of this?"

Jenny's eyes widen.

"I have a friend who has this *great* apartment," I say.

I watch the idea register, the different thoughts washing across Jenny's face like clouds across a clearing sky. She grabs my hand.

"*Could we*?" she says.

I shrug. "It'll cost a fortune," I say. "If you want to fly today."

Jenny raises an eyebrow. "Today?" she says, nodding. "Could we fly *today*?"

I smile. "Well, *yesterday*," I say. "*Officially*."

Jenny stares at me. Her eyes are shining. She actually looks quite mad. "I'd need my passport," she says. "I'd need to go home and get my passport and my purse, and some clothes."

"And a beach towel," I say. "And your sun-tan lotion,"

Jenny nods.

"We could rent a car," I say. "We could rent one of those ones you leave at the airport."

Jenny shakes her head dreamily. "Or a taxi," she says. "Who *gives* a fuck?"

We stare into each other's eyes as the idea takes its course.

"You don't mind though?" Jenny says.

I purse my lips and shake my head. "Actually I'm probably less keen on bumping into Nick than you are," I say.

Jenny nods slowly. "It's really mean though," she says. "What if no-one bails him?"

I shrug. "He'll fix it," I say. "He'll phone a friend, or his bank or one of his employees."

Jenny's eyes narrow. "Yeah," she says. "Oh, please let's do it." She grasps my hand so hard it hurts. "Let's get the fuck out of here!"

Last Minute Gestures

I glance in the rear-view mirror and pull the Punto over to the side of the road. I reach inside my jacket and hand Jenny the letter.

"Is that it?" she says, frowning at the folded paper.

I nod. "I didn't have any envelopes," I say.

Jenny shrugs and reaches for the door handle.

"Hang on," I say.

Jenny slumps back in her seat. "What now?" she says.

I pull my wallet from my rear pocket, and start to empty the contents onto my lap.

"What are you doing?" Jenny asks, a frown on her face.

I take the letter from her hand, refold it and slide it into my wallet so that only the word *Benoit* is showing.

Jenny nods. "That's radical," she says.

I shrug. "It makes the point," I say, handing her the wallet.

"OK," Jenny says, opening the door. "Number eleven you say?"

I nod. "And be quick," I say. "He's probably in and I don't want a scene."

As we drive away, Jenny buckles her belt. "So what did you say?" she asks.

I fidget, settling into my seat. "The pedals are really weird in this car," I say. "In the letter? Oh I just said how sorry I am, and that if he ever wants to forgive the fallible human being that I am to get in touch," I say.

Jenny nods. "But you never really accused him did you? I thought you said…"

I shake my head. "Nah, I didn't really. But I thought it. And Benoit thinks I did. It's quite karmic really."

Jenny snorts. "You like your karma, don't you," she says.

I pull a face. "I'm not really a believer," I say. "But things often seem to work out the way they should, despite everything."

"The way they should," Jenny repeats dubiously.

I pick up the London road and head north towards the A23.

After a minute or so, I add, "You know, when I was a kid I nicked loads of money, from my mother's purse."

Jenny rolls her head around, stretching her neck. "Yeah?" she says.

I nod. "This friend I had, I can't remember his name now, anyway, he encouraged me. We used to nick all sorts of stuff."

"But from your *parents*!" Jenny says, shocked.

"They never actually noticed," I say. "But my dad caught me with my mate spending loads of money in the amusement arcades."

"Shit," Jenny says. "What did he do?"

I shrug. "Not a lot really. He threatened to hit me with his belt," I say. "But he didn't actually do anything I don't think. I wasn't allowed to see the friend anymore though."

"Ah, loss of privileges," Jenny says. "My dad was hot on that too."

"The funny thing was though," I continue. "That the money we were spending, when he caught us... Well it wasn't stolen at all. My mate's mother gave it to us just before we went out."

Jenny laughs. "Really?"

I nod. "I thought there was something profound about that, even then," I say. "You know, being caught for the right crime but for the wrong reason."

"The birth of Mark's theory of karma," Jenny laughs.

I shrug.

By the time I reach the motorway, Jenny has slumped into her seat. She's been silent for nearly twenty minutes, so I start when she suddenly speaks. I had thought she was asleep.

"Put your foot down a bit," she says. "We'll never get there at this rate."

I frown and glance at the speedometer. "I'm doing seventy," I point out.

"Yeah," Jenny says with a sigh. "But everyone else is doing ninety, even the trucks are overtaking us."

I glance at her and frown. "Everyone else wasn't pulled from a car wreck four months ago," I say coldly.

"Oops," Jenny says.

"Whilst you were screwing," I add.

"Sorry," Jenny says. "That was dumb of me. Are you OK? Or do you want me to drive?"

I shake my head. "Nah, I'm fine really," I say.

I notice a mirage shimmering on the horizon and realise that it's turning into a hot day. I roll down my window, but the roar of a truck overtaking unnerves me, so I roll it back up again.

Jenny fiddles with the controls and with a puff of dust, cold air starts to stream from the vents on the dashboard.

"I was thinking," Jenny says, "about that coincidence."

I nod and wait for her to continue, but when she says nothing, I prompt her.

"Go on," I say.

Jenny sighs. "Nah, it's nothing," she says. "It's stupid."

I shake my head. "No, go on," I insist. "I'm interested."

Jenny rolls her head from side to side again. "It's just," she says slowly. "Well, you know, the way I conceived, at the same time as..." Her voice fades away.

I swallow. "At the same time as Steve died?" I say.

Jenny sighs and stretches her arms before her.

"Did you think that too then?" she says.

I nod. "I even considered reincarnation," I say, adding, "Well, considered isn't really the word. It crossed my mind, against my will."

Jenny snorts.

"I know," I say. "The weird workings of my mind."

Jenny snorts again. "No," she says. "I thought that too."

I drive for a while without speaking.

"It *is* strange though," I eventually say. "I mean the odds can't be that high can they?"

Jenny shrugs.

"Though, I suppose, if you think about it, the accident was probably a couple of hours before," I say.

"Before we started shagging, you mean," Jenny says. "Yeah. I thought of that too, but I know what you mean, it's like this can't really be just a random event, you know?"

"Exactly," I say. "And yet, apparently it is."

"I thought, you know, that if it had been a boy, I might have called him Steve," Jenny says.

I'm feeling tired and fragile from lack of sleep, and this thought suddenly makes me feel very raw, very emotional.

I screw up my eyes and concentrate on the road ahead. "That's a nice thought," I say.

"And, well, this isn't really the moment," Jenny says. "But I thought, well, you know how much you said you enjoyed your friends' kids."

I nod and swallow again.

"And how you won't be having any of your own," she continues.

I frown and grit my teeth. "Yes?" I say.

Jenny reaches out and squeezes my leg. "Well, I thought, maybe you'd accept to be godfather?" she says.

I nod but say nothing.

"Not in a religious way, but, well, it would be nice."

I nod and cast a watery glance at her. "Yeah," I say. "I'd like that."

I wipe my eyes, laugh, and then clear my throat. "Now, before you make me weep and *we* crash as well, maybe we could lighten it up a bit?"

Jenny laughs. "Sorry," she says.

"And stop saying sorry all the time," I say. "Do you have any idea how many times you apologise in a day?"

"I know," Jenny says. "Sorry?" she mugs.

I glance at her and wink.

"Music?" she says, reaching for the radio.

I nod. "If you can find anything," I say.

Jenny switches on the radio and hits the scan button a few times.

Finally the radio settles on a song I know. "Stop there," I say. "That's good." I drive for a few seconds trying to identify it.

"Hum. I know this too," Jenny says.

"You know who sings it?" I ask.

Jenny shakes her head. "Nope," she says. "It's lovely though."

I nod. "It's *Fleetwood Mac*," I say. "From *Tusk*."

Jenny nods. "John had that," she says. "Years ago."

I nod. "Everyone had that, years ago," I say. "This one's called *Over and Over*. But do you know who the singer is?"

Jenny cocks her head and listens to the radio for a moment. "No," she says. "It's somewhere in my mind, but..."

I laugh. "Her name's Stevie," I say.

"Stevie," Jenny repeats.

"Stevie Nicks," I say.

Jenny nods.

"Stevie," she says again.

"And Nick's" I say pointedly.

Once we get to Farnham, Jenny is remarkably efficient for which I am grateful. Though I know, logically, that Nick is back in Brighton, sitting in the Fiat in front of their house has my nerves on edge.

When Jenny throws a bag onto the back seat, I sigh with relief.

"Weird," she says, reaching for her seatbelt. "It gave me the creeps being back in the house."

I pull away across the drive. "Me too," I say.

"Yeah," Jenny says. "But I *lived* there for two years."

"You got everything though?" I ask.

Jenny nods. "I got the credit cards and my passport," she says. "Nothing else really matters."

"Good attitude," I say, driving past the point where we discovered the blood rushing from Tom's head. "Swimsuit?" I ask, trying to lighten the tone.

"Nah," Jenny laughs. "I think I need a new one. A special model for fat pregnant women."

"Maybe we should phone Tom," I say. "I don't know when he's leaving, but..."

"It'll have to be from a pay-phone I'm afraid," Jenny says.

I frown at her. "You forget your mobile?"

Jenny laughs and shakes her head "I left it in the back garden," she says.

"Shit!" I spit, glancing in the mirror and looking for somewhere to pull over.

But Jenny grabs my leg. "I left it on purpose," she says.

I stare at the road ahead and raise an eyebrow. "That way, Nick will think..." I say.

"That I never *did* get his message," Jenny finishes. "Plus, every time it rings I won't have to worry if it's him," she says.

I nod. "That's radical," I say.

Jenny nods and glances at her watch. "I know," she says.

"How are we doing for time?" I ask.

She nods. "It's all perfect really," she says. "An hour to get to Heathrow and two hours for check-in."

Close Brackets

Jenny drops her bag on the floor.

"Wow!" she exclaims. "What a great place to live."

I look around the apartment, but feel nothing. Though I dozed for most of the flight I feel numb with tiredness, and jet-lagged with the simple shock of suddenly being back in Nice.

My flat for some reason isn't speaking to me. It's saying nothing at all, except maybe, "I am an apartment. I need cleaning."

"I don't think my brain's caught up with my body yet," I say, shaking my head.

I cross the room and open the windows and shutters. Jenny follows me and peers down at the street below.

"Gosh you're really in the middle of everything here," she says.

The air is hot and clammy and the interior smells musty. I run a finger along the windowsill. "Everything's so dirty!" I say.

"Dusty," Jenny corrects me. "We'll clean it tomorrow."

I nod. "I'm just surprised though," I say. "It's been closed. I mean, where does the dust *come* from?"

I lead Jenny to the office-cum-spare-room and fold out the sofa bed.

"I should have some sheets somewhere," I tell her turning to leave.

She grabs my arm. "Mark, look, I'm *so* tired, really, I just need to sleep, kind of right now?" she says. "It's so warm anyway, really, lets sort out proper bedding tomorrow."

I nod. "Sure," I say, vaguely. "Suits me anyway, I'm not actually sure there *are* any clean sheets."

I return to the lounge. A group of drunken tourists are shouting in the street below, so I lean on the window ledge and watch for a while before closing the shutters again.

When I hear Jenny leave the bathroom and return to the office, I switch off the lights and sink onto the big red settee and try to reconnect with my place, with my stuff, with my own environment.

The glow from the street-lamps is shining through the shutters casting orange strips of light along the ceiling, and down below I can hear the rowdy group moving away into the distance.

The street falls silent, and I lie listening to the hum of this southern city whirring around me, a car alarm in the distance to the left, a moped buzzing madly up a hill far away to the right, chatter from a distant *brasserie*. The sounds are so different here.

The last time I was here was with Owen; a ten minute visit to pick up stuff for my trip to England, and to drop off...

Doubting my memory – it all seems so distant now – I glance over at the corner of the room. For a few seconds, I am unable to make out the form of Steve's saxophone, unable to spot the big black case lurking in the shadows. I actually feel a certain relief that it's not there, but then I spot it, peeking out from behind the speaker cabinet.

A profound sadness washes over me, as if a black hole has opened in the middle of the room, swirling and sucking me in.

It suddenly seems that the trip to Brighton has been pointless, that by returning here I have simply wiped it all out. And that pointlessness spreads and contaminates everything I think about until *everything* seems futile. My life itself seems pointless and absurd.

Steve's saxophone, Tom's saxophone, so many un-played instruments, so many bridges built, Hugo, Benoit, all of them. And then so much waiting and watching until it all crumbles away. *"Why bother?"*

I cross the room and kneel before the sax case. I gently turn it on its side, release the clasps and open the lid. *"Like opening a coffin,"* I think morbidly.

Sure enough, the inside of the box is lined in blood-red velvet, and nestling in the velvet, like a buried relic, is the gleaming saxophone.

I feel desperate and alone. For a moment I feel so bad I actually consider waking Jenny, just to be able to cry in her arms. But she's as exhausted as I am, and that – I logically reason – is probably all that's wrong with me.

That, and the fact that coming home has closed the brackets opened when Owen whisked me off to England. Suddenly it seems as if the previous sentence has been resumed, only I don't know how to finish it. I don't know how to finish any of it.

All the dilemmas of my life are still here to be faced. What to do, who to love, how to get through this thing we call life in some meaningful, or at least, less-than-awful way.

I stroke the saxophone. I had imagined Tom playing this, somehow making it *his*, somehow making it all OK. I imagined that Tom would delimit the past by opening a new paragraph for me, maybe even a whole new chapter.

I lift the sax and hold it in my arms, but it is cold and metallic. I wish I could have heard it; wish I could have known it alive in Steve's hands.

My eyes are misting and my mouth is filling with saliva so I put the sax back in the box, and unsteadily stand and walk through to the bedroom. I switch on the ceiling fan and throw myself on the bed.

The covers smell musty. I lie staring at the fan, watching as the white blades start hesitantly to turn, and I wait for its predictable, rhythmic creak to begin and for sleep to take me away, anywhere but here.

Here And There

The next morning, as they say, is a whole new day.

Unexpectedly, amazingly in fact, I wake up feeling bright and optimistic. I throw open the shutters and stare at the sheer brilliance of the light, the deep blue of the sky.

Jenny is still sleeping, so I dress quickly and head downstairs into the bustling streets.

The fish sellers on *Place St Francois* are hollering and the air is filled with market sounds and foody smells, and that unique, fading freshness that announces a scorching day to come.

I buy coffee and croissants, oranges and yoghurts, then I hurry back to wake Jenny up. I want to get out and about before it gets too hot to breathe.

Jenny is in the shower, so I wipe down the dusty table and set about making coffee.

"God!" she says, when she appears. "Food! Thank God!"

I smile at her. "Fresh croissant ma'am?" I ask.

Jenny crosses the room and rips off a chunk of croissant and pushes it hungrily into her mouth.

"I checked the cupboards," she says, her mouth full. "I was actually considering the tinned tuna!"

We drink strong black coffee and munch the croissants. When I squeeze the oranges, the zest makes my nose tingle.

"How come foreign food always tastes so much better?" Jenny asks. "I mean; it's not like we don't have croissants and coffee back home."

I nod. "I know," I say. "You forget, don't you?"

Jenny makes a mock *grrrr*, sound and rips off another bite of croissant with her teeth.

"I suppose it's just that the croissants were baked an hour ago by a real man, with real ingredients," I say.

Jenny nods. "And the coffee?" she asks. "I buy the best coffee they have, but it never tastes like this."

I shrug. "That too," I say. "They were roasting the beans in the shop. She ground this in front of me."

Jenny sips hers. "Being starving helps too I guess," she says. "Anyway, whatever the reason, it's bloody *lovely*."

I convince Jenny to leave the cleaning till later, and we wander through the shady streets, down towards the beach.

"It's such a different life here," Jenny says. "The way you just come out of your flat and everything's happening on the doorstep."

We round a corner, and the huge *Cours Saleya* market comes into view.

"And markets," she says. "Why don't we have vegetable markets in England anymore. Can you tell me that?"

We wander between the stalls, then along the seafront, and down onto the packed pebble beach where we squeeze our way between the towels, and tiptoe around the greased sizzling bodies to dip our heels in the Med.

"I must find my bathers," I say, as we walk back towards the house.

"I must buy some," Jenny says. "If I can find any big enough, in the land of the thin."

In front of the *Palais de Justice*, a pianist has set up in the middle of the square. He's playing the Brahms piano concerto beautifully.

"Can we sit over there and listen?" Jenny says nodding towards a bar.

Seated beneath the red awning Jenny sighs contentedly. "This was *such* a good idea," she says.

I laugh. "And surprisingly obvious really," I say.

Jenny nods. "God knows what you were doing in Brighton anyway," she says. "I mean; there's really no comparison."

I nod thoughtfully and look out across the sun-drenched square.

"I know what you mean," I say. "And in some ways... In *most* ways in fact, you're right."

"But?" Jenny says.

I shrug. "But Brighton has things going for it too," I say.

Jenny nods. "Brighton's nice," she says. "With the sea and the beach and everything... But I'd still say here's better. I mean what does Brighton have that Nice doesn't?"

I smile at her. "That's because you're English," I say. "You don't see it."

"You're English too," Jenny points out.

I laugh. "Yeah, I mean you live there all the time," I say. "So there are things you don't notice."

"Like?" Jenny says.

I shrug. "Like people wearing the first thing they found this morning, because it's the weekend and it just *doesn't matter*," I say.

Jenny frowns and looks around.

"And people with reggae plaits in their hair and pierced noses, and men walking down the street wearing leather chaps and teddy-bear backpacks."

Jenny smiles.

"And literally thousands of gay men who are fairly happy about who they are," I say. "And plumbers who ask if you or your *partner* can be in around three."

Jenny nods. "I see what you mean," she says. "It's the culture you miss. The relaxed easy-going..."

"Look at Tom," I interrupt. "He's a pure product of Brighton."

Jenny nods. "Tom's lovely," she says.

I nod. "And he doesn't *exist* here," I say. "He couldn't."

Jenny sighs and wrinkles her nose. "I guess," she says, looking around. "He's with Antonio now, right?"

I nod. "I'll phone him at some point I suppose," I say. Then I shrug. "Then again, there's not much point."

Jenny smiles sympathetically at me. "I really thought that was going to work out," she says. "For you two I mean."

I snort sadly. "Me too," I say. "Stupid and selfish really," I say. "To just assume that Tom's relationship with Antonio was of no importance."

"Will you go back?" Jenny asks. "Or do you think you'll stay here now?"

I shrug and think for a while. "I don't know really," I say. "I need both I think."

Jenny nods. "I can understand that," she says.

"The trouble is organising it," I say.

Jenny wrinkles her nose. "Organising it?"

"I mean, finding a way of earning a living that lets me do both, finding a way of having a relationship that lets me do both," I say. "I guess it's a lot to ask."

Jenny shrugs. "Tom goes back and forth," she says. "It *could* happen."

I smile. "Yeah," I say, thoughtfully. "Back to Tom. Sacré Tom!"

Jenny smiles. "Sacré Tom!" she repeats.

"Funny to think he's probably only about a hundred miles that way," I say nodding towards the east.

Jenny nods.

"Maybe I *should* phone him," I say. "Then again..." I shrug. "I have trouble seeing Tom as a mate really. And I don't even *like* Antonio."

"I need to phone my mother," Jenny says. "She'll be hysterical by now."

I nod. "So we go back, clean the apartment and while you phone home, I'll make lunch," I say.

Jenny nods and lifts her handbag from the back of the chair. "OK," she says.

"And then it's siesta time," I say.

Jenny grimaces. "I'm not sure about that," she says. "I'm not sleepy yet."

I laugh. "You will be," I say. "Once the thermometer hits thirty-five."

Thus slips by the best part of a week. Simple shopping excursions, cups of strong black coffee, and long sweaty siestas.

Isabelle brings back Paloma, my cat. With her purring and rolling around, the apartment feels a little more like home.

We take the train to Antibes – Jenny is too pregnant for motorbikes – and we swim for the first time at the little sandy beach near the port.

On Friday, we take the train again, but this time in the other direction, to Ventimiglia, the first town after the border.

The journey is gorgeous, and the train's plunging in and out of tunnels with its now-you-see-it, now-you-don't views of the

Mediterranean is simply stunning.

"Next stop Italy," I tell Jenny as the train lurches out of Menton.

"Borders are so weird aren't they," she says shaking her head.

I nod. "I know. Every time I go to Ventimiglia I think that. The fact that there's like, just this line; and a baby born on one side speaks Italian, and on the other side, French."

Jenny nods. After a pause, she says, "Actually, I was wondering, I mean, I'm not sure how it would work, but I wondered, well, if I stayed here. Do you think I could have the baby here?"

I smile and shrug. "I don't know," I say. "But it would be really good... If it's doable."

"I mean," Jenny continues. "I could rent a holiday flat or something. I bet they're cheap after the summer. I wouldn't have to be under your feet all the time."

I shrug. "We'll see," I say. "I'll ask Isabelle if you want, find out how it works. She's a nurse."

The train rumbles into a tunnel and we sit listening to the roar.

When we burst into sunlight again, Jenny leans over and peers at the beach below. "It's just so beautiful," she says, shaking her head in wonder, then sitting back in her seat. "I guess it's just because it's so different being here... But I've hardly thought about Nick at all."

I nod. "He must be out by now," I say.

Jenny shakes her head. "Weird," she says. "It seems so far away now. I'm surprised he hasn't been in touch with my mum though."

Rumbling and squealing, the train trundles through another, shorter tunnel.

"*Buongiorno Italia*," I say as we come into the daylight.

Jenny leans out and looks up at the hill on the left. "Funny," she says. "It actually looks different too."

I nod. "Greenhouses instead of hotels," I say.

Ventimiglia market is a mad frenzy of dodgy deals.

The official market traders are outnumbered two-to-one by beautifully built North Africans selling counterfeits of everything I never wished for.

"If you ever wanted one of those awful *Louis-Vuitton* handbags, now's your moment," I tell Jenny.

The nearest trader apparently overhears and grabs my arm. "You want Vuitton?" he says. "I do you good price. Very good price."

I actually have to shake my elbow to get him to release his grip.

"They're very aggressive," Jenny laughs.

"I know," I say. "Avoid eye contact or you're done for."

Despite Jenny's assertion that, "*Those things never work once you get them home*," I buy a miracle tin opener from an overly cute Italian demonstrator.

Jenny finds another cheap swimming costume, and I manage to replace my wallet with a new model. It has the advantage of having a big chain connecting it to my belt loop.

"You won't lose that in a hurry," Jenny laughs.

Down on the seafront we choose a small restaurant on a wooden platform overhanging the beach, and order beers and panini sandwiches.

"It's such an amazing place to live," Jenny says again. "I mean you really have it all here, don't you."

I laugh and look out at the sea. "Yeah," I say with a sigh.

Jenny touches my hand. "You OK?" she asks.

I nod. "Just a moment of melancholy," I say. "It doesn't mean anything. A passing cloud."

Jenny frowns at me.

"Look!" I say, forcing a grin. "It's gone!"

Beneath the faded *Gini* parasol, we quietly eat our sandwiches and drink our beer and watch the sun beat down on the beach below.

"The men on that beach," Jenny points out, "all have really long trunks, and really short legs."

I grin and nod. "You're right," I say. "How funny."

"Cute though," Jenny says.

I nod. "Yeah, cute."

"You're not into Italians much are you?" she says.

I shrug and sip at my beer. "Actually I think they're unbelievably gorgeous," I say. "It's just the only Italian men I have ever slept with were either suicidal that they were gay, or pretending they were straight."

"Antonio seems OK though," Jenny says.

I snort lightly. "Yeah," I say. "Maybe."

Jenny pulls a grimace. "Sorry," she says. "Shouldn't have mentioned the A word."

I shrug. "Nah, it's fine," I say. "Hey, shall we be real pigs and order desert?"

Jenny's eyes flash. "Do you think they have profiteroles? I *love* profiteroles."

I wink at her. "Dunno," I say, "but I certainly intend to find out."

"Oh my God," Jenny says forking the first one into her mouth. "If you hear any strange noises, it'll just be me... Having an orgasm."

Sottopassaggio

Around five we head back up to the station. We stop en-route to pick up some cheap bottles of Martini.

There's a wait for the train, so we sit in the little café on platform one and drink another round of cappuccinos. The waiter smilingly serves us, then returns to a deck chair at the far end of the bar where he resumes reading his newspaper.

Jenny nods at him. "It's a hard life," she says.

I laugh. "Yeah," I say.

"It's so easy to forget," Jenny says. "Living somewhere like England. You forget how relaxed other people's lives can be, you know?"

I nod.

"Especially in the hea..." Jenny freezes mid sentence. Her mouth drops.

"Oh my God!" she exclaims.

I frown at her.

She smiles madly and stares into the middle distance.

"What?" I ask. "What is it?"

"It moved," she says. "The baby, oh my God! It moved!"

I grin broadly. "Is that the first time?"

Jenny nods. "Yeah!" she says, wide eyed. "Wow, that's so weird. Gosh." She pulls a face and bites her bottom lip. "It's a bit *freaky* actually. Like having an alien inside."

I grimace. "Is it moving now? Is *she* moving," I correct myself, anxious to banish the idea that it's an alien.

Jenny pauses then shakes her head. "No," she says. "Just a one off."

She laughs and nods. "Wow though!" she says.

"I expect there'll be lots more of that," I say. "Did you think any more about names?"

Jenny shrugs. "I liked the Stevie idea, I mean, I liked the idea of the link, but the Nicks part kind of put me off. Depending how things work out, I may well want to try and forget that particular aspect of things."

"Yeah," I agree. "I thought it was a bit dodgy."

"I actually like Catherine," Jenny says. "Or Sarah."

"Catherine will become Kate I guess," I say. "Kate bush, Kate Winslett, Katey Boyle…"

"And Sarah?"

I grimace and shrug. "Sarah Ferguson? Sarah… Sarah Lee's Black Forest Gateau?" I shrug. "Actually there's another Fleetwood Mac link there. On the same album we heard the other day there's a song called Sarah. It was *the* big hit as I recall."

I glance at my watch. "But we better make a move," I say. "The train will be here in a bit."

Jenny pulls her bag towards her and stretches.

I nod towards the underpass. "Platform numéro quattro," I say.

Jenny nods and stands, placing a hand on her belly. "Sottopassaggio," she says, reading the sign above the underpass. "Isn't Italian beautiful?"

I nod. "It means exactly the same thing though," I say. "Underpass."

Jenny takes my arm. "Yeah," she says, starting to walk. "I know, and I expect Italians probably think *underpass* sounds more exotic, but I still prefer *Sottopassaggio*."

As we descend into the tiled tunnel the temperature drops. Involuntarily I shiver. "It's cold down here," I say, my voice echoing off the tiled walls.

Pools of sunlight illuminate the tunnel at each set of stairs. We wander arm in arm towards the far end, the bottles clinking in the carrier bag.

"Hey, here come the alcoholics!" I laugh, shaking the bag.

Jenny squeezes my arm. "Don't joke about that," she says.

I pull a face. "Sorry," I mutter.

"So how far away did you say Tom…" Jenny glances up the first flight of stairs and pauses. She looks like she's listening for some distant sound.

"The baby again?" I ask.

Jenny shakes her head but continues to peer up the stairwell. I follow her gaze. The aura of evening sunlight at the top is beautiful and I wish I had my camera. Thinking that Jenny has got the wrong platform, I tug on her arm.

"Our train's platform four," I say nodding forwards. "Down the end."

At the top, silhouetted against the evening sunlight, a figure has appeared.

"I know!" Jenny says, in an irritated tone. "Wait!"

I glance at her, and then back up at the figure, now heading towards us.

"Isn't that…?" Jenny says.

As the figure comes closer I see it's a man. He's carrying a bag over his shoulder. He continues down until only his spiky hair remains silhouetted against the orange sky.

I shudder.

Jenny says his name first. "*Tom?*"

He pauses, now only one step above us. I stare, mouth open, speechless.

Tom takes the final step down to our level. He looks pale and drawn, so washed-out in fact, that for a moment, I doubt that it *is* him.

His expression is wide-eyed but emotionless. He looks frowningly at Jenny, then at myself. He drops the heavy green army bag from his shoulder to the ground, and silently stands before us. Then he looks from Jenny's face to my own, and then back again over and over.

I put down my bottle-filled carrier bag and step towards him. I watch as his lips thin, his forehead wrinkles and his cheeks start to distort. A tear runs from the corner of his eye.

"Tom?" I say, moving forward and wrapping my arms around him.

At first his body remains rigid, but then, with a jerk and a shudder, he stiffens, and then collapses against me.

"You?" he gasps, his body shuddering as he emits a sob. "How?" he breathes.

Jenny steps forward, and rests a hand on each of our backs. "Jesus Tom!" she says.

A train rumbles overhead – *our* train.

We lead Tom back though the underpass and order fresh cups of coffee at the café.

The Italian waiter laughs and says something I make no attempt at understanding, but take to mean, "*You changed your minds then.*"

Tom disappears to the bathroom and eventually reappears looking recomposed, but his eyes have an air of madness, a certain crazy stare that I have never seen before.

He sits opposite, alternately running a finger across his pierced eyebrow or stroking his beard.

"This is madness," he says, shaking his head. "You know that this is mad, right?"

I sigh and nod at him. "It *is* pretty crazy," I say.

Tom snorts and shakes his head. "You know the phrase," he asks, his voice trembling a little again, "*A sight for sore eyes?*" He lifts a trembling hand to cover his mouth.

Jenny tuts sympathetically. "Oh *Tom*," she says.

He shakes his head. "I'm sorry," he says. "I've had such a bad few days, I don't know..." He swallows hard. "If I had thought this was possible... If I had believed I might bump into you here, today, right now, I would have prayed for it," he says. "It's incredible."

"But why are you here?" I say. "Where are you going?"

Tom shakes his head. "Why am *I* here?" he says.

I shrug. "We came over to Nice to get away from all that hassle," I explain. "You know, Nick and everything. And then, today, well, we just went to the market, here, in Vingtimiglia."

Tom nods. "I'm going to Nice. I thought I'd try and get an early flight home."

Jenny strokes Tom's arm. She glances at me and catches my eye. Her regard is profound and communicating. It says that she knows what I need to know, and she knows that I can't be the one to ask the question.

"And Antonio?" she says.

Tom shakes his head slowly. "He'll notice that I've gone in a few days," he says sourly. He stares at the table for a while, then swallows and continues. "His parents turned up. It's was so... *Humiliating*," he says.

I glance at Jenny; she shrugs discreetly.

Tom shakes his head again. He scrunches up his eyes, fighting back tears. "He made me stay in a hotel," he says. "I barely saw him. I had no idea anyone could be so ashamed. I had no idea anyone could be so ashamed *of me.*"

"His parents don't know then," I say.

Tom shakes his head. "I don't think Antonio *himself* knows," he says. "I offered to be discreet you know? But he said I'm too gay... He said I'm an embarrassment."

Tom's face crumples. A fresh set of tears runs down his cheeks. He shakes his head dolefully. "I've never been treated like that in my life," he says.

I feel close to tears myself. I reach out and wipe Tom's cheek with the back of my hand.

Jenny pulls a tissue from her bag and hands it to him.

"I'm sorry," he says taking a deep breath. "I'm a bit overwrought. I didn't sleep the last couple of nights. I kept waiting for him to realise, I kept thinking he'd come, that he'd say sorry or something, you know?"

Tom wipes his nose again, and then snorts sadly. "I thought we were going to fix the details of the move," he says. "Not organise a break-up."

Jenny rubs Tom's back again. "Well, you'll probably sort it all out," she says. "Things are rarely as bad as they seem."

Tom shakes his head slowly. "I may be a bit too gay, but I'm no drama queen," he says. He swallows hard and looks up towards the roof, blinking back the last of the tears. Then he reaches out across the table and lays one hand on Jenny's and the other on mine.

"And now you two!" he says. "I mean, what on earth is *that* all about?"

After It's Over

On the journey back, the three of us slip into a stunned silence. I don't know what the others are thinking about, but I can guess. Tom looks pale and slightly crazed. I imagine he's still chewing over his last few days with Antonio. Jenny has a hand on her stomach and she's staring out of the window at the fading light. She'll be thinking about her baby, where to have it, how to organise things, what to do next.

Me? I'm trying to resist telling Tom how much I love him. Seeing him vulnerable, and hearing about how badly he's been treated, hearing the uncomprehending hurt in his voice has cracked my heart right open. Strangely, I'm also fixating on the sleeping arrangements. There are two beds in the apartment, so Tom is going to be sleeping with Jenny or with myself, and that thought, the relish that I feel about the simple idea of finally sharing my bed with Tom is inappropriate and selfish, but I feel it all the same.

As we roll out of Menton, Jenny turns from the window and smiles at Tom.

"Are you OK Tom?" she says.

Tom nods. "A bit in shock I guess," he says. "I feel a bit like my brain is overloaded. Like it has just sort of shut down."

"Do you want to talk about it all or..."

Tom shakes his head. "Nah, not really," he says. "There's not so much to say... I mean, sometimes you're trying to work out what happened. But *this time*?" he shrugs. "This is one of those occasions where you feel like you already knew, but just didn't let yourself realise."

I frown at him. "Really?" I say. "I'm surprised. I thought you and Antonio were quite solid."

Tom shrugs. "I'm good at ignoring stuff," he says. He shakes his head. "Too good. It's dumb, but I always do it. I always stick my head in the sand. I never realise what's happening till after it's over."

Jenny leans over and touches his knee. "We all do that Tom," she says. "Don't give yourself a hard time about it."

Tom shrugs. "Yeah, it's just that, well, ever since..." he looks at me. "Actually ever since that conversation we had together about his supposedly straight ex... you know, that Hugo bloke, well I knew that there was a problem we needed to deal with. But I just ignored it."

A train passes in the other direction causing a stunning whack as its slipstream hits ours.

I wait until the quiet returns, and then say, "But you can't fix other people; believe me, I've tried."

Tom nods. "Yeah, I could have tried to address it though, instead of just being surprised when it all falls apart."

Jenny smiles sadly. "Italians," she says, nodding at me meaningfully.

"Yeah," I say. "We were talking about just this just an hour ago."

"Maybe if I could have got him away," Tom says. "Maybe if I could have got him out of Italy, like we planned."

I nod. "With time, and patience maybe. But you know, he was in England, he was in Brighton when he was telling us how straight his ex was."

Tom nods. "He was so proud of that. Anyway, he wasn't ever going to move," he says. "I was actually considering moving to Italy instead."

A ticket inspector slides the door open. "Vos Billets s'il vous plaît," he says.

We hold up our tickets to be clipped and watch as he inspects, clips them and moves on.

"New wallet," Tom says. "With a chain this time!"

I nod and smile as I slip it back into my rear pocket. "Yeah," I say. "I bought it in Ventimiglia today. The old one caused that much anguish."

Jenny nods meaningfully. "Especially for Benoit."

I shoot her a glare. I've never told Tom about my relationship with Benoit, and now is not the moment. She pulls a grimace showing she understands this.

Tom frowns. "Benoit? John and Jean's mad photographer friend?"

I nod. "Yeah... It's a long story," I say.

Tom shrugs and looks out of the window but just as he turns, we enter a tunnel. He sighs heavily and looks back at me.

Suddenly what he just said registers. "*Mad*?" I say.

Tom grimaces. "Not very PC of me, sorry," he says. "I used to quite fancy him actually. He's lovely as long as he takes his meds."

I frown. "I'm sorry, I don't..."

Tom shrugs. "Sorry, I thought... Never mind. It's not for me to say really."

I shake my head. "No," I say. "Please, Tom. I know Benoit quite well and I knew there was something, but... What's actually wrong with him?"

Tom grimaces. "Sorry, I shouldn't have said anything. He's, you know, what do they call it? Manic depressive? Only there's another term for it nowadays."

Jenny nods. "Bipolar disorder."

"Yeah," Tom says. "That's it. He's lovely most of the time, but well, when he's manic he's a handful; he goes quite wild. Plus he'll shag anything that moves."

I bite my lip and avoid looking at Jenny. "And when he's depressed?"

Tom shrugs. "You don't see him at all when he's down. Sometimes for months."

"Right," I say.

Another story that becomes clear only after it's over. "Why don't people ever tell you this stuff whilst it's happening," I wonder.

"I didn't know you were friends with him," Tom says. "I'm sorry, please don't tell him I said..."

I interrupt him with a reassuring smile. "I haven't seen him for months," I say.

The Big Picture

Jenny pushes past me. "Bagsy the toilet," she says.

"Go for it!" I laugh.

"God you have a cat," Tom says, handing me his bag and sweeping Paloma into his arms.

I close the door and laugh. "A very *demanding* cat," I say.

Tom lifts Paloma into the air and rubs her nose against his. She purrs appreciatively.

"I love cats. I used to have one," he says. "We called her Riley. Because she lived the life of Riley."

"Yeah?" I say. "Paloma does OK too," I say, stroking the cat's head. "Don't you Paloma."

"She's sweet," Tom says. "Aren't you Paloma?"

I nod. "They're a tie though," I say. "It's lucky my friend was able to look after her."

Tom nods and puts the cat gently down. "I know," he says. "My mum ended up with mine. Though it didn't stop *her* doing anything. She used to drive all over with that poor mog." He shakes his head sadly at the memory.

I pull a doubting expression. "If you carried that one to the corner-shop she'd have a heart attack," I say.

Jenny reappears from the bathroom. "Anyone want tea?" she says, "Or are we breaking open the Martini?"

I pull a bottle from the carrier bag and head through to the kitchen. "Martini for me," I say.

"Yeah," Tom says. "Me too. A good strong one."

I stand in the kitchen and pause, listening. From the lounge I can hear Jenny and Tom talking quietly. It seems as if I have been here before, doing exactly this, as if Jenny and Tom have already been next door waiting for Martinis.

Maybe it's just because it feels natural, normal that they should be here. Maybe it's just the déjà-vu thing, my brain sorting away memories faster than it is processing the present, or maybe déjà-vu is really our momentary perception that what the scientists say is true, that time *isn't* linear.

I pull ice-cubes from the tray and think about our chance meeting with Tom, retracing the events in my mind. Didn't Jenny freeze just *before* Tom appeared? "Wait," she had said. "Look." But there had been nothing to look at; nothing to wait *for*.

Why would she do that unless she saw something? And if Jenny saw Tom before I did, then were we in the same moment at all?

Just for a second a strange image fills my mind, an image of the planet as seen from afar. I see ripples of shifting time rolling across the surface and a vast web of connections and events, a network of secret tubes running, like wormholes back and forth through space and time, linking our lives and the lives of our parents and the lives of future generations, of our every act and every other.

It's as if there are secret passages forcing destiny in ways we don't understand and for a split second my life seems to be not an isolated thing, but a logical manifestation of every event that ever occurred, a mathematical *result* of the complex ricochets of the entire shifting sands of human history.

I shiver, and then as quickly as it came, the feeling passes. I frown and pick up the drinks.

When I enter the lounge, Tom is crouched in the middle of the floor. The saxophone case lies open before him.

He looks up at me frowning. "You have a sax," he says.

I bite my lip and put the drinks down on the coffee table. I take a breath and stare at the gleaming instrument.

"Yeah," I say quietly. "It was Steve's."

Tom nods and lifts the sax from the case. "I remember now," he says. "You mentioned it."

I nod and shrug.

"It's beautiful," Tom says reverently. "It's a *Selmer*."

I squint at him and nod gently. "Is that *good* then?" I ask.

Tom snorts. "It's the *best*!" he says. "I bet it sounds lovely."

I shrug again. "I don't know," I say. My voice is foggy so I cough to clear my throat. "I never heard it," I explain.

Tom moves the mouthpiece towards his lips, then pauses and

glances back at me.

"Do you mind?" he asks. "Only, I've been really missing mine. Antonio was always complaining about my practicing, so in the end I stopped bringing it."

My eyes are tearing and my chest feels so tight, I can barely breath.

Tom bites his lip and lowers the saxophone, but I shake my head.

"No," I say. "Please…"

Tom raises an eyebrow and lifts the instrument again. "You sure?" he says. "It's just, well… It's a *Selmer*."

I nod gently and slide to the floor beside him.

Jenny who is seated behind me lays a hand on my shoulder.

"Go ahead Tom," I say. "It's all yours."

Epilogue

I can see the sun, orange, no, *red* through my eyelids.

I push my toes down through the layer of scorched sand into the damp, humid layers below. Against my chest, Sarah is wriggling and cooing gorgeously, and behind me the jazz band is playing old Fleetwood Mac songs.

I raise myself on one elbow, and glance back up the beach.

The sight of Steve wearing his baggy brown suit and his orange seventies shirt makes me smile. He winks at me and jazzes up his rift a little for my benefit.

I turn back and see Sarah standing, pulling herself up onto my chest. She lies on my stomach and rubs her nose against mine. It tickles. She makes me sneeze.

I open my eyes with a splutter and focus cross-eyed on Paloma's furry chin. She has crawled onto my stomach and is head-butting me; she wants food.

I gently push her to one side and rub the cat-hairs from my face. I stare at the ceiling and listen to the sounds of Sunday.

Outside I can hear rain gently tapping against the windowsill. Upstairs in Jenny's apartment, I can hear Sarah screaming madly, and beyond that I can just make out Jenny's gentle yet exasperated voice as she tries to calm her.

I can hear the gurgling of the central heating, and from the office I can hear Tom playing the same dreadful jazz rift he has been trying to learn for the last month. Over and over he plays the same soaring screaming sequence; over and over he stumbles at exactly the same point. I lie and listen and wait... *There*! It's still wrong. It still hurts my ears. It stops.

I wait for him to start over, and roll my eyes and smile as I imagine his red face. I stretch languorously in the bed and then snuggle against Paloma.

I lie and wait for the magical moment when the heat of Tom's body against my back, when the feeling of his arms enveloping me, will announce the beginning of Sunday proper.

I smile and listen to the screaming baby and Tom's endless saxophone rift and Paloma's purring and the rain outside.

Then I push my toes down into the sand. It feels cool and dark and refreshing. Against my chest, Sarah is wriggling and cooing gorgeously, and behind me Steve and Tom are playing old Fleetwood Mac songs together.

And the sun is *red* and hot against my eyelids.

THE END

Also Available

Good Thing, Bad Thing

A Novel
By Nick Alexander

On holiday with new boyfriend Tom, Mark – the hero from the best-selling novels, *fifty Reasons to Say goodbye* and *Sottopassaggio* – heads off to rural Italy for a spot of camping.
When the ruggedly seductive Dante invites them onto his farmland the lovers think they have struck lucky, but there is more to Dante than meets the eye – much more.
Thoroughly bewitched, Tom, all innocence, appears blind to Dante's dark side... Racked with suspicion, it is Mark who notices as their holiday starts to spin slowly but very surely out of control – and it is Mark, alone, who can maybe save the day...

Good Thing, Bad Thing is a story of choices; an exploration of the relationship between understanding and forgiveness, and an investigation of the fact that life is rarely quite as bad – or as good – as it seems. Above all *Good Thing, Bad Thing* is another cracking adventure for gay everyman Mark.

"Spooky, and emotionally turbulent – yet profoundly comedic, this third novel in a captivating trilogy is a roller-coaster literary treasure all on its own. But do yourself a favour, and treat yourself to its two prequels as soon as you can..." – Richard Labonte, Book Marks

Part of the Fifty Reasons Series:
Vol III – Good Thing Bad Thing,
Vol IV – Better Than Easy, Vol V – Sleight Of Hand.

The Case Of The Missing Boyfriend

A Novel
By Nick Alexander

C.C. is nearly forty and other than her name (which she hates so much she can't bring herself to use it) everything about her life appears to be wonderful: she has a high powered job in advertising, a great flat in Primrose Hill, and a wild bunch of friends to spend her weekends with. And yet she feels like the Titanic – slowly, inexorably, and against all expectation, sinking.

For despite her indisputable success, C.C. would rather be shovelling shit on a farm than selling it to the masses – would rather be snuggling on the sofa with The Missing Boyfriend than playing star fag-hag in London's latest coke-spots.

But opportunities to find The Missing Boyfriend are rarer than an original metaphor, and CC's body-clock is ticking so loudly that at times she can barely hear her mother wittering on about her own Moroccan boyfriend.

Could her best friend be right? Could her past really be preventing her from moving on? And if she unlocks that particular box, will the horrors within simply drift away and leave her free? Or will they sink her?

If she can shake off the past and learn to trust again, will she stop attracting freaks and find The Missing Boyfriend? Or will she just end up tethered and gagged at the bottom of the stairs?

"A bittersweet, bang-up-to-date take on the eternal quest for love."
– Rupert Smith (author of Man's World).

.

Lightning Source UK Ltd.
Milton Keynes UK
UKOW06f1624100716

278049UK00025B/818/P